fighting

a peacock springs novel

book two

Jordana Blake

Just Vibes Media, LLC

Copyright © 2025 by Jordana Blake

www.jordanablakebooks.com

just vibes media, llc*

Paperback ISBN: 979-8-9985325-0-4

Digital ISBN: 979-8-9985325-1-1

Library of Congress Cataloging-in-Publication Data available upon request

Line and Copy Editor: Beth Lawton, VB Edits

Proof Reading: Emilie Mortati, Glitter Penned Edits

Cover Illustration: Sonia Garragoux, @artbysoniagx

Cover Design & Typography: Jordan Burns, @joburns.designs

❀ Formatted with Vellum

dear reader,

The following story is the product of my undying love for TV/movies of the late 1990s and early 2000s and psychology. Within these pages *fighting* examines the push and pull between who we are and who others believe us to be.

Writing 'Romantic traum-com' requires finding the humor in even the most challenging experiences. It has been said that comedy is the sum of tragedy plus time. I've never been great at math, so I can't say what the *correct amount* of time is to laugh at something tragic, please be advised the following sensitive subjects are included:

Secondary trauma from being a helping professional related to:

- Interpersonal Violence (IPV) the subset of Domestic Violence (DV) which happens between romantic partners
- Sexual Harassment, Molestation, and Assault

Direct trauma related to:

- Stalking and harassment
- Slut Shaming
- Racialized/Ethnic Stereotyping

Open door sex scenes, frank discourse around cannabis, alcohol use, and explicit language.

Please note there are multiple ways to experience real-life events and I have done my best, alongside sensitivity readers, to do it justice. Though you may not relate–it does not make it untrue. Additionally, the main characters have frank conversations around unearned reputations, including past experiences with antisemitism and racism. **The author does not approve of the derogatory statements. These moments do not reflect my thoughts on members of the Jewish American or Filipino American communities.** It is my hope that the team of sensitivity readers employed have ensured that the story you'll read treats those topics properly.

What began as my thirsting over Manny Jacinto's portrayal of Jason Mendoza in The Good Place™ morphed into a journey through the Filipino and Filipino Diaspora romance community. Please be sure to check out the resources in the back for Own Voices stories and other ways to support their community.

While I hope you love my imaginary friends, your mental health should always come first.

Please be kind to your mind,

Jordana

dicktionary

come & see our (pea)cocks

Chapter 12

Chapter 18

Chapter 32

Chapter 33

Chapter 43

Epilogue

i wrote this for:

younger me, Amanda Beth, and loud little girls everywhere

one
Nessa

Present | Labor Day Weekend

"PEOPLE, PEOPLE," Jim Kelly, mayor of Peacock Springs and town veterinarian, calls from the makeshift dais in front of the floor-to-ceiling mirrors in the dance studio. He runs his hands through his wiry hair and adjusts his tortoise-shell glasses. He's wearing charcoal-gray scrubs covered in tufts of pet hair, clearly having come straight from work. Unceremoniously flipping a binder open, he tries again to quiet the room.

This school year, meetings moved from the local bar and restaurant, The Featherweight, to Lily Long's dance studio. Like most changes in a tiny town, it has taken some getting used to.

Now that Lily is seated in her new place up front, I can't join her, so I crane my neck, searching for another friend to sit with. My roommate, Delia, is in the back of the room, looking two seconds away from falling asleep after a long weekend tending bar. She gives a quick wave, but I know she's not moving.

Where is everyone? I check again, finding my dad and brother Shua, but neither of my other two siblings are anywhere in sight.

"We'll start with last week's business," Jim says. "Then we'll move into establishing committee leads for the upcoming Sunflower Festival. From there, we'll discuss the upcoming sale of the Morgans' full real estate portfolio, including the undeveloped lands on the north side of town." Clearing his throat, he peers at someone at the back of the room, though I can't tell who it is from this angle. "Once we're finished, we'll open the floor to new business."

Beside me, a warm, solid body slides into the open seat, and a knee knocks mine. Without turning my head, I can make out a pair of cognac loafers and a large, well-manicured hand splayed over a thigh clad in black jeans.

It must be my lucky night. I groan internally and shift away from the man I haven't been able to avoid in the months since his sister's wedding.

Though I attempt to put space between us, the irritatingly attractive man I do not want to want leans closer.

"Quit it," I hiss when Mateo spreads his legs a bit wider, causing his thigh to graze mine.

With a fake yawn, he stretches his left arm out and drapes it over my chair. Now that he's exposed his ribs, I jab an elbow into his side, eliciting a yelp.

Don't laugh, don't laugh, don't laugh, I repeat to myself while trying to muffle the sound with my palm.

"Excuse me, Miss Rabin. Would you like to share what you find so funny?" Jim chides from the dais.

"It's Doctor Rabin," Mateo says before I can respond.

Well, damn.

"Sorry." I half-heartedly apologize.

"Don't be like that, Ivy," Mateo whispers. "I hoped I'd see you tonight. Can we talk after the meeting?"

While Jim moves on to the plans for this fall's Sunflower Fest, I try to tune out the electricity that prickles my skin because of the man at my side.

Clearly ignoring the vibes I'm giving off, Mateo rests his arm across my chair again, distracting me enough to cause me to miss which committee Jim is filling. I put my hand up, intending to ask him to repeat himself.

Rather than call on me, he grins and jots a note in his notebook. "Wonderful. Nessa Rabin will lead the volunteer teams this year. Who is willing to co-chair with her?"

I stare hard at Lily, begging her with my eyes to say yes. Come on, come on, don't let me get stuck with someone who has gross breath or is going to try to set me up with their grandson.

"Perfect. She'll be paired with Mateo Santos-Manolo," Jim announces, banging the gavel on the podium.

Oh no.

"Looks like I've got time to grow on you, Ivy," Mateo teases, giving me the boyish grin that did me in the one and only time we slept together. The grin that's a little lopsided and makes his deep dimples pop.

"Quit calling me that," I snap.

"You called yourself that." Chin lifted, he faces the front of the room again.

"Last order of business is the Morgan property divestment," Jim says from the podium.

"Good riddance," I grumble under my breath.

Beside me, Mateo snickers.

As Jim titters with excitement, he glances at the dark corner again.

Interesting. Do we have a surprise guest?

"In the coming weeks, Caleb Reynolds will be in town. He plans to present his development plans for the north side once he's gathered the necessary information. Please be kind and keep your gawking to a minimum while he's in town."

"Un-fucking-believable. Is this a Dickens novel?" I grumble. Apparently the ghosts of past mistakes have come to haunt me. This one in the form of my ex.

Is it just me, or is it getting harder to breathe?

"Fuck that guy." Mateo leans closer. "Not happening." He leaves tiny puffs of air on my neck. His lips nearly skim my ear, stirring feelings I'm not interested in revisiting.

"What do you have in mind—"

Before I can finish the question, he jumps to his feet.

"Mr. Santos-Manolo, can we help with something?" Jim asks, his tone stodgy.

Mateo adjusts the leather band of his wristwatch and clears his throat. "Yes, Jim. In fact, you can. As you know, I am a developer myself, and I'm familiar with the work the Reynolds Group does."

Jim continues to glance at that darker corner.

"They're from the city. Are we sure they're really the right group for a town like ours?" He lifts both brows. "I'd appreciate the opportunity to provide my own proposal. As a lifelong resident of this town, I want to ensure we keep the integrity and history of this place intact."

The room breaks into a round of applause, and on the other side of the room, his parents, Susan and Eddie, nod in approval.

"Call my office and schedule an appointment. We can talk about it then," Jim hollers over the din of the crowd.

Movement in my periphery catches my attention, and I turn in time to see Caleb step out from the dark corner. With Caleb "Satan's Bikini Waxer" Reynolds the Third lurking nearby, suddenly being this close to Mateo is a comfort. Not that I'd tell him that.

This is the first time I've seen him in years. Standing at six feet tall, with thick blond hair and wearing a navy suit, he looks every bit as devilish as my name for him.

He still looks like the boy I met at the Skull and Cross fraternity party, where he played up his family's rumored billions and their key place in society.

We dated through graduate school and while I completed a doctoral program in psychology. The longer we were together, the more dysfunctional, selfish, and possessive he proved himself

4

to be. I squirm in my seat; my head drops and my muscles tense at the shameful memory. The old urge to withdraw from confronting the irony returns. I am a fraud. Despite focusing my academics and career on supporting healthy intimate relationships, I lingered in a toxic relationship out of convenience.

Standing in my hometown, Caleb looks equally out of place as I felt with him.

His family regularly made comments about my parents' background that left me uneasy. They'd toss in what they deemed compliments about my blond hair and tiny nose. The underlying meaning? In their eyes, I don't look Jewish. And they assumed that because my family is secular, it shouldn't be a big deal to give up our holidays. Couldn't I get on board with things like being married in their church, no rabbi needed? Couldn't I pretend my last name meant that I'm distantly related to a former prime minister? Because a connection like that would elevate my status for their optics.

The worst part was that Caleb didn't have any issue with any of it at all.

The Reynoldses wanted me to give up my identity and become a trophy on his arm. I had worked too hard to agree to that and slowly distanced myself. Eventually blocking his number and breaking all contact. Not that it stopped him from getting a new phone number and trying again. Ignoring him had worked for a bit, but somehow, he's back like the cold sore he is.

The meeting wraps in a blur and people file out.

I grab my purse from under the seat and glare at my festival co-chair. "Why would you do that?"

He's co-chairing a town event with me and trying to outbid the most narcissistic group of gentrifiers in the country? What is his goal here?

His wide smile only highlights his beautiful bone structure and makes that damn dimple pop. His brown eyes glimmer, and his thick jet-black hair hangs just long enough to be unruly in a '90s teen heartthrob kind of way.

I clench my fist to stop myself from brushing it away from his eyes.

Mateo chuckles, the low rumble vibrating through me. "There's your pal…"

"Satan's Bikini Waxer," I bite out.

Just the sound of Caleb's smarmy voice over the crowd makes my hackles rise. I need a shower. I feel dirty breathing the same air as him.

"Bikini Waxes? I thought you were vehemently against those. Did you have a change of heart? I would love to see that," Caleb says as he appears at the end of the aisle, wearing an oily smile.

Pulling me close, Mateo holds out a hand. "Mateo Santos-Manolo. We were supposed to meet for drinks this summer when I was representing Merrick Paul on the Park Ave project. It's nice to finally meet you." His tone is terse, belying his words. "However, I'd prefer if you didn't talk about my girlfriend's pubes. Seems a little inappropriate, my dude."

Rankled by what looks like the start of a pissing contest, I try to step away. But he squeezes me closer to his side.

I bite my tongue. *Girlfriend? What the hell?* Sexist Satan here, though, will probably respect the request coming from him, since a woman equates to property in his mind.

I thought we didn't believe in hell. How am I already here?

As if sent by God himself, my brother walks by, giving me an excuse to free myself from Mateo's grasp.

"Joshua, wait up!" I yell, but my brain is shouting *oh-em-gee, kill me now.*

I follow Shua to where Aba—Dad—and Tal are standing close, talking. Aba pulls me into a bear hug. "Motek! Do my ears deceive me, sweetie? Or did Mateo just call you his girlfriend while speaking to… the one you call, em"—he arches his brows—"Ha'Sah'tahn?"

My dad has been in the states for over thirty-five years, but he often slips between languages when he's emotional or confused.

Laughing, I nod and hug him tighter. "I'll walk you all home. I can explain." I link arms with him and peer over my shoulder to where Grant, Jim, Caleb, and Mateo are still talking. "I'll explain what I know, at least."

As we head out into the cool night air, I pull out my phone and send a quick text.

––––––

NESSA:

I am NOT pretending to be your girlfriend.

BAD IDEA:

Who said anything about pretending?

two
Mateo

Three Months Ago | Memorial Day Weekend

HOPING to make it to the bar unnoticed, I weave between tables quickly. The white tablecloths are adorned with low taper candles and floral centerpieces. The place really is beautiful.

Tonight is my baby sister's rehearsal dinner, and my number one goal is dodging aunts and uncles and town meddlers. I'm in no mood to deal with all the questions and assumptions. My life in Manhattan is amazing, and its distance from Peacock Springs and small-town gossip is one of many reasons why.

I hold out my rocks glass, the oversized ice cube clinking, and catch the server's eye. With a nod, he slides the top-shelf bottle to me. I cringe as I examine the bottle he cracked open on my first visit to the bar. From the look of it, I've polished off a good quarter of the fifteen-hundred-dollar tequila.

"Shit," I mutter as I dig my wallet out of my pocket. I drop a black card onto the shiny surface and tell him to charge this to me rather than the bride and groom. His name is Ross, according to the gold tag pinned to his shirt. Or is it Russ? It's hard to tell from here. The world has gone a little hazy.

Either way, I ask Ross/Russ to put this on my card so that Nanay, a.k.a. my very sweet but strict Filipino mother, does not have a heart attack the night before Stefanie and Lee's wedding.

The last thing I need is to cause my little sister any additional headaches.

But the tequila is a must if I'm going to survive the weekend and play my part. In the family, I'm the handsome devil without a brain who can get any girl he wants. The man who stumbled into a high-salaried career that isn't in healthcare—a detail that every nurse, doctor, and physician's assistant in the room will remind me of. Tatay, my dad, and his sisters, my titas, tease me about being one of only a couple of grandkids who don't wear scrubs to work.

Stef doesn't either, but they don't give her shit since she's in education. She's taking care of kids' minds.

I scoff at the phrase I've heard a million times.

Not one of them understands that I have a vision. I'm not as stupid as they think I am. I only have what I do because my grandparents sacrificed comfort so that my parents could have choices, which in turn allowed me to have a choice. And I'm making the most of what my American upbringing gave me.

As for the playboy part, that's an incorrect label, though I don't bother to correct people who want to believe it. I just refuse to settle for anything less than the best. Have you seen me in this suit? It's called confidence, babe.

Speaking of the best, my sister's friends are top-notch, two of whom are approaching the bar now.

My friends, unfortunately, seem to be of the fair-weather variety. Other than Liam, who's around here somewhere with his partner.

I'm not trying to be an eavesdropper, but when I hear something like "you need to relax," I can't help but lean in.

"You played caretaker at the bachelorette weekend," Delia says

9

to Nessa, who's a couple of inches shorter than her, even in heels. "Now let's get you a drink. It's your turn to let loose."

I turn, being sure to smile in that way that makes my dimples pop, and say, "I can offer you top shelf tequila if that will sway you."

"Yes!" Delia cries, while Nessa mutters her half-hearted acceptance.

Delia bounces on her toes and glances around the room before her eyes land on the bartender. He meets her gaze before shaking his head and returns to counting his tips.

With nobody watching the bar, Delia reaches one long arm over and grabs two glasses and the salt dish. Placing the goods before her and Nessa, she brandishes a triumphant smile.

"Hey, Matty," Delia says. "Truth or dare?"

I smirk. "What about truth or drink?"

With a nod, she elbows Nessa, who is assessing her pointy manicure and doing her best to ignore me. Her nails look like claws. Yikes.

"Fine." Nessa heaves out a breath, and before I know it, her lips curl up in a smirk. "Me first. How often do you wash your sheets, playboy?"

"That's easy." I rest one forearm on the bar and cross my ankles. "The morning after company or once a week. I'm not a heathen. My cleaner comes on Fridays." I give a simple shrug. "Okay, Doc. My turn."

Her nostrils flare in annoyance.

Maybe I'm sick, but the sight sends a bolt of excitement up my spine. I love riling her up. "Where is the strangest place you've flicked the bean, Dr. Rabin?" I tease, using the name of her podcast on sex and relationships. Hosting 'Flicking the Bean with Dr. Rabin' is only one of the many hats she wears as a shrink.

She picks up her glass and downs the tequila, then narrows her eyes on me. "Have you ever sexted the wrong person?"

With a laugh, I shake my head. "No, never."

Delia clears her throat, breaking our banter, and I turn her way. I don't want her to pull Nessa from me just yet.

"Have you ever considered kissing Jim Kelly just to see if he'd react?"

"I'd rather kiss a peacock," Delia says.

Nessa giggles. She actually giggles.

It's light and airy, so unlike the harsh tone I am usually met with.

I sip and savor the way they good-naturedly tease one another and fall into another fit of laughter.

During her freshman year of high school, the little genius was in my eleventh-grade English lit class. While she was ahead of her grade, I was repeating the course. That's when I realized that getting a rise out of her was more fun than being ignored.

I hold my smile, though in this moment, I can't help but think about one story I can recall from that year. The one about the sad clown named Pagliacci.

Pagliacci, out of costume, goes to the doctor because he's depressed—which I am not; I'm just not thrilled about this weekend's events.

Anyhow, the doctor tells him to go to see the clown, Pagliacci, who is performing in town that night, suggesting that it will cheer him up. That's when the punchline hits. He is the clown.

That's what I do at family functions. I smile. I avoid worrying my parents. I ensure everyone else is doing okay.

Our game continues as the room thins out, going from after-party to after-the-after-party status.

"My turn," Nessa shouts over the music, pouring a refill for us both. "Marry, kiss, or kill the bridesmaids."

"No fair," I tease. "Lily Long is already taken, and Delia Shane here has that weird thing going with Seth Whitter."

The women simultaneously guffaw.

"That would be like kissing my brother. No, thanks." Delia downs the last of her drink and claps it against the bar with a soft thud. "On that note," she says, pointing at Nessa, then me. "I'm out. Good night, kids. Drink water and get some rest. We have makeup and golf bright and early tomorrow."

"Looks like you're going to have to marry, kiss, and kill me, Matty," Nessa teases, her face split in a wide smile.

In that moment, something inside me shifts. I don't know about marriage, but yeah, I'm pretty sure I'd like to kiss her, even if she would kill me for it.

She licks at the salt on the rim of her glass, then sips her tequila, the move far sexier than she means for it to be, I'm sure.

I grab her stool and yank it closer to mine. "Last question. Ever see *Cruel Intentions?*"

Nessa swallows thickly, her eyes locked on mine. Her lips part, and she exhales a small puff of salt air. That soft, wet, pink tongue slowly grazes her lower lip. She angles closer, and her long blond hair slides over one shoulder, curving around her gorgeous, full tit.

I lean in, head lowered. "To be clear, I mean kissing you good night on your other pair of lips. I promise you the best kiss good night you'll ever have."

Her pupils blow wide. "Nobody has ever..."

I dip my head and bring my mouth to the sensitive spot below her ear. "Then let me show you what you've been missing. Nobody has to know. It'll be a little favor between friends." I punctuate the suggestion with a nip at the spot where her pulse is jumping.

She pulls her shoulders back, her breathing shallow. "We're not friends. But let's go."

Tipsy enough to be out of character, but not so drunk to be unaware of the implication, I wrap an arm around her and pick up the bottle of tequila, then guide her to the elevator.

three
Nessa

Three Months Ago | Memorial Day Weekend

SOMEWHERE BETWEEN THE orgasms and when I passed out in Mateo's bed, my phone's battery died—something I never let happen.

With a huff, I plug it into the charger on the bedside table in my own hotel room, then scurry to the bathroom to take the world's fastest body shower.

I'm gathering the embroidered button-down shirt Stef gifted me for getting-ready photos as the rapid-fire dinging of my phone sends piercing pains through my head.

Last night's clothes tossed on the floor, I pick up the device, finding dozens of unread text messages, too many emails to count —ninety percent of which are probably from stores and blogs I follow—and thirteen calendar reminders. Great. Nothing urgent.

I open our group chat and type out a message before jumping in the shower.

Group Chat: Bad Bitches
[Stef Santos-Manolo, Lily Long, Delia Shane, Nessa Rabin]

13

> Overslept. Getting in the shower. Will be up shortly.

IT CONTINUES to chime through my shower, but I don't bother to check. Only once I've finished and am drying off do I scroll through the messages.

STEF:

> I'll rearrange hair appointments. No worries!

LILY:

> Some worries. Susan's not as chill as the bridezilla here...

DELIA:

> She's right. Stef is chill and her mom is not. Hurry-ish.

I'M WRAPPING myself in my towel when another text comes through. This one in a separate thread.

SATAN'S BIKINI WAXER:

> Come on, Ness. Can we catch up over coffee?

I delete that message. If I don't acknowledge it, then it didn't happen, right?

Last night was the first night I've spent with another man since I ended things with Caleb. Another man who just so happened to use his fingers, lips, and tongue to make me come multiple times.

No need to ever think about Caleb the selfish limp-dick jerk again.

Except, as I slide my bra on, my nipples graze the cups and

tingle into peaks again.

Dammit. Don't think about last night either.

With a shake of my head, I snag my leggings off the bed. I slip them on and button up the adorable bridesmaid shirt. I'm just sliding my phone into my belt bag when another text pops up, bringing up the three previous texts from my middle sibling.

TAL:

Aba is giving me a hard time about the pronouns.
AGAIN.

Can you please talk to him?

Where are you?

You never take this long to reply...

NESSA:

Stef's wedding weekend. You know this.

For now, ignore Dad.

I'll see what I can do this week.

TAL:

Best big sister.

NESSA:

Screenshot to torture Shae with later

With a shake of my head, I step out into the hall and let the heavy metallic door thunk shut behind me. My voice is taut as I grumble, "You're fucking twenty, Tal. Talk to your own parents." While my hand is still perched on my belt bag zipper, the damn thing vibrates again, jolting me back to the present.

732-848-0609:

We exchanged numbers last night

See you at the altar. I'll be the best-looking one ;)

I choke on a laugh; he did not think that was cute. Ugh, I gave Mateo my number. Cool. With a sigh, I create a new contact and label it Bad Idea.

NESSA:

Sorry, who is this?

BAD IDEA:

You know who this is.

oh, I know what you need.

The elevator doors open, and I step in. There are a few women scattered around the tiny stainless-steel box, and any one of them could be related to Stef, so on the off chance that the image is risqué, I don't open the text thread.

It dings again as I step out and stride toward the double doors with the gold plaque embossed with Bridal Suite. With a flair for the dramatic, I enter, flinging the curtain of dark blond hair that hangs down to my waist over a shoulder.

"Good morning, ladies—" My enthusiastic greeting gets cut off when the blazing sunlight streaming in from the floor-to-ceiling windows blinds me. Wincing, I slide my black mirrored sunglasses over my eyes. Thank god the suite is outfitted with a coffee bar.

I fill a mug of coffee, sugar, and cream, then slide onto the chaise lounge beside Lily.

"How did you sleep?" The second the words are out, a queasy rush comes over me. Pressing my coffee into her hand, I jump up, then scurry for the bathroom.

When I'm done emptying the contents of my stomach, Lily enters with a hand towel and a tiny plastic cup of mouthwash from the sink in the room. Great. I haven't been hungover like this since my years at Harvard.

More ringing. Is that in my head? No, it's texts. Why is my ringer on?

BAD IDEA:

[goofy face selfie]

Come on, Ivy Out of My League

It was nice to see you have some fun.

NESSA:

Ivy Out of My League?

BAD IDEA:

<screenshot of contact card>

NESSA:

<eye roll emoji> Last night was a mistake. It will never happen again.

"Can I kill the best man?" I groan to Lily.

She blinks. "I mean, I'd prefer you... oh, you mean the other one." She's piecing it together in real time.

"Delia and I had a lot of tequila and played a game with Mateo. Or I did? I think she was there for a bit." I groan. "And I ended up sleeping in Mateo's room. So, anyway..." I heave out a breath. "River said he now gets 'relationship privileges,' and that if I didn't tell you, he would. He kind of... found me there this morning?" My voice squeaks on the last bit.

Slumping my head against the wall, I slide my sunglasses back on so I can wallow with at least a modicum of privacy.

"So what? You were in his hotel room? And that's a big secret...?" She's really not getting this.

"Come on, babe. Please do not make me say it. You can put the pieces together." I nudge her.

"Oh. *Oh*. Wait *what?*" Her voice gets a little too loud, her excitement taking hold.

17

I shush her. For the sake of my head, but also because I do not need the half-dozen members of the Santos-Manolo family on the other side of the wall knowing what we were up to last night.

"River said that if he knows, then you get to know. So now I told you. Okay?" I roll my head against the wall and sigh. "This means he can leave me alone with the whole *he's over keeping secrets* thing."

In fairness to River, he did just unburden a pretty big one from Lily's ex-husband. Holding onto a secret for ten years would make me hate them too.

"But you are going to tell Delia and Stef too, right?" Her eyes widen in a silent plea.

"Yes, but later. It's Stef's wedding day. Can you text your man? Let him know you know?"

She pulls out her phone, taps out a text, then looks up at me. "Done." As she slips her phone back into the pocket of her black joggers, she steps over to the in-bathroom sink. Wet washcloth in hand, she wipes the sweat from my brow.

"Let's get some carbs in you. Maybe some electrolytes?"

It's so weird, the way our roles have reversed.

There's a light knock on the door, and Delia slides inside, giving a soft smile. "I forgot how little you've been drinking these days. I should have stopped you sooner. But..." Her lips tick up on one side. "It seemed like you were having fun. You okay? What can I do?"

My upchuck reflexes kick back in, and I turn to say hello to the porcelain gods. Lily holds my hair and rubs circles on my back while instructing Delia to go down to the lobby for medicine and a sports drink.

Delia holds up the oversized tote I hauled up here with me. "No need. Knowing Nessa, there's a hangover kit in here. Which of the many little bags in here is designated for a situation like this?"

"The bright pink one," I groan as I wipe my mouth with the washcloth.

"Hang tight." She digs through the bag, pulling out cubes for sewing kits, headaches, bumps and bruises, and extra cards for gifts in the event that someone forgets. "Good lord, Nessa. What do you have in case of a nuclear attack?"

"That's the shiny one," I joke. "Zombie apocalypse is neon green." I hang my head and heave a sigh. "Fuck it." Glasses on again, I pull my shoulders back. "Don't tell Stef because today's not about me, but—"

The door creaks open, cutting off my confession, and the bride-to-be appears.

"Don't tell Stef what? That you and Matty drunk giggled at the bar, then stumbled into his room together? Or what happened after that?" she says, one brow arched.

All I can do is blink at her.

She huffs. "I'm a middle school teacher who's marrying another teacher. You think we don't notice things?"

Shrugging, I say, "Welp, now River doesn't have to whine about keeping it a secret, I guess. We can discuss this another time. Like never. Now go relax." I wave a dismissive hand. "Today is for you. It's your wedding day."

"True, and I also have no interest in hearing about my brother's sex life. Just, please tell me you know what you're getting into with him." Her tone is sweet, but her mouth is turned down in a concerned frown. "I love him, but he's an idiot. I don't think he takes anything seriously."

My head pounds, making it hard to keep up with the conversation.

"I don't want her to get her hopes up," Delia says. "Caleb really messed with her head. I don't want to see her heart get broken again."

"Please, we don't use the devil's name," I say, eyes closed. "As for your brother, I want to take a bath in bleach, then drink it.

This will not be happening again." Head lowered into my hands, I tune them out and wait for the room to stop spinning.

———

"FUCKING FLAWLESS." I nod, looking one last time at the work Delia did to make it look like I slept. "Damn, girl. When are you quitting your job at the bar? You need to do hair and makeup professionally. You have talent."

"As soon as the Salvatores are willing to hire me, I guess? I won't compete with the mob," she teases.

We huddle together with bouquets in hand—tiny sprays of white roses to complement Stef's dress. Her larger bouquet is full of blues and purples that coordinate perfectly with our dusty blue dresses, each a different cut to flatter our individual figures.

Thank god she didn't force me to wear something more fitting for Delia's tall, lithe figure or Lily's toned feminine curves.

The bride's American style ballgown is gorgeous, but her Maria Clara terno—the traditional Filipino sleeved bolero—is the star of the show.

In minutes, she'll head down the aisle to Lee Carter, a dead ringer for her teen TV crush. The four of us stand together for the last time as a group of single women.

I soak in the moment, so appreciative of the love these friends show me.

Stef's tan skin, the same golden-brown shade as her brothers, causes my mind to flash back to last night. But I shake the image away, determined to be present in this moment. Her deep brown eyes glow with soft tears, her hand in mine, with Delia's and Lily's joining. Somewhere in the distance, a slight click suggests the cameras are capturing our huddle.

"Delia's first," the coordinator calls.

An ethereal instrumental pop song provides the tempo for her trip down the aisle, an uplifting melody that people in the crowd mouth the words to.

At close to a foot taller than me and with dark blond waves, Delia is every bit a Barbie at first glance. Given her stature and figure, she's in a silky column gown with a cowl neck and halter strap. She's stunning. Her old Hollywood style waves and the deep side part add to the vintage glamour.

"Nessa's next. Then the maid of honor—" The coordinator's brows lift, and she scans the space beside me, where Lily was just standing.

I turn in a slow circle, finding her peeking through a panel of windows to one side of the doors. Her chocolate eyes are glassy as she watches the men lined up by the altar. I pop my arm around her waist and lean in. "You got this."

When she turns in to hug me, her off-the-shoulder sweetheart neckline sheath gown lightly swishes my toes. The thigh-high slit sweeps wide, giving her a seductive quality.

She swallows thickly, nodding, as the coordinator guides me to my place. Like I practiced last night, I walk slowly toward Delia. It's impossible not to take in the splendor of the room as I go. The men all look incredible in their navy suits. Of course, Mateo has his eyes locked on me. The millionaire playboy who has never committed to anyone or anything looks like a delicious mistake I can't afford to repeat.

As I walk in time with the music, his attention burns into me. His smirk is wicked, and the wink he gives me makes my heart flutter in a way it shouldn't. After everything with Caleb, I've decided the best way to protect myself from being fooled again is to maintain my independence. Shoulders back, bouquet low, I glide to the music and do the only thing that comes naturally to me. I plaster on a bright smile and focus on the task at hand.

four

Mateo

2 Months Ago | Summer

MANHATTAN IN JULY is sticky and humid, leaving my clothes fitting a bit too snugly. Stuck in something ill-fitting really sums up how I feel. Even if I undo the top button, it's hard to breathe. When I moved to the city, I was fascinated by how it smelled like the dollar pizza slices sold in tiny corner shops. Now all I notice is trash sizzling on the sidewalks. The hustle of people down the streets and below, inside subway cars, used to make me feel as though I was part of something. Today, I'm positive if I stood in the middle of an intersection and screamed, I'd get honked at and nothing else. Over time, or maybe it happened overnight, every part of the city experience I once celebrated faded. By no longer looking up in fascination, I'm confronted by one facet after another of a blurry puzzle I used to fit into.

Nothing about New York City feels the same since my night with Nessa. Too often, I stare longingly at her contact in my phone, trying to concoct reasons to text her. I went out. Tried to meet other women. Get my mind off her. But all I did was compare them to her, noting all the ways they didn't measure up. I don't even recognize myself anymore.

Tonight, I'm once again entertaining clients to court business for someone else's benefit. As I sit in a high-quality leather armchair, waiting for this guy and his crew to arrive, I pull out my phone to dig further into his background. As I peruse his social media, I come across a photo that instantly has my blood running cold. It's her, with my client.

It's an older photo, from what I can tell. The two of them are standing in a brick courtyard. Ivy Out of My League. That's how Nessa put herself into my phone. Though based on her texts the next day, she doesn't remember. I spent the next twenty-four hours calling her Ivy.

I'm still stewing over the image when my client texts that he can't make it because the *pussy here is fire.*

Great, wonderful.

> MATEO:
>
> I don't understand how you dated him.
>
> <screenshot of Caleb Reynolds's text >
>
> He was clearly there because his daddy donated a few buildings.

I pull up the ride share app and order a car, then cash out with an extra generous tip to expense to the company.

While I wait, my phone buzzes.

I'm ecstatic that she actually replied.

> IVY:
>
> Satan's Bikini Waxer?

> MATEO:
>
> You dated him <eyes emoji>

> IVY:
>
> Ugh, don't remind me.

I'm too tipsy to restrain myself the way I probably should, so once I'm in the back seat of the car, I switch over to FaceTime.

To my absolute shock, she picks up, though by the way she's glaring, she's not thrilled about it. "Video too now? Why?"

"I'm happy to see you too, Ivy." My grin stretches from ear to ear, I think. I'm feeling the buzz a little more as we speed down FDR parkway.

"Cute." With a roll of her eyes, she props her phone up on what looks like her desk, if the papers and the laptop are any indication.

I point over her shoulder at the framed diplomas proudly displaying the name of the infamous school, making her scowl.

As if she thinks I'll believe she's unbothered by my teasing, she removes the claw clip from her hair and shakes out the long, golden tresses.

Damn, I love getting a reaction out of her. There's no stopping my preening now. The smug satisfaction on my face and tilt of my head are visible in the tiny video chat bubble, making me realize that I haven't felt this way since the last time I saw her. My stomach flutters and my skin tingles at the memories that flit through my mind. If I allowed myself to really think about how long this kind of happiness has been missing from my life, I could admit it's her voice that's brought it on and not the liquor.

With a shake of my head, I will those thoughts away.

"Why are you calling? Looks like you had so much fun with Satan. But were you not able to close tonight?"

Her irritation makes my pulse speed up, and an uncomfortable heat washes over me. Just thinking about Caleb and his brush-off makes me anxious about work tomorrow.

If I can keep her talking until I get inside, maybe I can force it out of my mind for good tonight. Maybe I can get a good night's sleep. Or maybe I'll do what I've done every night since Stef's wedding. I'll lay on my back, staring at the ceiling, telling myself not to think about my night with Nessa until I can't stop thinking about it and fuck my fist.

Mind fuzzy, I struggle to find a topic that doesn't involve her fuckhead of an ex. Finally, I clear my throat and blurt, "I need your help."

Anything to keep her on the phone.

"Was the STI test positive? Just go back to the doctor and get medication."

I let out a sardonic laugh. "You're hilarious. No, I'm trying to get Stef and Lee to house-swap with me. I'm over the city. If I can get your buddy Caleb—"

"Satan," she hisses. "We do not invoke the devil's name. Ever. And he's not my buddy."

"Fine. Anyway, if I can get him to close this Park Ave deal, then I can take a sabbatical and give Stef my place."

"So you said," she sasses.

God, I love that sassy mouth. Damn. The things I want to do to it again.

"Keep being mean to me. It just turns me on." I wink.

She rolls her eyes. "Do you need something, or can I go?" The sass is off the charts.

"Nah, I'm good." I give her a big, dopey grin. "You go. Try to have some fun again, Ivy."

"I'm hanging up now," she singsongs an instant before the screen turns black.

For several minutes after the call ends, my heart continues to beat wildly. Every cell in my body is wide awake and adrenaline courses through me like I've just finished a marathon. This woman is clearly igniting that spark I've been missing. I'll do everything I can to be near her and find my drive again.

———

FOR WEEKS, it's been one canceled meeting after another. Don't get me started on all the unanswered emails. Still, I haven't broken into the Reynolds party circle. I've tried my usual tactics—event tickets, the hottest reservations, private entrance to pop-ups—but nothing is working. It's impossible to impress a person whose name has always opened every door.

I've discussed this in biweekly meetings. I've tried to pass this up the line. However, according to Chip Merrick, in my position here, there's no reason I should need support. Apparently, I'm senior enough that even after I have checked every box on our list of standard approaches and come up with several of my own, I'm still expected to make it happen.

When I asked for someone with more seniority to reach out, providing a draft message with the request it wasn't to Chip's liking, so I had to revise it. Again and again, he sent it back with suggestions, and before he could approve it, he was gone for two weeks on vacation. Now, it's time for another check-in, but, fuck, am I over this.

I'm done working for a man who confuses teachable moments with hanging me out to dry. I'm over sitting in these crowded, loud, overpriced places, praying that a tool like Caleb Reynolds will bother to show up.

I'm burned out. The magic of New York City has evaporated. I no longer know what I'm chasing or why. I'm so lost and defeated that I'm about to burn my life to the ground just to feel something again.

"Boss man," I say as I knock on his open doorframe.

He nods and waves me in, and I close the door behind me.

I drop into a chair and heave out a long breath. "I need a fucking break, Chip."

"Matty, you close this pending deal with Reynolds, and you can take the rest of the year off for all I fucking care. Just get them to sign over the Park Ave luxury apartments, and I'll sign off on your sabbatical."

My gut twists. "It's not going to happen. He's dodged me all summer, and nothing we've put in front of him is good enough in his mind." It kills me to do it, but I know when to fold.

"That's not the can-do attitude we expect around here." He straightens and laces his fingers on top of his desk. "This negativity isn't good for team morale. Let's review what you've done again."

I shake my head. "We need to pivot. Maybe put someone else on this account and let me try my hand elsewhere. I've exhausted all my resources."

"That isn't your decision to make. I don't understand why you are giving up."

Blood simmering, I grit my teeth. "In the past, you've let other people take a rotation when the Reynoldses weren't cracking. Why not me?"

"This isn't about anyone else. It's about you and only you." His tone is now sharp.

"I'm just say—"

"No. You're not. If you can't do this, then you're done." His acidic words land hard, the vein in his forehead protruding. "You have one hour to clean out your office and get out. You've been making excuses for months now. And this pathetic attempt to cast blame on others? It's beyond unacceptable."

His anger has cooled to ice.

"And don't forget about the noncompete clause in your contract. If you so much as sneeze in the direction of my clients, I will bury you in legal fees. You're done in this city. Now, get the fuck out of my office."

Numb with shock, I stand. It's an out-of-body experience. Like I'm hovering in the corner, watching the scene unfold. Finally, I find enough sense to say, "Please forward all the parting documents to my legal team. We'll look them over and get back to you."

With that, I stride from the room and pack up my things.

WITH A GROWL, I slam the bank box down on the marble island in the penthouse I've come to loathe for how cold and empty it feels and take inventory of my life.

I can easily live off the dividends of my investments, thank fuck. I can thank Susan Santos-Manolo for that. She would never let me spend recklessly. I have everything I need. Yet I have nothing I want.

Everything is going to be fine.

I repeat the phrase, willing myself to believe it. It's no use. It's overpowered by other voices. Voices that remind me that I'm nothing but a good-time person, not a serious person. It started in high school; I never got great grades, but I excelled in sports and with friends. This continued in college and then through my twenties in the city. Now, in my early thirties, it's become frustrating.

I might have plenty now, but the blue-collar kid raised by immigrants in a small town is still in here. Maybe if I can find him again, those stuck feelings will go away.

Maybe some interaction with Nessa will help. Just being around her energizes me.

Fuck yeah. I know exactly how to pull this off.

MATEO:

Did you find an apartment yet?

STEF:

Not any good ones. There are a few maybes on the list.

MATEO:

How does a semester-long house-swap sound?

STEF:

Like the start of a Christmas movie or a bad
prank, TBH.

MATEO:

I'm taking time off between jobs and don't want
to stay with Mom.

It would be a huge favor to me.

STEF:

Lee and I can live in your penthouse? For free?
As a favor to you?

MATEO:

Y U P

STEF:

Okay, twist my arm. We're in.

five
Mateo

Present | Labor Day Weekend

IVY:

I am NOT pretending to be your girlfriend.

MATEO:

Who said anything about pretending?

IVY:

OK. I am not your girlfriend.

MATEO:

Can we please talk?

AS NESSA RUNS OFF, I shake my head.

What the hell, man? Did I really say *pubes*? In public? The man *does* send texts to potential business associates using phrases like *pussy is fire*, so maybe it's fitting.

What was probably more ridiculous was the way I invaded his personal space, jaw and muscles tense like I was about to brawl, and blurted out a claim to a woman who has no interest in me.

Caleb sneers, "Trouble with that one is common. Don't waste your time."

"Well, you are the expert." Though I'm referring to all the time I wasted on the asshole, I keep my tone light.

It's obvious by his cocky smirk that he doesn't catch on.

Jim weaves through the crowd, ignoring elderly constituents vying for his attention, focus fixed on us.

At the same time, another man steps into the group, looking as formidable as always. The six-foot-four brick house of a man crosses his arms over his chest, causing every muscle to show under his fitted Peacock Springs Fire Department shirt.

Head dropped back, I bark out a laugh. I have been in town for less than a day, and already, I can claim responsibility for a fight between Jim and Liam. Classic.

"Caleb, meet Liam Kelly. He's one of Peacock Springs' Bravest, and my oldest friend," I say, using an overly friendly tone. "You've probably heard about him from his brother."

"Can't say I have." Caleb assesses Jim, eyes narrowed.

"Hey, little brother," Liam says, pulling Jim in for a side hug.

"We share a birthday," his twin grumbles as he bats him away, surreptitiously side-eyeing me.

This is so perfect. This is what I need. Something comfortable and familiar.

"Why don't we get out of here?" Jim says, steering Caleb away from Liam and me. "We can go over any outstanding business before your trip back to the city."

As they depart, we smile and wave, shouting, "Bye! Have fun! Be safe, sweetheart!" among other motherly phrases, until we're laughing raucously.

"Come on, Matty." Liam slaps my back. "Let's help Lily collect the folding chairs."

He heads for the rolling cart while I start folding.

"Did you tell me you were coming tonight?" he asks as he slides two chairs onto the arms that hold them in place on the cart.

"No. Surprise! I'm back, baby." I toss both arms out and wiggle my fingers.

"What do you mean 'I'm back'?" He mimics my playful tone.

"I mean Stef is a genius who's going back to school for her PhD." I give a half-hearted eye roll.

"Nerd Alert," Liam teases.

"Right." I slide two more chairs onto the cart and dust off my hands, scanning the cleared-out room.

"You guys are lifesavers. Thank you," Lily squeals as she steps out of her closet-sized office.

"Any time, Lils. I'm here for the rest of the year, and I'm always happy to help you."

"Oh, wow. That's amazing. I'm so happy to hear that," she stammers. "Does that—oh my god." She huffs like she's annoyed with her inability to string a coherent thought together.

"Stef and Lee took the penthouse, and while she's living large, I'm going to house-sit for her." I shrug.

"Oh, I love it. We're so lucky to have you home."

Her excited tone and constant motion make her hard to follow, so I'm surprised when she wraps her arms around me in a friendly hug.

"Also, goodbye." She makes a shooing motion with her hands. "I want to get out of here, and I'm sure my dog is anxious for a walk. You have to leave so I can lock up."

With placating smiles and quick goodbyes, we make our way onto the street. When we hit the center square, I stop and turn slowly, taking in the full downtown view. Instantly, my body relaxes. Just being here is alleviating some of the tension I accumulated in the city.

"Are you on duty tonight?" I ask when I find Liam observing me like I'm a lost tourist.

"No, but I was going to work out before heading home. What's up?"

"Can I join?" The words are tentative. It's ridiculous, really. I've known this guy my whole life. I know it's fine.

Liam takes a half step closer and puts a hand on my forehead. With a slight humming sound, he grabs my wrist and stares at his watch like he's taking my pulse.

"Why the hell are you acting like such a weirdo?" He drops my arm. "Come on, let's go."

NESSA STILL HASN'T RESPONDED by the time Liam and I are finished. My little white lie means I need to make things right, so I try to call, but after a single ring, it goes to voicemail. My shoulders slump in response. Shit. I should not let a declined call fuck with my head.

Before I can pocket my phone and force my thoughts elsewhere, the device buzzes in my hand.

Poison Ivy, my adjustment to her contact, flashes on the screen, and my heart rate picks up.

"Sorry," she says when I accept the call. "I've been busy with my parents. I thought it was my alarm."

"No worries. I'm leaving the fire station. How 'bout I swing by to walk you home?"

"Fine."

"Great, give me a couple of minutes, okay?"

When she doesn't respond, I pull the phone away and realize the call has been disconnected. She's back to normal, I see.

Even so, I smile. She can act as unaffected as she wants, but I've gotten under her skin.

The historic American colonial, with its large rectangular façade, is beautiful, if not a little worn. Its entrance is flanked by symmetrical lines of windows, the shutters of which are embellished with faded black horse-drawn carriages. The weathered storm door has a matching buggy emblem too. It's frozen in time, looking well-maintained but at least as old as I am.

The part of my brain that's always evaluating properties takes over, immediately working to assess the property value.

This house is at least two stories, maybe three if the windows at the top aren't just dormers. Though it could also be a walkable attic. I'm examining the immaculate landscaping of the Rabins' lot and the late summer blooms when the storm door slams.

"Why are you skulking around?" Nessa stomps down the brick walkway, full of fuck-off attitude.

There she is. My favorite firecracker. "I was just about to knock." I flash a winning grin her way.

The huff she lets out reminds me of the loch ness monster. Hmm. I'll stow that nickname away for later. Along with the sound comes a realization that I'd let her pull me under and drown me any day.

six
Nessa

"I'M NOT PRETENDING to date you." Hands on my hips, I lift my chin.

"I'm going to convince you to date me." He winks. The asshole *winks*. "Don't worry about that part."

Head tossed back, I groan. God, why won't he just go away?

"Satan is determined," he says. "Liam said Jim's already collected political donations. So, while I'm no 'esteemed billionaire'"—he uses air quotes, the humor softening me slightly—"I am real competition for him."

That's all it takes to go rigid again. Competition?

As if he can read my mind, he shrinks in on himself a little. "I mean when it comes to the land deal part."

I hum and head for the sidewalk. "You're really serious about that?"

With a nod, he matches my stride. "Growing up, I struggled with school. I'm sure you know that. But in New York, things just clicked. I get when and where to reinvest. So I've been careful with my money. And I figured that if I intervened when it comes to you, that might encourage him to keep his distance. You know? Because word is he's hell-bent on talking to you too."

A shiver racks through me. No thank you.

"What's wrong?" He surveys me, his brows pulled low in concern.

I stop short and cross my arms over my chest. "I don't want Caleb anywhere near me. I have nothing left to say to him. His family members are antisemitic turds. He cheated. All the time. Even while he tried to convince me to drop out of school and marry him. Like it was a tradeoff. I'd be extended the honor of being part of his family and allowed to enjoy the luxuries that come with the name—things I didn't even want—and in return, he could have extra-curricular sex with whoever the fuck he wanted. Bringing up your wealth does no good if you're trying to win me over. When I left Boston, he started to play games like this. It's just a power move. He'll get bored..."

I huff a breath to shut myself up. Shit. I said far more than I meant to. More than I've even told my friends.

"So," he says, giving the respect of not responding to my rant, "I thought, why not keep up appearances? Stick with the *stay away from my girl* message? Men like him, who don't listen to women, will listen to other men. It's shitty, I know, but I can help."

Peering up at me through thick dark lashes, with his hands in the pockets of his black jeans, he looks almost boyish. "Common enemies have made for stranger bedfellows, Ivy."

That's where he loses me. Scoffing, I pull up short. "Do not expect to get anywhere near a bed with me again, jackass." Taking off again, I pick up my pace. "I. Am. Not. Dating. You. We'll have to keep in touch to work on the Sunflower Fest. That's it."

His expression is distant, his smile half-hearted. "Whatever you say. How about I take you to dinner one night this week? To discuss the festival."

My stomach sinks. Dammit. We really do have to plan. "How about I come to you? Although, I'm thinking it would be better to just 'break up'"—with a grin, I throw back his air quotes—"with you publicly and be done with both of you."

"Sorry, babe. You're going to have to stick this festival thing out." With a smirk, he places a hand on my lower back and steers me toward home.

———

"CORDELIA DANIELLE SHANE, get your ass out here. Right. Now. DEFCON, um, five? The worst one," I shout, sounding more like my mother than I'd like to admit. But the next words come out as a high-pitched whine. "I need you."

Delia is the only person I trust to play therapist for me. Except, of course, my actual therapist.

Emerging slowly from her bedroom, she rubs her eyes, then takes in my disastrous state—hair up in a messy pile on my head, bra strap slipping below one sleeve.

"Were you mentally at town hall tonight?" I whine, pulling out one of the island stools.

Delia opens the fridge and then faces me, holding a bottle of white wine.

I give a soft nod, accepting the gesture.

She pours two glasses and slides one across the island, lips twitching. "Maybe? I was physically there for a while, but I snuck out to go to bed early since it's my night off. That plan was foiled when you came in screeching my full name, *Mom*."

I drop my head to the island and groan. "I suck. Sorry. Do you want to go back to bed?"

She lifts a shoulder. "You've got me here. Hit me with it. It's not like you to cry wolf."

"Caleb and Mateo are competing to buy Grant Morgan's properties and the undeveloped farmland on the north side of town."

"See?" She points a finger at me, eyes wide. "Actual. Serious. Shit."

For a long moment, we sit in the silence, sipping our drinks. Delia knows by now that I plan my words carefully.

"The good news is that the dick confetti was the final straw," I say.

Dick confetti, as in the package we sent to Lily's ex-husband and his wife, making sure they understood what a bag of dicks they were for hurting Lily.

Our mutual acceptance that some stories aren't shared bonded us. Sure, it means she has no context for why Mateo has been on my shit list since I was fourteen but it also means I accept that her middle school falling out with Landan Sherman is good enough. Tack on that Landan dated Grant but waited to sleep with him after he married Lily, she's the living embodiment of a pick-me girl.

I'd love to pry—again—but I have to let Delia come to me in her own time if I want the same courtesy. So instead, I quickly add, "I only wish I could have hit her in the face with a vibrator the way Seth got walloped at the bridal shower."

Silently, she holds out her glass, and we clink and sip quietly.

"Satan's set his target on our town for his next gentrification project. Now Mateo is my only hope to prevent personality-free houses with overpriced amenities from destroying our culture. Plus, they'll decimate anything nature-related."

"Didn't realize you were so passionately against housing expansion." Delia cocks an eyebrow.

"No, this is Satan's way of trying to get close to me. And now Mateo has swooped in, claiming he's my boyfriend, yammering about how he doesn't want to hear Caleb talking about my pubic hair styling ever again—"

"Your what?" She throws her head back and cackles.

"Yeah, um. That's where the moniker came from. You know? Satan's Bikini Waxer? He was so obsessed with 'aesthetics,' and I was young and dumb, so I let him talk me into trying it, but it hurt." I avert my gaze, cheeks heating. Why am I suddenly the one spilling my guts?

"But I've seen you in a bikini. It's not like..." Delia huffs.

"Correct," I say. "I'm not rocking the '70s bush, but... I feel better when I look like an adult, which means I don't remove all my body hair."

"That makes sense. What the fuck is wrong with men? You're allowed to—wait, hold on. Don't distract me with beauty things. Didn't Mateo just show up? He's been here a matter of hours, and he's already telling people you're an item?"

"Yep." I sag against the cool countertop. "He thinks that by claiming me, Satan will back off. Like if he pisses around me, marking his territory, the asshole will respect it."

"Hey, even stupid gets it right sometimes." She chuckles at her own joke.

I blow out a long breath. "Mom is out of town for work, which means I need to put in extra work with Dad while also co-leading the Sunflower Fest. With Mateo. I do not have time to deal with a dick-measuring contest too."

She gives me a sympathetic smile.

Pinching the stem of my wineglass, I lower my focus to the table and clear my throat, eager to shift this conversation away from men.

"Want a sibling update? Way more interesting if you ask me," I deflect.

Delia pauses, eyeing me, but eventually nods.

"Tal has decided to use they/them pronouns."

"Good for them," she says, her tone light. "Do they plan to change their name?"

"No, Tal is a genderless name. But Dad Gabe is having a field day with semantics. His first language was gendered. The conversations are driving everyone up a wall."

Biting her lip, Delia nearly whispers, "Is your dad...?" She shakes her head and starts again. "Do you get the impression it's about the queerness of it all?"

"Oh—" I suck in a breath. "No, no. Not at all. Since going into private practice, he's focused on the legal spiderweb around parental rights for same-sex couples, legal name changes, and all kinds of affirming paperwork. This is all failed attempts to make jokes or debate for fun."

Taking a fortifying sip, I give Delia a soft, nervous smile.

"Want the tea on Shae?"

"Always." She smiles brightly.

"From the look of her socials, I'm convinced that she's back to her party girl ways. Any time I bring it up, she scoffs and moves on. She talks about her work a lot, but then it's just parties."

"Isn't she in public relations?"

Delia finishes her wine and turns to the sink, muttering.

"What was that?"

"Nothing," she says, turning back holding two glasses of tap water. "She's twenty-five, and you aren't her mom," she adds weakly.

"Yeah, but our parents basically grew up on Mars. I get every phone call. They unload every stressor on me. I do not have time to babysit Mateo too."

"Maybe you can let him babysit you." She waggles her blond brows as she sips her water.

I stand and push in my stool with a little too much force. "Maybe when you tell me the real story with Landan."

The glass hits the counter with a wallop. Mid storm-out, Delia pauses and glares at me over her shoulder. "Low blow."

"Nighty night." I wave as she heads toward her bedroom.

Eventually, I will wear her down. Something happened, and it's making me crazy. Everyone is making me crazy.

I wipe down the counters, put my cup in the dishwasher, and head to my room. There's really only one way to get myself over this and off to sleep.

I scroll through my e-reader until I find a passage in one of my favorite stories, then change into my silky nightshirt. I don't need Mateo to babysit me, or for anything else. I can take care of myself. In more than one way.

I reach into my bedside drawer for my trusty vibrator and proceed to do just that: take care of myself.

seven
Mateo

"HOW'S UNPACKING GOING?" Phone on speaker, I give myself a quick appraisal in the mirror, considering whether I should change my shirt.

"What do you want me to do with all these suits?" Lee shouts in the background.

"Improve your style? When you aren't painting and Nerd Alert isn't studying, why don't you get dressed up and take her out? I can give you a list of the best restaurants around the city."

"Thanks, but no thanks. We aren't all multi-millionaires, *my dude*. We're going to be eating ketchup sandwiches while looking out at the park through these two-story windows." He says *my dude* mockingly, and laughs silently. I love his 'little brother' stuff.

"No, we're not," my sister chides.

"She giving you the same look our mom does when she's annoyed?" I tease.

"You mean the glare and shake of her head, followed by an eye roll? Yes, she—" He yelps, and the sound is followed by a squeal, then a giggle from her.

I roll my own eyes. "I'm still here, guys. Can you keep the honeymoon antics to a minimum for a moment?"

I'm met with muffled sounds, followed by a second of silence. When the noises resume, Stef sounds closer, like she's talking directly into the device.

"Anything new going on with you?" she asks, her footsteps clicking against the wood floors.

I groan. "First, please promise me you brought your own sheets."

She barks out a laugh. "Yes, we will use our own bedding, manchild."

"Wonderful, next... have you heard from Nessa lately? She's supposed to be here soon—"

"Hope you brought your own sheets to my house, Mateo," my sister says, throwing my words back at me.

"Har-har. Yes, I also have a new mattress being delivered this week."

"No," she whines.

There's no stopping my laughter. She had to be expecting me to make upgrades.

"If you really hate it, I'll keep it. Don't worry." I shrug like she can see me.

My grandparents busted their asses to get to America, and I'm continuing the momentum, working hard to give my family nice things. It's that simple.

"So back to me." I flop down on her sitcom sofa and snag the remote. Once SportsCenter is playing on mute, I rest my socked feet on the coffee table and lean back. "Have you talked to Nessa?"

"Nope, why?" Her voice laced with hesitation.

"She hasn't told you that she's my girlfriend?"

She huffs a breath like I'm the world's biggest idiot—as usual.

"Stef, I want her to see that I've changed. I'm over picking up random women at bars. Have been since your wedding."

"Wow. You've been celibate for a whole... three months?" she says, mocking me.

43

"What counts as 'celibate'? Like, only sex, or are we talking kissing—"

Stef cries, "I take it back. TMI. Don't tell me."

With a sigh, I rough a hand down my face. *Be sincere, dude.* "I tried, hoping I'd get over her. But I couldn't close. I missed Nessa."

She lets out a long *aw*, and I have to question if I'm actually virtuous. It would be an amazing upset against that asshole Caleb to win the property bid and the girl.

"I want to start my own firm, and why not begin with the property on the north side of town? There isn't any stopping the expansion. We have a housing shortage, but we don't need to go with big, splashy, overpriced cookie-cutter houses to make things nice. Plus, Peacock Springs is my home—I'd rather the land be developed by a local than a nepotism-fueled manchild, wouldn't you?"

"You'd rather it be developed by a manchild fueled by chicken adobo from his mommy, huh?" she teases.

"Hey, you leave Mom's cooking out of this," I cry, debating whether it's too early to dig into the leftovers. "Anyway, like I was saying..." I really lay this on thick for my sister's amusement. Or my own. Same difference. "I need to know what Nessa told you about us before I see her. Spill it, girlfriend," I say, affecting a feminine lilt.

"There's no tea to spill. She thinks what she always has. That you're a dumb playboy who thinks too highly of himself and has too much money—"

"And who's amazing in bed and made her come—"

"La-la-la. I can't hear you," she shrieks. Though a moment later, her tone softens. "You're really hung up on her, aren't you?"

My heart thumps heavily in my chest. "Yeah. I am. And I'll win her over eventually. Just you wait and see."

"There's my delusionally confident big brother."

"I could do it, you know. If I wanted to." I huff. "I could be a good boyfriend. I'm a good brother, aren't I?"

44

Sighing, she finally relents. "You are a great brother. You know I tease you because I can... and also, you are an idiot."

"But a great one."

"Back to your question," she says, her tone gentle. "Nessa did not mention that the two of you are dating. More importantly, can you really outbid him? That asshole really hurt her. I'd love for someone to chase him out of town."

Chuckling, I reply. "You're in my apartment. Look around. Need I say more?"

"Touché. What comes next?"

"I'm going to make her fall in love with me."

———

MATEO:

You sure I can't take you some place nice for dinner before this meeting?

IVY:

No thanks.

MATEO:

I promise to be a gentleman.

Please <hands pressed together emoji>

IVY:

I'm tired. Let's just get this over with.

THAT LAST TEXT is like a knife to the gut. Just what every man wants to hear, that she wants to get it over with.

———

SHE'S HERE.

She's standing on the porch, her hair pulled up in two light bulb-looking knots on top of her head, though the ends cascade down her back.

Yeah, I'm studying her from the window. So what?

With a steadying breath, I open the door and step to the side, inviting her in.

She unbuttons her gray peacoat, and I take it from her and hang it in the front closet.

"It's gotten chilly so fast. I feel like this happens every September. One day, it's summer, and the next, boom, pull out the winter gear."

Her voice is casual, flippant, like she's trying to come across as unaffected by my presence. But her outfit gives her away. And damn, this girl is absolutely trying to kill me. She's wearing a soft pink silk slip dress with an oversized light gray cable-knit cardigan wrapped around her shoulders. She's been here a million times—it's my sister's house, after all—so out of habit, she bends down and unties her combat boots, giving me a view of the seam on the back of her sheer black tights and lifting her skirt ever so slightly. Fuck me; seriously. Please fuck me.

"So." I choke back the need clawing up my throat. The last thing I want is to come on too strong. My goal tonight is to impress this woman. "What's on the agenda tonight?"

"First, dinner. Where do you want to order from? Or, I'm a great cook," she practically purrs.

Fuck, she's cruel. I inhale, willing my dick to stand down.

"Cooking involves knives, though, and I would hate to slip and stab you if you got too annoying. Though that would get rid of this pesky problem of being around you too much." She flutters her lashes and pouts her glossy lips.

A hearty laugh erupts from my lungs. This girl is going to be the end of me, and I'm here for it. Fuck, I'm down bad.

"There's a new spot a few towns over. We could go out," I prod.

For a split second, her confident mask drops, and uncertainty flickers behind her eyes. As quickly as it appeared, though, it's gone.

"Forget it," I say with a dismissive wave. "How about pizza? I have Mariano's pulled up online already. Do you want toppings? Apps? Zerts?"

She screws up her face in disgust. "Apps? Zerts? You can't say the full words?"

"You don't know the show?" I clutch my chest, incensed. How is this possible?

"Oh lord, here we go again. Mateo's latest obsession. Please enlighten me. But wait until the pizza is here. Whatever you get will be fine. Plus a small house salad."

I cock a brow. "Anything?"

"Whatever." She inspects her nails, looking bored.

"Anchovies?"

"Why not?" She finally meets my eyes, her expression deadpan. "When we visited my grandparents, they ordered theirs with tuna and corn. Apparently, it's popular there. You cannot gross me out, dude. I've had to eat corn and tuna pizza."

My stomach rolls. Yuck. "Okay, so pineapple and ham it is."

With a lift of one shoulder, she blinks once. "Like I said—whatever is fine."

Half an hour later, the delivery guy has dropped off two pizzas, one with ham and pineapple and the other classic Margherita, along with her house salad.

We put on a rerun and dig in. Nessa's legs are tucked under her on the couch, her skirt falling above the knee and exposing a hint of her satiny thighs. With any luck, having a full belly will brighten her mood. When the third episode wraps and the *do you wish to continue watching?* screen loads, it's time to try again.

"What do we have to do for the festival?" I ask.

She eyes the giant binder sitting on the coffee table. Jim, generously, dropped the massive thing off earlier. "I assume it's in there. Have you not looked yet?"

Is she seriously irritated that I haven't read the binder? It's just a binder. We've been to this thing a million times.

"No. Why would I? Why do what's already been done before?" I smirk.

She leans forward to grab the enormous thing, the movement causing her sweater to glide down her shoulder and expose her creamy skin.

A cluster of dark brown birthmarks peek out, and a hazy memory comes to me. I'm back in the hotel room with her that night, with her silky slip dress in my hands, my body pressed to hers against the hotel door as we fumble with the keys. Kissing her along each of the four spots, asking her whether she realized how sexy they were. Asking if she knew about the old wives' tales, how they mean she's a take-charge person. The moment we stepped inside, she took the comment as an invitation to take her dress off. She stayed like that, in her underwear and heels, making jokes and verbal jabs, while touching me, kissing me. The most delicious mix of teasing.

I shake my head and stand, yanking on the collar of my shirt. "I need a water. Want one?" I open the freezer and stick my head in farther than necessary, desperate to cool down.

Okay, time to try and get some points on the board.

I fill two glasses, then snag the ball cap off the island, pull it on, and head back to the living room, turning my usual swagger up a notch. Once I've set our waters on gray and white marble coasters, I slow my movements to ensure she's looking at me, then I straighten and slowly turn the cap backward.

Her pupils dilate. Dope, the playing field is leveling out.

Her sweater still hangs off one shoulder, the cut of the dress beneath it highlighting the ample curve of her breasts. It's impossible not to look.

Before I can force my gaze away, her expression turns to a glare. It's more than that, really. The woman straight-up incinerates me with her eyes.

"So," she says, adjusting her sweater. "It looks like we should make sure that the usual groups plan to set up their booths, which is just a simple email. Can you handle that?"

Does she really think I can't complete such a simple task? I have built a portfolio worth hundreds of millions of dollars, but when I'm in Peacock Springs, I'm just Stef's dumb older brother. As if the kids here were so smart. They called me Jeremy Lin. First of all, resembling a pro basketball player is not an insult. And second, they couldn't even tease me in a way that made sense. That guy is Taiwanese. I'm Filipino. Not the same place.

With a chuckle, I settle on the couch. "I can try, but you'll have to help me find the website."

"Only know how to navigate to sports and things in incognito mode?" She smirks.

"I knew you were still thinking about my sexual preferences."

A flush creeps from her chest up her neck and into her cheeks.

"I see what you're playing at, coming here in this sweet, flirty little dress." I skim a finger lightly over one thin strap, and her breath hitches.

"We can go as slow as you want. Tease me all you like, but you already know..." I angle in and bring my mouth to her ear. "I like when you tease me. And I'm patient. You'll be back, and until then, I'll be here. Sending emails." It takes everything in me not to kiss her on the cheek and instead simply lift the binder from her lap.

With that, I turn away with a silent prayer that I've left her wanting more. If only a tiny bit.

eight

Nessa

IF HE THINKS I can't tell what flirtatious game he's playing, he's mistaken. Time to level up.

I pull my shoulders back and, being sure my chest brushes his, slide off the couch. As I strut to the door, I peer over my shoulder and give him a tiny wave. "Thanks for dinner, Mateo." I slip one foot into a boot, then the other. "I look forward to seeing those very professional emails from you."

I step out into the chilly evening, leaving my coat unbuttoned. The rush of cold air is exactly what I need after that moment.

As I start for home, I whip out my phone.

SISTER CHAT [NESSA, SHAE, TAL]

NESSA:

> Tal, should we change this chat name? Sibling Chat already exists, but Shua is part of that group.

TAL CHANGED THE CHAT NAME TO JOSH-FREE ZONE
SHAE:

> He's going to shit a brick if he sees that.

SHAE CHANGED THE CHAT NAME TO SHUA-
FREE ZONE
TAL CHANGED THE CHAT NAME TO JOSH-
FREE ZONE
SHAE CHANGED THE CHAT NAME TO SHUA-
FREE ZONE
TAL CHANGED THE CHAT NAME TO JOSH-
FREE ZONE
NESSA CHANGED THE CHAT NAME TO 18+ SIBS

NESSA:

You two can fight over his name another time. I
need your help with Mom.

TAL:

Not it. Aba will insist on going into a grammar
story for me, and I have no patience for his shit
right now.

SHAE:

Tagging in <high five emoji>

TAL:

<prayer hands emoji>

SHAE:

I got you, Tall

SHAE:

Tall

SHAE:

T A L

SHAE:

Damn it, why doesn't autocorrect know my own
sister's name?

NESSA:

Sibling

TAL:

Sibling

51

SHAE:

Ugh... I'm going to stop fucking things up someday, I promise. Just... not tonight. Okay, Tally Wally?

TAL:

<black heart emoji>

U R my favorite hot mess, Shae.

AS I'M ABOUT to put my phone away, it vibrates in my hand.

BAD IDEA:

Admit it. That was fun.

I'm fighting a smile as another message appears. This one instantly wipes the expression from my face and sends a shudder through me.

SATAN'S BIKINI WAXER:

Loving the coquettish look, babe.

Why don't you come over and talk with me? I'm staying at the Bumble Bee.

I roll my eyes at his intentional misnaming of the Honeybee Inn. I will not be goaded into a reply. If I give an inch, he'll take miles. And years of my life. I've been down this road before; his reasonable side, the innocuous request that is hard to say no to. However, once I drop the boundaries it's taken ages to build, he's a snowball down a mountain. I won't let the avalanche crush me again. Not with him. Not with any man.

I pull the sides of my coat together over my torso and continue on. What have I posted on social recently that could have him calling me coquettish? I have been leaning into this trend a little.

Maybe that's all he means? Maybe I'm reading too deeply into a casual comment.

Or maybe I'm not. Because just then, a familiar silver sports car passes me, slowing. It turns, looking like it would be circling back. But before it can pull around again, a luxury SUV slows beside me, its window lowering.

"Get in the car," Mateo calls, looking far too good in that backward cap for my liking.

I groan. "Did someone forget to tell me it's jackass night?"

"Get in. It's going to storm any second."

Head tipped back, I survey the clouds overhead. They do look a little angry. "Don't worry, I'm a wicked bitch, emphasis on the *b*. I won't melt."

"Nessa, please." His voice drops lower. His protective tone is deeper and commanding, unfamiliar yet comfortable. It's like wearing a man's hoodie. The shudder that follows is nothing like the one that hit me at the sight of Caleb's text. This one is primal and confusing.

Looking in the open window, I chide him. "You'd kill anyone who treated Stef this way."

He sighs, his expression going serious. "I got a cryptic text from Caleb. I was worried about you."

With a huff, I round his SUV and climb in. "What did yours say?"

"Mine? Does that mean you got one too?" The hissed question reveals his panic. "Answer me, knucklehead," he says, sounding slightly more comfortable now that I'm in the car.

"Knucklehead?" Chuckling, I set my bag on the floor between my feet. I pull the door shut and reach for my seat belt. "Okay, talk."

"He is a creep. He said if you were really my girl, you wouldn't be walking home alone at night. Dressed this way." He grazes my wrist, continuing on to my palm, taking his time examining each of my fingers. With a long breath out, he places my hand over the gearshift, then rests his on top.

"His text to me was about how I looked too," I admit, flustered enough to let my guard down. "Shouldn't I call the police or something? Most of the stalking victims I've seen in the hospital clinic..." I press my lips together, leaving it at that. My patients' lives are just that. Theirs. It's not my place to share.

Mateo lifts his hand from mine and uses those same light touches across my jaw. He turns my face toward him and winks—like actually acts like this is a normal gesture for a grown-ass man to make—then leans in.

He buries his face in my hair, his lips mere millimeters from my ear. His breath is a soft puff as he giggles.

"I think that asshole just drove by and saw you looking pissy as you got in the car. Then he saw us kissing and making up. I'm telling you, girl, you might be book smart, but I know people. He's not only fucking with you; he's taunting me."

My stomach sinks. "What do you mean?"

Pulling his hat off, he leans back, then he scrubs a hand down his face. "I gave Stef and Lee my place in the city so she wouldn't have to worry about paying rent while she's at school. They're already on a tight budget, and I did really well at Merrick Paul. Like... well, like there are a lot of commas in my bank balance, okay? I have real estate holdings all over the country that continue to pay monthly returns. While I liked working on large-scale deals, it was exhausting. I asked to take a sabbatical. My boss told me I could, but only after I closed a Park Ave deal with the Reynolds Group. It's why I asked about him this spring. Caleb was the person I needed to wine and dine to get the deal signed, but he dodged me all summer. Ultimately, when I couldn't close, I couldn't take a leave. So I quit."

"Quit?" My nose wrinkles. Something smells fishy.

"Semantics." He waves a dismissive hand.

I cross my arms over my chest, but when I feel my breasts rise,

I uncross them. Brow furrowed, I correct him. "So you were fired."

"Mutually beneficial termination of working arrangement," he counters. "When I found out that he was poking around here, I couldn't believe the... the... what the fuck is that word?"

"Audacity?"

He shakes his head. "Nah, that doesn't sound right. Whatever. He's a dickhead. I hate him as much as you do."

My stomach twists and my head pounds. Rubbing my temples, I quietly say, "Doubtful."

"Well, he's clearly fucking with us both, but I'm not backing down. I'm here to keep you, and this town, safe from that asshole."

I suck in a breath at that admission.

Yes, Mateo is gorgeous. Yes, he was great in bed. But that was it. I can't stand him, and I don't trust him. Yet goose bumps erupted along every inch of my skin in response to his statement, not to mention the heat pooling low in my belly.

It's hormones. And proximity. We've spent too much time together. Nobody protects me. I protect people. It's not real. This cannot be real.

"How do you plan to do that, exactly, Matty?" I ask, desperate to focus on anything to slow the flutters.

He holds up a finger. "You are going to date me." A second finger. "We are going to wow the town with the best Sunflower Fest ever." A third. "The Morgans will accept my offer." His lips curl in a wicked smile. "I am going to be a hometown hero, and you'll be swept off your feet. And you better believe nothing will stop me from succeeding. It's only a matter of time before you see it, brainiac."

"So we're just like Pinky and the Brain," I chuckle.

He squeezes my hand, which is still draped over the gearshift. "Well, Brain, what do you say? What do you want to do tonight?"

This is not supposed to be so endearing. With a roll of my

eyes, I give in and finish the cartoon catchphrase, my voice squeaking as I say, "Try to take over the world?"

"Atta girl. Now let me get you home." He signals and pulls onto the quiet street, and two minutes later, he's pulling into my driveway.

When I grasp the door handle, he clutches my wrist and yanks my hand away. Then he climbs out and jogs around the front of the SUV. On my side now, he opens the door with an over-the-top bow.

Tipping an invisible cap, he says, "Milady."

And I can't help the tiny laugh that escapes from my lips.

Oh fuck, my head and hormones just declared war.

nine
Mateo

"FINE, I'LL READ THE ASSIGNMENT," I say while flipping open the textbook-thick binder on the coffee table.

As I skim the contents, one thing is immediately clear: I was correct—nearly nothing has changed. The vendor list for the Sunflower Fest could have been written in 1985. And when I turn another yellowed page and read the date, a chuckle escapes my lips. September 23,1985.

Prudence Cleary still owns the tea and tarot shop.

Meanwhile, the Salvatores, rumored mafia family, own the salon, Curl Up & Dye, as well as the butcher shop and mechanic garage.

Landan Sherman's mom, Amelia, still runs the Honeybee Inn with her best friend.

River Hendrix is the latest to run The Featherweight. His girlfriend Lily Long took over the dance studio.

Pippa Whitter, who is my age, and her younger brother Seth—Stef's age—are listed as the bookstore co-owners. Grabbing my phone, I tap out a text.

MATEO:

Hey, lil broski, I need the dirt on Pages. Who is in charge? <photo of business list>

LEE:

Both, but Seth is attached. Pip does a bunch of traveling. But I'd include her in emails if I were you.

MATEO:

Sweet. Anything else I should know about?

LEE:

Aren't you getting the Peacock Springer text chain of town gossip?

It has been quiet. Did they take me off because we moved?

MATEO:

Did they take you off? How will you survive without your gossip texts?

LEE:

<eyes emoji>

MATEO:

<eyes emoji>

I KNOCK out the entire list of returning vendors with hours to spare before Nessa gets out of work, so I figure I'll surprise her by getting proactive. I follow the socials of several counties surrounding Peacock Springs as well as small businesses and groups, checking for connections. I'm working on finding an in with my favorite local garage band, Ishtar's Temple, when my phone rings.

I straighten and stretch my back, then pick up the device, grinning when *Poison Ivy* flashes on the screen. It's only four. I figured I wouldn't hear from her for at least another hour. It's probably a pocket dial. Regardless, I pick up.

As I raise the phone to my ear, she's grumbling.

"I can't believe I'm fucking calling him for help, but"—she gasps—"ugh, oh fuck. Hello."

"Hello there, killer. What can I do for you?" I tease.

"My car. It's dead. It's a million years old, the windows still have to actually be rolled down by hand, and it's got a cassette tape player, but it's mine, dammit. And it's dead. Gone. And I'm stranded at the stupid clinic in Pennsylvania. I haven't had luck with a rideshare, and I..." She clears her throat, and her next words come out quickly and quietly, as if they're painful. "I need help."

Grinning, I pocket my wallet and keys, though I can't help but tease her.

"Sorry, what was that last part? I couldn't quite hear you." I suppress a chuckle as I step into my motorcycle boots. Once I've slipped on my favorite royal blue bomber jacket and coordinating baseball cap, I step out and close the door quietly.

"I. Need. Help," she grits through her teeth.

"Oh, Ivy. Why didn't you just say so? Do you want me to look up the bus schedule for you?" I slide into the driver's seat and thank my remote start for not giving anything away.

"You're the worst," she grumbles.

A thrill zips up my spine. "Don't stress, gorgeous. I'm on my way," I say as the phone switches to Bluetooth and the plinking of the turn signal gives away that I'm in the car. There's a tense silence when the perfect distraction hits me.

"Is that my name in your phone? The worst?"

"No."

"Is it Best I Ever Had?"

"Ugh, gross. No."

"Number One Pussy-Eater with a trophy emoji?"

She snorts, the sound making the phone line crackle. "Yep. How did you know? But it's written in emojis. So it's the weird laughing cat face, a tongue, and the trophy. A few gold medals too."

I can't help but laugh along. It's true that my tongue does not disappoint.

"But really," she says, "it's just a picture of the desert, because when I think of you, I dry up."

Her snappy retort is missing its usual heat, betraying her increased anxiety, so I switch to a soothing tone.

"Hey, Nessie, I'm already on the way. Just tell me what name you saved me under in your contacts. Since you know you're Ivy in mine. Are just as creative for yourself?"

She exhales, then mumbles in a language I don't understand. Finally, she says, "Brain emoji, trash can emoji."

"That's not it. You don't actually think I'm stupid. Don't do that." What others think of my intellect may be an insecurity of mine, but I know better. "No, you want to call me a man whore. Or some other sex-positive passive-aggressive term."

"You're right. It's the…" Her hesitation gives enough space for my heartbeat to skyrocket.

"It's what?" The question nudges her along and she rushes out a reply.

"I was going for a germs emoji joke, and then I couldn't do it. Doesn't feel right to tease about STIs—"

"Something I am regularly tested for and currently do not have, and I've shown you the paperwork. Don't forget," I interject before this can linger.

"Even if you did, plenty of folks do and they care for their health and that of their partner."

I chuckle. "Anyhow, I'm clear. So it must have been another guy you ran out on after you smothered him with that tight little cunt of yours."

If it wasn't for the call display on the dashboard, I'd have thought we'd been disconnected. Is she hurt? Is someone there?

Finally, she whispers, "Fuck you, asshole. I'd only ever been with two guys before you and your fancy tequila. My reputation is based on what I do without even a shred of the truth, and yet in comparison to your body count, I'm still considered a dirty little slut."

My stomach twists at the anger in her voice. "Looks like I struck a nerve. But while we're on the subject, since when do you judge someone's body count?"

"Not someone's. Yours. Only yours," she grits between her teeth.

"Aw. I like when you're jealous. I also like when you're with me, and since I'm here, which level are you on?"

"You can't get in. It's staff only."

"Do you want to head down to the street level? Or do you want to keep chatting from here?" I tease, swallowing back how angry I am.

The anger is because of her admission. I'm pissed that no matter what she has done, it's what she appears to do that causes folks to talk. The anger comes from knowing that the first time someone centered her pleasure was during our night together.

Well, it's also a little focused on how she could walk away from that night and still compare me to her ex. I scrub a hand down my face and play with the radio dials until I find a good song.

My heartbeat thumps to the beat of a rock song and my fingers tap in time on the steering wheel while I impatiently watch the pedestrian doorway. Two minutes later, her mass of blond hair appears, flying in the wind.

Nessa's adorable light pink boucle jacket stands out in angry contrast to the black leather heeled boots and bag. Sort of like how the anger across her face is the polar opposite of the halo of light around her head.

As she approaches, I step out to open her door, flooded with a mix of emotions I can't follow.

I can only assume the feeling is mutual when Nessa slams into me with a very uncharacteristic hug. I wrap my arms around her and squeeze her tight, relishing the palpable electric current between us. After another second, her tensed muscles relax and something resets between us.

She blinks back emotion as she pulls away.

I cup her cheeks, swiping my thumbs over her silken skin. Nessa is not one for crying, jealousy, or fear. Yet she appears to be combating all of those when I look into her amber eyes.

"Ivy, breathe with me. It's just a car. You'll fix it."

She gives me a terse nod. "I'm fine. I don't know why I'm overreacting. I must be tired." She moves my hands from her face and heads toward the passenger door.

"I owe you. Thank you for coming to get me." She slumps against the seat as I close the door behind her. When I climb into my own seat, she looks relieved enough that I aim for the bleachers.

"Then be my girlfriend." I flash her my most charismatic smile. It causes her to tense, so I soften my face, hoping to convey my sincerity and concern. "Publicly at least? Until the Reynolds Group leaves town? I'll feel better. An assumed relationship will give you another layer of protection."

As she adjusts the seat belt, she huffs out, "Fine, but there will be rules."

ten
Mateo

THE WORD "RULES" causes me to puff out my cheeks before expelling my breath. Rules? Why can't we just go with the flow? I hate rules.

She pulls a notebook from her tote, then a pen, tapping impatiently.

"What happened to your car?" If I can keep her from making rules, it'll be so much better.

"It won't turn on. I don't know. AAA said they can't come out today." She shrugs, fidgeting with her hands.

"Gabe's old car, right?" It's from the late eighties. Maybe the early nineties.

"Yeah, but we can't all go out and buy whatever we want all the time." She lowers her head, her focus fixed on her hands. "I could do that stuff I make good enough money. The problem is Ema."

"E. Mah?"

"E-Ma. Don't you know I use the Hebrew words for mom and dad?"

"No shit, me too. Well, not Hebrew. I use Tagalog. We call our parents Nanay and Tatay." I huff a laugh. "I guess you probably know that, being so close to Stef."

I lean on the console between us, my arm brushing hers.

"Ema and Aba." She nods once.

"So, what about your Ema?"

"She's been on some giant work assignment, and she's barely around lately. It's like, without her around, everybody comes to me when they need something. There was the time Shae drank too much, and I covered her ambulance cost. Tal needed help with textbooks last semester, and I didn't want to worry our parents... and..." She shrugs.

"Oldest child steps up," I say. "True that. True that."

"I love supporting my siblings, helping them when I can, but I was saving that money for car repairs. Unfortunately, the car has decided it's time to be put to rest."

"If you woke up tomorrow and your dream car was parked in your driveway, what would it be?" I glance at her before returning my eyes to the road.

She's begun to finger-comb her hair, pulling three strands out and starting a tiny braid. Her hands tremble through the motion and her voice shakes as she firmly shoots me down. "Mateo, absolutely not. No."

"What if it was just a rental? While you figure it out?" I push because I never know when to quit.

She wets her lips, and now I can't help but think of kissing her. I want to fight with her and take care of her. It's a compulsion that continues to bubble inside me.

Her protest comes out in the cutest little whine, her gaze on her shoes. "No. Please don't offer to pay for things."

"No extravagant gifts. Got it. Then here's my final offer," I say, using a game show host tone. "Mateo will be Nessa's personal chauffer until other arrangements can be secured."

Tapping her lips, Nessa lets out a soft "hmm" and shifts in her seat. "I can just call you at the drop of a hat and you'll come running? Go anywhere?"

Her eyes have lifted again, meeting mine briefly. The golden threads through the soft brown irises twinkle with the return of the mischievous girl.

When she puts it that way, my cock twitches, eager to scream "fuck yes. Use me."

"Yep. Exactly," I say, though my throat's gone dry. I reach for a water bottle, but the cupholder is empty.

Perky and beaming a wide, toothy smile, she agrees. "Sounds fun. Now, back to the rules."

With a groan, I drop my head back against the seat.

"Rule number one: No seeing other women."

I chuckle. Pausing to consider whether to turn it around on her, suggesting she not see other men. But I can't think of the last time anyone talked about Nessa dating. Not to mention her comment about the number of men she's been with. Does she date?

Setting aside the serious question, I use this opportunity to make these "rules" as ridiculous as I find the concept.

"Fine. Rule number two: When we're in public, you must say at least one nice thing to me or about me."

Her lips kick up on one side. "Can I still be mean the rest of the time?" The earnestness is adorable.

"Actually, I'd prefer it." I reach across the car in an attempt to hold her hand.

She pulls back. "Rule number three: No unnecessary touching or kissing."

"What makes it necessary?" I push back.

She ignores me. "Four: What's the story with your sister?"

"What do you mean?" Lips pressed together, I study her, hoping her expression will help explain the question.

"In most romance books, when a person is in a relationship with their best friend's sibling, they keep the friend in the dark until the friendship suffers. I don't want that to happen."

I frown, confused. "This isn't a book."

"Right. Also, those aren't fake dating situations. In those

scenarios, everyone knows about the relationship. That's the point. To get the antagonist—in this case Caleb—off the back of the person faking it—me," Nessa says, her pen tapping noisily on the page.

"This is way too complicated to be a book," I tease her.

Her face twitches, betraying a tiny smirk. "Never read an eight-character why choose before, I see." The wicked expression falls quick, along with her voice. "Since Caleb, I don't date. Been pretty clear on the fact that I don't plan to, either. Everyone is going to have questions that I do not want to answer."

"Why?"

Breezing past my question, she continues. "They aren't going to believe that somehow, months after I randomly hook up with you—someone I've actively avoided since high school—I've changed my stance on dating... so I guess rule number four is that if one of us adds to the story, we go along with it?"

"Oh. My. God. Nessa, you want me to 'yes, and' you?" I grin and clap my hands once before returning them to the wheel.

"Oh no. Are you telling me you are an improv comic?" She shudders.

"Don't judge. Think about the movies and TV shows I love— the actors are all graduates of a few elite improv schools. I tried to take classes in New York, but my work schedule got in the way. Still, I was an audience member every chance I had."

She hums, one brow cocked, but doesn't say anything.

An unfamiliar wave of nervousness runs through me. "What?"

"Just trying to fit this new, extremely uncool information into the picture I have of cool, playboy Mateo," she teases.

"Uncool? Please. First, it was cool, and second, it was mad fun." I scoff. "Fun? That gets me thinking. Rule number five: Nessa must do something that is fun and just for herself at least once a week." Feeling smug, I wait for the fight, but she just continues to scratch the notes on her page.

"Fine." She taps the end of her pen against the paper. "Now there's just one last thing to do to make it official."

I arch a mocking brow. "You want me to change my Facebook status?"

"No, someone will have to text the Springer." She sighs.

Perfect.

"Don't worry. I have just the brother for the job. He loves that thing."

PEACOCK SPRINGER:

Alert! Insiders confirm that love is blooming between the Sunflower Fest co-chairs.

eleven

Nessa

IT'S BEEN a week since Mateo became my personal driver. During our time together, he's filled me in on the progress he's made with the festival. He's already reached out to the entire group of festival vendors and started on a secret plan. He's saved my ass, honestly. I did not want to take this on once I saw how much was expected of us. But once something has my name on it, I won't let it fail.

Between the on-demand chauffeuring and weekly Sunflower Fest planning sessions that often end in watching an old show or movie, I've started to really enjoy our time together. Worse, Delia might have been right when she suggested letting someone "babysit" me. Not that I'd ever tell her that.

And not that I actually want someone fussing over me. I'm fine.

"So..." Mateo drums his fingers on the steering wheel, his demeanor uncharacteristically nervous. "I know we still have a lot to do for the festival, but I need to take the week off to work on my pitch and meet with some investors and the bank. Do you think you can tackle the rescue folks meeting? It shouldn't be too crazy."

Why is he stressed about asking me to do something very clearly spelled out in my responsibilities as the co-chair?

I try my best to keep the snappy tone in my voice so he doesn't suspect anything, though I fail miserably. "Yeah. Why? Would that be a problem?"

"Did you take a gummy at work by accident?" He quirks an eyebrow at me.

I raise a hand, fingers—tipped with black-painted nails—clutching a vibrant green vape pen, and take a deep inhale. With a slow exhale, I blow the vapors his way, then playfully give him the middle finger.

"I've been working on this 'being chill' thing you keep going on about. It seemed like it would be on your approved list. Oh," I say as we pass the mall, "can we stop for soft pretzels and cinnamon buns?" I make my best attempt at giving puppy dog eyes.

"You going full Loch Ness on me tonight?"

"Nope, just think I deserve a little treat."

"Can't fight that logic." He eases into the parking lot, then leads me by the hand to the food court, where we order one item from each food stall. A hot dog, Bourbon Chicken from the Chinese takeaway place, guava and cheese empanada, fries with chocolate shakes for dipping, and, of course, the originally requested soft pretzel and cinnamon bun.

While we sit across from one another, I pull out the research I've been working on for my relationship podcast, *Flicking the Bean with Rabin*, and leaf through a pile of recent listener questions and Reddit Q&A conversations.

I need a distraction. And maybe I want to rile him up a little. Pretend the man across from me isn't affecting me. Maintain an aloof but flirty attitude, just to poke at him. Because despite my best efforts, that goofy grin he plastered on and his obnoxious ability to go with the flow and still succeed effortlessly are drawing me in.

My plan to ignore him is foiled when he slides into the chair beside me.

"Better angle for the shake and fries," he offers in explanation.

"Uh-huh. Whatever." I shift in my chair, putting some distance between us, and continue to read.

The universe is working against me. I turn the page, and a slew of printed comments about cock rings slides out from the folder and into his lap.

"It's for a listener question."

I reach out a hand for my papers, but he holds it out of reach and laughs. The bastard *laughs* at how I work to research before discussing a topic on air.

"It's funny to you that I prepare?" Heat barrels through me, and not the good kind.

"I don't know, preparing by using the opinions of others doesn't seem authentic. Did you and Satan not try these kinds of things? You were together for years."

I clear my throat and wait.

Mateo scratches his cheek.

Come on, dude. We established months ago that you're the only person to have gone down on me. Does that question sound ridiculous yet?

Hackles officially raised, I grit my teeth. "You think that Mister God's Gift to Women would deign to do anything that was not self-serving?"

"Okay." He grimaces. "You mentioned you were with another guy, right? What about him?"

Apprehension skitters through me. Why the hell am I talking about this with him? But with a sigh, I go on. "Just once at sleepaway camp. I was a CIT. It was a few pumps and over in a locked shower stall after the campers went to sleep one night. Nothing too exciting." I pull my shoulders back and straighten the papers in front of me. "Ugh, this is why you are 'Bad Idea.'"

"Did you just call me 'Bad Idea'? Dope. Yo—did you know she's got a Filipino dad and European mom? We could make our own little Olivias if..." His eyes go wide, and he snaps his mouth shut.

Pretending he didn't just suggest a future where we have children together, I close my folder and shove it back into my bag. "Can we just go?"

"Hold on, Ivy." He grabs my hand, stopping me from slinging my bag onto my shoulder. "Hold on. It just hit me." He leans in close and whispers, like maybe he believes I should be embarrassed by what he's about to say. "I was the first person you slept with after him."

"Great job, Detective. That is exactly what I told you. Directly," I retort.

If I could use magic to make his head to explode, I would. I want to cause him pain without touching him. I want to destroy him for bringing this shit up when I'm trying to be the easy-going version of myself.

"Let it go," I growl.

This is getting too close to the part of my story I've only ever shared with my therapist. The part I hoped to leave behind in Boston, along with night sweats and the self-doubt that comes from gaslighting.

I'm supposed to be an expert. Yet I missed the signs in my own life.

"Huh?" He looks dumbfounded, which infuriates and frustrates me, even if it's no surprise.

"Let's. Go," I say, enunciating each syllable.

"Where are we going?"

I've run out of patience. Grabbing his wrist, I drag him through the hallway, making a beeline for Oliver's Gifts.

Oliver's is where tweens and teens go to giggle over low-quality and inexpensive sex toys, flavored condoms, and lube. I prefer purchasing from boutiques—queer or women-owned companies that support ethical porn—but we're here, and I'm desperate to keep from letting that conversation ruin my mood. So I drag him directly to the back of the store to a display case.

"All right, Mister Big Shot. What do you have experience with?" I zero in on him, daring him to talk.

"Does it matter? You said what we have isn't like that." He crosses his arms, smug.

I mimic his stance and glare back.

With a huff, he storms to the front of the store and picks up a basket. He barely looks as he drops item after item into it. Fuzzy cotton candy–pink handcuffs, a water bottle shaped like a veiny penis, a cheap vibrator shaped like a gummy bear, another shaped like a frog, sex position dice, and a deep-throat numbing spray.

Then there's a black ashtray with a tarot card style decoration embossed with an image of a cat smoking a joint and the words *the stoner*. A Twilight tumbler with a straw. A stack of Team Jacob merch. As I watch, my mood shifts. Whether from my plant medicine or his silly shopping spree, I'm not sure.

"Oh my god, are you serious?" I'm struggling to suppress my laughter.

"I heard you were Team Jacob, Nessie." He stops in front of me, his eyes sparkling with mischief.

"It's true. Jacob had the better abs. And complexion…" I blush at the admission, hoping he doesn't catch on to the double meaning there.

"Let's go, little monster." He places an arm around my shoulder and steers me toward the cashier. He purchases everything in the basket, plus a cock ring. "For research," he says, giving a wink.

As we climb back into the car, he silently sets the bag on my lap. We remain quiet as he drives, the silence somehow more stressful than the teasing.

It shouldn't be, not for someone in my line of work. Therapists have to allow space for patients to speak. I'm used to uncomfortable silences, but I really dislike being waited out like this.

Finally unable to take it anymore, I say, "I know you have money to throw around and all that, but why did you go shopping like a teen boy?"

He shrugs and laughs. "Why not? I thought the rule was that I'm supposed to encourage you to have fun."

twelve

Mateo

MATEO:

How's the research going?

IVY:

You think I'd use that stuff?

MATEO:

Visualize with me...

Nessa, wearing her teen idol T-shirt, chugging electrolytes from the veiny straw between rounds with each of the toys.

IVY:

Uh, okay. The only part you have correct is that I'm walking around with Taylor Lautner's face plastered to my chest.

MATEO:

That's fair. You are classy. How about this vibrator instead? <Link to Lelo Inez>

IVY:

OH! ONLY $20K? Sure. I'll go order that right now. <smirk emoji>

Are you more of a gold or silver person?

IVY:

<middle finger emoji x2>

MATEO:

One of each?

Never mind, I'll pick.

Expect a package soon.

IVY:

You did not!!!

MATEO:

Guess you'll find out <wink emoji>

———

CAN I send her a twenty-thousand-dollar vibrator just because? I can.

Would it be reasonable? Not even close.

Plus, now that I've sent her the link, I've removed the element of surprise.

Instead, I find something better and choose rush shipping.

Then I watch the status updates, tracking the package from pending to shipping.

From the warehouse to the first postal stop, then another.

After another few days, it's arrived in the US.

Next, it's with the local mail carrier. It's delivered to her house on Dragonfly Lane.

It'll be waiting for her on her doorstep when I drop her off after work.

The whole way home, I work overtime to put a lid on my enthusiasm. I'm giddy, amped up like a puppy with zoomies. But I don't want to ruin the surprise.

It only took a couple of days to discover that the key to unlocking playful Nessa was a great playlist. As a man who grew up surrounded by people who loved to break out the karaoke machine at parties, I've been training for this my whole life.

I distract her from my giddiness by putting on a playlist full of high-energy girlie pop artists. My smiles don't raise suspicion since I'm also belting out bangers.

In the car like this, she becomes my favorite version of Nessa. She's a series of perfect contradictions: tough, feminine, empathetic, and brilliant, while also being biting and sarcastic. And she takes no shit.

"How is my pop princess today?" I'm cheesing hard; I can't help it.

"Obsessed with this playlist and, actually, kind of relaxed." She sighs, her lips tipping up, but before I can respond, she snaps straight and says, "And that is not because of your cheap gag gift sex toys. Don't even."

"Of course not, princess. Only the best for you." I glance her way and give her a wink.

"Oh no. No." She groans, turning the music down. "Princess will not be the nickname you use."

"All right, how about cutie?"

She cringes.

"Babydoll?"

"Hell no."

"How about I just stick with Ivy?"

On that, she relents and then does a double take. "Wait. You didn't."

"What did I do?" I keep my eyes on the road as I merge into traffic. "Or not do?"

"You didn't buy that five-figure vibrator you texted me, did you?" She hides her face in her hands. This is so cute. She's afraid of what I might say.

"No way. I'm far too economical for that. I am much better at hunting for subtle luxury." I can't help but let that last part slip. The anticipation is killing me.

"What?" she asks, fast and sharp.

"What?" I reply, brow cocked. "I guess you'll find out."

Much sooner than she realizes.

———

IT TAKES two hours for Nessa to come pounding on my door like the four horsemen of the apocalypse have arrived.

Like a predator, I'm ready to go in for the kill.

The first thing she'll see is my wardrobe change: light gray sweatpants slung low so the waistband of my boxer briefs is on display. No shirt. The nervous energy had me doing pushups to keep myself busy, and it got too sweaty.

Slowly, I pull the door open and rest an arm against the frame.

"Fancy seeing you here." I can no longer contain my smile, knowing that dimple she pretends not to love is on full display.

The tiny tornado I'm met with is adorable. With one arm around a cardboard box, she pushes me back into the house and stomps in behind me.

"What... the... fuck—"

I steal the words from her mouth with a kiss as fiery as her entrance. After waiting seventeen weeks and a day—not that I'm counting—to kiss her again, I can't resist any longer.

She must feel it too, because she kisses me back just as fervently. I graze her lower lip with my teeth and lightly nip. She swipes back with a press of her tongue, and we continue to devour each other in a frenzy.

She's terrifying in the best way. I cannot keep my wits about me with her. She's soft and pliant, yet she fights me for control with her own intensity. Powerful and so fucking beautiful.

"Tell me what's on your research list, Ivy." I press open-mouthed kisses to her neck, then nip at her earlobe. From there, I kiss and lick and bite my way down to the pulse point at the base of her throat.

Back pressed against the closet door, she wraps one leg around me. I palm her ass and lift, and she clutches the back of my head. The way her fingers comb my hair and mix between soft scratches and yanks sends electricity through me.

"You. Infuriating. Immature. Insufferable. Man," she says between kisses. "You think you can just send me a full catalog of products, and then what?"

Without breaking contact, I stumble to the living room. She slides down my body, slow enough to slightly rub herself over the growing tent in my pants.

"Sit." She points at the couch, and as I soon as I do, she shoves the box at me.

"Then what? I hoped you'd show up here mad as hell. Which you did. I hoped you'd be too angry and turned on to restrain yourself. Like you've been. We didn't even break a rule. This is necessary touching. You were doing something fun, just for yourself."

I grasp her arm and pull her onto the couch beside me, then draw a light line along her jaw and tilt her face so our eyes meet.

"If everything goes according to my plan, I'm one screaming match from finding out what's on your list." I bite my knuckles and consider pushing this a bit farther.

"Once I start to check those boxes, you'll be all"—I raise the pitch of my voice—"oh, Matty. This was so much better than having to think about rules or ex-boyfriends."

I kiss the tip of her nose and pull back, making sure to give her my best smolder, then I take a calculated risk.

Returning my voice to its normal register, I say, "We can benefit from this fake relationship."

"Listen, Scarecrow, if you only had a brain, this would be so much easier. Let me use words that you can understand. This. Is. A. Terrible. Idea."

Swallowing the hit to my pride, I feign disinterest and look down at my watch. "Right on time. Listen to me for a minute here, killer. You said you've only been with three men. You don't want to date and won't while we're faking this thing anyway. So take advantage of me. Form your own opinions. It's a win-win for your brand; you'll improve your podcast. Then, by going back for seconds with me, it keeps your precious body count down."

Bringing up body counts was a gamble. A long shot for sure. But based on the ice replacing the fire in her eyes, I went bust.

Rearing back, she flashes both middle fingers at me. "Fuck off, asshole. Next, you'll ask me how many blow jobs I've given or make that stupid fucking joke again."

My gut plummets. What joke?

"God, sleeping with you was the worst mistake I've ever made."

She stands and scrambles for the door. Before I can get to her, she's stepping into her warm, furry boots and slamming the door behind her.

Shit. I can't let her walk home alone.

I dart to the kitchen, where I left my shirt, then stuff my feet into my sneakers. "Nessa, wait," I call, still tugging the shirt over my head. "Hold up a minute. Can I—"

She pops in one earbud, then the other. As she stalks away, she sings along to the song. I'm trying to catch the lyrics, but all I hear is the word *poison* over and over.

She's so fucking cute, even when she's probably plotting my murder. I follow several steps behind her the whole way. Her light pink coat sways as she dances. Her long, thick blond hair is in these adorable big French braid pigtails. And her smile is larger with each passing house. Instead of pushing it farther, I just soak up the sight of her.

Once she's inside her house, I make my way toward the park before looping around town and heading home to sleep.

When I get into bed, all I can think about are those kisses, causing me to end another day fucking my fist with visions of her in my head. Except this time, her citrus vanilla scent lingers on me.

thirteen
Nessa

I FIND Lily and Delia sitting at the kitchen table drinking tea when I get home, so I grab myself a mug and join them.

Right away, the topic turns to Seth and the bookstore. According to the girls, he's been spending more time hanging around the bar and avoiding the store as much as he can while Rosie, the flower shop owner next door, is training the person taking over. Delia's been trying to get information about the new owner, but every time she brings it up, he sort of growls and then glazes over.

"I'm worried about him. He's quieter than usual. Which is saying something." Delia lifts one shoulder. "I'll figure it out eventually."

From there, Lily gushes about how well things are going at the dance studio. "Registration roll over from the surrounding towns is great," she says, her smile bright. "I've had this wild influx from a local college. The students remember me from my influencing days, I guess. They even asked if I could put together a workshop on content planning and creation, that kind of stuff. It's been fun to watch them carve out a niche and help them get started."

In typical Lily fashion, the more excited she is, the faster the words spill from her.

"What about you?" She props her chin on her hand and homes in on me. "You've been spending a lot of time with Mateo lately. The Springer claims you're dating." Her eyes flash with mischief. "Are you dating Stef's brother? What about everything you said after you left Boston? Or after you hooked up with Matty? And what's with the personal chauffeur service?"

Delia looks at Lily, wide-eyed, and I swallow a large gulp of tea. I regret it half a second later when it burns my tongue. I open my mouth and inhale sharply for relief, then let out a noisy exhale.

"Yeah," Delia says. "I barely see you lately. What's going on there?"

"Shit stirrer," I balk, imagining a world where I exact revenge by mixing Nair in her shampoo.

I couldn't, though. I love her too much.

With a sigh, I gently spin my mug on the tabletop. "Hmm. Let's see. He's still annoying, but Satan is worse. That man is creepy. Matty and I are working on the festival together anyway, so we thought maybe we could scare Satan off by letting him think I'm spoken for." Head tilted, I shift in Lily's direction. "Speaking of which, can I go over things for the studio and The Featherweight with you while I have you? Would love to check those boxes."

"Remember last year when River visited me in Vermont? Before things started with us for real?" Lily beams.

Perfect. Delia surely has more questions, but they'll have to wait. Lily is in control of the conversation again.

"He and I agree that fall in New England is so romantic." She clasps her hands in front of her. "We want to do it again, but the right way. Anyhow, we're going up for a few days and plan to pick up a ton of fresh syrup. Which means the Maple Porter will return to the menu."

I waggle my brows. "Bring me some extra, and we'll do a big brunch soon."

"You got it!" She taps something in her phone, then flashes the screen, showing a note that reads *bring back extra syrup for Nessa* on the multi-day Vermont Trip line.

"Jim said that the folks from Harebrained Helpers are going to have a flock of adoptable pets for us," I tell Delia. "Apparently, a new volunteer didn't check the tags when putting some of the bunnies back, and they multiplied, you know, like rabbits. Could we hold a few overflow pets here before the event?"

Before she can answer, an alarm blares, interrupting us.

Lily taps her phone's screen, silencing the ear-piercing sound. "Gotta run." She stands. "And in case you planned to ask me about housing animals next, I'll pass. Pete would likely not take well to sharing his space. But maybe there's space at Stef's? Ask Mateo."

I stand and sink into her embrace, so grateful for my framily.

I love my siblings, but the kind of sisterhood I share with my friends is special in so many ways.

"Thanks, Lils. If we need the space, I'll be sure to check."

My smile may be a little too bright, but thankfully she's got her face buried in her phone as she shuffles to the door.

Once the door snicks shut behind her, Delia laughs and shakes her head at me.

"What are you going to do now?" She's definitely both entertained and afraid.

I smirk. "Well, we're co-chairs. He's got a responsibility to help with anything he can. Seems like a reasonable thing for a man living alone to help with, don't you think?"

"You wouldn't be going to this much trouble if you weren't enjoying it." Brows lifted, she peers at me over the top of her mug.

I mimic the expression. The staring contest goes on a bit too long and I "accidentally" graze her leg, hitting that spot that makes her laugh. Boom, winner.

"Whatever you say, D." Looks like I need to email Jim and the head of Harebrained to follow up.

She huffs a laugh. "Sure." She elongates the word, then says, "This is all an act, for Caleb, who isn't even around right now. Whatever you say."

I wave her off, having moved on to thoughts of what I'm going to say to Jim. Oh, yes, Jimmy, ole boy. I have the perfect place to house those animals. My "boyfriend" has loads of free space. I've got to make sure people believe we're in this together, of course.

———

SATURDAY AFTERNOON, I walk up to Mateo's house and find an unfamiliar car in the driveway. He's outside, wearing a pair of dark gray chinos and a deep plum-colored button-down. He's walking my way, doing that key swinging thing, charming me and irritating me in equal parts with his swaggering entrance. He needs to stop approaching me like every encounter is some sort of movie moment.

"Think fast, Ivy." He launches the keys at me.

Though I flinch, I manage to catch them. I look down at the series of interlocked rings engraved on the key fob, then peer back at the forest green convertible.

"New car?" I frown.

"Nah. I pulled it out to make space in my garage and figured you could drive it while you figure out what to do about your busted one. I love being your chauffeur, but this way you don't have to rely on me all the time. You deserve reliable transportation," he says.

He uses one hand to rub the back of his neck, a nervous tick, but his eyes are glowing.

In quick succession, butterflies take flight in my stomach, but in a matter of heartbeats, they plummet, and dread takes over. An extravagant gift like this could be a trojan horse.

Pulling out my phone, I quickly tap the make and model of the car into the browser.

Once I've hit enter, I suck in a sharp breath.

"You just so happened to own Elle Woods's car from the *Legally Blonde 2*?" I snap my head up and blink. Being around this man causes my pulse to thump everywhere. This is no coincidence. He knows I idolize her. We share an alma mater, and we're both girly blondes, with personal characteristics that cause people to underestimate intelligence.

The package he had delivered a few days ago included two extremely beautifully crafted and discreet pieces of jewelry. A set of pink silicone stacked bracelets connected by a delicate rose gold chain engraved with *Ivy* and a necklace adorned with a long, skinny pendant. It didn't take long to discover the power button. After that, I assumed that luxury cuffs and a vibrator were the height of amazing and inappropriate gifts from him—and no, I did not return them; the box I left at his house was full of the toys he purchased at the mall—but I was so, so wrong.

Circling the car while I fiddle with the bracelets, I focus on self-talk to calm my raw nerves. A gift like this doesn't have to be a trap. Even so, there's a voice in the back of my head reminding me that he's a rich real estate guy, trying to solve my problems with fancy gifts. Why would he do it if not to ensure that I'll owe him?

"Happy coincidence," he says with a dismissive wave.

Forcing a breath in and out, I accept the car—for the moment.

"It's got all-wheel drive, so it's safe to drive in the snow. Do me a favor: drive this for the next few weeks so I know you can get places safely while I'm in and out of meetings."

When I narrow my eyes at him in response, he crosses his arms over his chest, causing his muscles to pull his fitted dress shirt even tighter.

I roll through the options in my head. I could argue with him, which could be fun. Or I could accept the offer graciously and drive this sexy little convertible while I figure out my next steps.

I hum and tap my lips to hide a smirk.

"Either way, we're rolling up to dinner in this tonight. I reserved the private dining room at The Featherweight. The council wants to discuss the festival and the north side sale, so give me a little spin." He holds a finger up and twirls it. "Let's see how you clean up, and let's head out."

As I do a quick spin, he makes a loud hum while holding his chin like he's thinking hard. Eyes darting from one spot to another, like they're not sure where to linger, he loosens his collar and lets out a sigh.

If I can't hide my giggles, I can at least turn away. I walk to the driver's side and peer through the window.

The moment I open the door to slide behind the steering wheel, all my indecision evaporates. The soft leather is stitched like an engraving over the doors, steering wheel, and center console accents. This car is sexy. Damn.

When Mateo finally lowers himself into the seat next to me, I give him a quick wink.

"How's my passenger princess?" I tease. "How can we service you tonight?"

"We?" His eyebrows rise.

"That's it? No jokes about servicing you? Wow, this must be a powerful car. I like her." I slide a hand over the leather once more, barely holding back a purr of appreciation.

"Yes. We're a team now. You're right; I deserve the fancy Elle car." I turn the engine on and rev it once for good measure before backing out and heading to River's place.

When we slow to navigate the center of town, Mateo hits a button that lowers the gray top, making it extremely easy to be spotted. This is the first time since the Springer's announcement that we've been seen out together.

"Windows down and heat on in the fall is the best." He leans forward and taps a button on the console. "There. Your seat warmer is on now. You'll be super comfortable and also get the breeze and the sunlight."

I side-eye him quickly, then force my focus back to the road. I hate to admit it, but it's perfect. Cozy.

He once again insists on opening my door, even though I'm the driver. So while I wait for him to round the hood, I flip down the visor and use the mirror to reapply my lip gloss.

Delia has a point. *For someone who is not interested in dating Mateo, you sure seem to be interested in flirting with him, annoying him, and looking good around him.* I close my eyes, desperate to shut down the little voice in my head that is making this something it absolutely is not.

My door opens, and with a half-bow, Mateo extends a hand.

Biting back a grin, I take it and let him guide me out. My outfit tonight is cozy but feels extremely sexy. The cropped sweater with a mock neck is a rich cranberry. My breasts are well contained, but it's not possible to ever hide their size. The sliver of my midriff that shows when I move my arms is flirty without drawing overt attention. The A-line windowpane plaid skirt that falls to just above my knee balances things well, creating an hourglass shape and making things overall less scandalous. The neutral colors balance well with the color of the top. I finished the look off with my trusty Docs and high socks slouched over like the '80s.

Hand in hand, we cross the gravel parking lot and ascend the stone walkway to the hostess stand. Kyle, Delia's least favorite server, is working the front of house tonight. She must be thrilled; this keeps him out of her hair.

"Nessa. Great to see you." He greets me with open arms.

For a moment, Mateo's hold on my hand tightens, but he quickly releases me.

"Aw," Kyle says. "Guess this is why I could never convince you to have a drink with me. Who is the lucky gentleman?" He extends a hand.

My date tonight returns the gesture, grasping Kyle's hand firmly. "Mateo Santos-Manolo. Wish I could say I'm sorry she never said yes." He steps back and pulls me into his side.

Remembering to play nice, I force myself to relax against him. Warmth radiates between us, eliminating any chill in the fall air.

"We're joining the council tonight," I say. "Delia said we're upstairs. Is that still the plan?"

"Absolutely. It's the smaller dining room." He holds out an arm, gesturing for us to head that way. "River's already up there too. Let me know what you want from the bar, and I'll send someone up with your drinks while you wait."

"Perfect. Sparkling water with lemon. And for you?" I ask Mateo through long, fluttering lashes.

"Aw, Ivy." He drops a kiss on the crown of my head. "A scotch old enough to order its own scotch, please."

I bite back a laugh. There is no way Kyle will understand the request, so I grab my phone and shoot Delia a text.

NESSA:

Mateo just told Kyle he wants a 21-year-old scotch, but I doubt he understood him.

DELIA:

Correct, he just asked me for "old scotch."

You only want sparkling water with lemon?

NESSA:

I knew he could get that right <upside

DELIA:

No alcohol? For this dinner?

NESSA:

Nothing strong. I need to keep my wits.

DELIA:

Red or white?

NESSA:

Surprise me.

A few minutes after we're seated, our drinks arrive. Despite Kyle's claim about River waiting up here, he's nowhere to be found. And I'm not going to knock on that office door. He and Lily have been unable to keep their hands off each other, and I'm not interested in catching him with his pants down.

fourteen
Mateo

IT'S amazing what the team did in here. Below the chair rail lining the room, the walls are painted a creamy off white. Above it, they've applied a whimsical floral paper. The fixtures are all black iron and wood. The table is one of those resin-filled raw-edge pieces, the legs and chairs an old gold. Gold mercury glass votives in clusters filled with flameless candles decorate the top. This is really a step up from the old days.

Nessa is smirking and nudging me under the table as River and Lily enter. When I take them in, I fake a cough to cover my laugh. River's green shirt is untucked, while Lily keeps tugging on her skirt to adjust it.

"Heard you'd be up here waiting. Looks like we were wrong." Nessa breaks into a wicked smirk.

"Oh, uh. We were," River stammers. "But we had to run upstairs to the apartment to make sure things are in order for when my brother comes home for Christmas,"

Lily, pink cheeked, bursts into laughter. "They don't buy it, darling."

Kissing her temple and sweeping her hair back, he whispers, "I knew that, but I was trying to not give them what they wanted. I save that for you." He punctuates the statement by playfully grabbing at her ass.

That move only causes her to have to adjust her skirt all over again.

"Speaking of knowing things." River pulls out a seat for her beside Nessa. "I swear when I had my accidental front-row seat to your—" River clears his throat.

Lily perks up and takes over for him. "Your supposed one-time-only pre-wedding festivities."

"Darling," River says, his tone laced with hesitant devotion.

"What? We all know you walked in on them."

With a smug sigh, River says, "I guess congratulations are in order. I could tell you were smitten then. Called it when I said there'd be a repeat. Pony up, darling." He opens his palm, and she drops a bill onto it.

He looks at Nessa, then at me again, and I start to sweat. Will she contradict him?

Before he can go on, the door to the private dining space opens.

"Okay, lovebirds. Enough for now." Prudence enters with the strong floral and spicy scent of her tea shop following her. "We need to talk before the others join us." She eyes us conspiratorially. "What can we do to scare this man away? Nessa, that's your territory. What does Satan hate? Last-minute menu changes? Mateo, how are the meetings with the bank going? Do you need additional investors?"

As she digs through her enormous bag of items, the usually rock-solid woman's hands tremble. She mutters to herself, peering over her shoulder at the door.

Something feels off. Yet part of me questions if I'm projecting. Maybe she's changed with age?

A moment after that thought crosses my mind, River reaches a hand out to her, affirming my concern.

Pru locks eyes with Nessa, her face shifting from red with fury to white as a ghost, then green with nausea. "I knew his ancestors in Massachusetts. I don't like them."

Confident that I finally have my moment to one-up Caleb, I say, "There's nothing to worry about, ladies. If anything, we have the home court advantage."

This is the meeting I've been waiting all summer for, a blessed second chance to prove myself while also telling Merrick Paul off.

Jim Kelly enters, his face fixed in an apologetic frown. "Caleb can't make both this meeting and another he and I have scheduled and has requested to combine. I know this isn't ideal, but he's down at the bar having a drink, so we'll go over a few things up here first, then bring him in to join us." His tone is decisive. This isn't a question but a command.

Beside me, Nessa stiffens. With none of her usual grace, she pushes the chair back and rushes toward the door.

"Excuse me, just need to go to the ladies' room," she says with a trembling voice.

Lily meets my eye across the table, and I tip my head toward the door in silent request.

She blinks in confusion. River nods and lifts his chin, then leans over and whispers in her ear. A second later, Lily stands and excuses herself as well.

Once he's rounded the table, I stand to shake Jim's hand and make eye contact. Given the twins' relationship challenges and my known alliance with Liam, I aim to stroke his ego. "Finally, I'm with the good twin," I tease, clapping him on the shoulder. "Women," I sigh. "Always need to go to the bathroom together. Am I right?" It goes against my beliefs to say such a thing, but his hearty laugh signals that I'm playing to his nature.

"We can always adjust. Maybe just us gentlemen and a bottle of scotch?" Jim suggests with an oily smirk.

"As much as I love that idea, Lily and Prudence are council members. We can't really exclude them like that." I eye River, hoping he understands that I set him up for an assist.

"Plus, Lily and dark alcohol do not mix. Remember the proposal? We only got her to stop calling you Narc a few months ago. Let's not undo the progress," River adds.

I sag in relief, grateful for the support.

"Fair point, gents. Please..." He waves his hand toward the table.

As I settle in my chair, Nessa's phone vibrates from where she's left it on her chair. When it buzzes for the third time in a row, I finally peer over at it.

GROUP CHAT: BAD BITCHES [STEF CARTER, LILY LONG, DELIA SHANE, NESSA RABIN]
DELIA:

Douche Bag The Turd is here

STEF:

What's happening? He's where?

LILY:

Jim just told us. Can you get some dirt for us?
<prayer hand emoji>

DELIA:

<salute emoji>

STEF:

He's at The Featherweight?

When the ladies return to the table, Nessa has steeled her face and applied deep red lipstick. She looks gorgeous. It also looks like that tiny bit of her midriff is completely hidden. I stand and pull out her chair, wanting to show her all the ways I can be a true gentleman. As I help move her seat back toward our table, I lean down and whisper in her ear.

"The lipstick is a bold power move, but you don't have to cover up for him. He doesn't have the right to tell you what to do anymore, Poison Ivy." I'm about to leave a light kiss on her temple when she goes rigid again.

As I ease back into my seat, I can't help but catch the smallest hint of a smirk.

"Thanks for your patience," she says to the table. "Just needed to freshen up a bit. Of course, we want to keep things as streamlined as possible for you. However, given the evening was going to be partially social and partially business, let's spend a few minutes catching up first."

Prudence's usual stoicism is back in place, but there's a subtle flicker of approval in her eyes.

"Jim," Lily says, seamlessly jumping into small talk. "When Pete stayed with your boarding team, he came home so well-behaved. Please tell me your secrets."

Jim's expression brightens, and he launches into a monologue about tailoring training styles for the disposition of individual breeds.

"That makes a lot of sense," Nessa says. "It's similar to the way we approach diagnoses for different types of patients."

"I thought your job was to talk about masturbating on air." Jim gives a slimy smile and laughs at his own joke.

Irritated on her behalf, I squeeze her hand and angle forward.

"Have you ever listened to her podcast? Dude, she's incredible. And that's only one facet of what she does. She's an ivy league–educated doctor of psychology with a focus on human sexual development. Her specialty isn't even pleasure; it's trauma processing." I huff a sharp laugh. "Outside of the podcast, she's everywhere: an emergency room response unit, meeting private clients, and a monthly virtual meeting for her book research. Does she talk about the fun stuff too? Hell yeah, because that's the best way to make conversation about the harder topics more approachable."

I squeeze her hand again, preventing her from pulling away to pick her nails, the action meant to reassure her that I'm not letting this stand.

"She's got to make jokes and puns. How could she not when her last name rhymes with bean and people call female

94

masturbation flicking the bean? She's marketing serious work in an approachable and stigma-free way because of men like you and me who benefit from the Madonna-whore complex." I brush my thumb over her knuckles, hoping she hears my sincere admiration. She's a powerhouse.

When I finally shut up, the room is silent, and every eye is wide and locked on me. Though Prudence looks to be doing her best to keep her lips from twitching.

And the woman beside me, the one whose opinion is the only one I care about, watches, jaw slack and a mixture of amusement, awe, and maybe confusion in her expression.

"Did I cover it well enough?" I ask with a wink at Nessa.

"While we're all here," I say, focusing on Jim again, "Nessa and I should use this moment to update you on the progress we've made for Sunflower Fest. We've got all the usual vendors secured, and contracts are coming in. There's no shortage of options for new booths either. We've been hitting the pavement and meeting with the folks from Woodbury, Mount Sunhope, and Pikesville as well."

I pick up my rocks glass and give it a swirl, building my command of the conversation.

"A few of the local colleges have asked about attending to raise money for fundraisers and charitable events. We plan to review the options later this week. Would love to share the top candidates with you all before we make the final selection." I break out into a grin, knowing that in a matter of minutes, I've both defended my lady and successfully shocked her.

"Good, good." Jim nods thoughtfully. "If I can do anything else, let me know. Oh, wonderful. Looks like Caleb is headed up. Let's review the rules of the pitch meeting."

fifteen
Nessa

GROUP CHAT: BAD BITCHES [STEF CARTER, LILY LONG, DELIA SHANE, NESSA RABIN]

LILY:

<face is hot emojij> Is it just me, or is it suddenly extremely hot in here?

Delia, send up some ice for the burn Mateo just gave Jim <eyes emoji>

DELIA:

???

LILY:

Mateo just took Jim down about 8 pegs while defending Nessa.

I think someone is smitten.

STEF:

Oh, my brother is a smitten kitten, all right.

(NESSA HAS LEFT THE GROUP CHAT)
(DELIA HAS ADDED NESSA TO THE GROUP CHAT)
(NESSA HAS LEFT THE GROUP CHAT)

———

NOPE. I can't do it.

When Caleb entered the small dining room, the scent of his cologne hit my nose, causing my body to go haywire.

First came the stomach cramps, a sweaty brow, and clammy skin. I tried to sip my cold water, forgetting it was bubbly. The fizz did not mix well with my situation, and I was about to regurgitate bile.

Somewhere, my rational brain identified the panic attack, but that didn't stop me from feeling like I was dying. No, instead, I'm currently storming down the steps of The Featherweight, ignoring everyone. I slam the door to the sport car and begin to speed out of the parking lot. In the rearview, I see Mateo outside chasing after me.

Rather than wait for him, I toss up a peace sign and tear out of the lot. *Sorry, I can't handle anyone seeing me spiral.* I'm winding my way through town when I decide I need to step away from this.

I need to get out of here. I need to be someone else for a night, someone who's fun and carefree. Someone who isn't stressed about her responsibilities. I know just the person. Using Bluetooth, I call Shae.

"You up for a drink tonight?" I ask when she answers. "I can pick you up in about an hour and a half."

"I would, but tonight is not the night. My boss just gave me a lecture about taking my work more seriously, and you know how much I love this job. I can't mess it up. What about Thursday?"

I hang up, there's no point. Thirty seconds later, a text notification appears on the console, and a robotic voice reads the message aloud.

"Shae sent a text message that says, 'Okay, bitch. Thanks for being proud of me for taking something seriously.' Would you like to reply?"

"Nope. Thanks, robot," I say.

The phone rings next, and I decline before even checking the display. I don't want to discuss anything with anyone right now. As I come up to the sole traffic light in town and slow to a stop, I decline yet another call.

The light is still red when the passenger door flies open and Mateo hops in. Great.

"You can't lose me that easily. Plus, I really can't have you destroying this priceless gem." He grins at me.

"Go away, Matty." I'm fuming, but he's looking at me like I'm an adorable little bunny.

"What happened back there?" His gaze lingers, like he's examining me.

Hit with a wave of shame for my outburst, my cheeks heat. I'm not sure how much I want to share.

Professional Nessa would tell me to be vulnerable and give Mateo a chance to prove that he's not like my ex. Unfortunately, Impulsive Nessa is in the driver's seat tonight, and she simply glares at him.

Finally, the light turns green, and I accelerate a little too hard, causing the tires to squeal. Tentatively, Mateo reaches one hand out, but he stops just short of touching my shoulder before retreating. I'm thankful for the space, and yet I long to feel comforted.

His words are slow and careful, almost fearful, when he says, "I have a few more weeks, right? You aren't calling this? We'll keep this up through the festival and keep working together?"

"Yeah, sure. Then you can run off and forget me and that any of this happened." I inhale deeply, holding back a scoff. I pull into Stef's driveway and throw the gearshift into park.

Mateo cups my chin and tips my face in his direction. "Never. There is no way I'd forget you. You're one of a kind, Nessa. Always have been. I couldn't forget you if I was an old Lolo in khakis up to my armpits and a short sleeve button-down open to my undershirt."

I frown, confused by the end of that statement.

"Even when I'm an old man, like my Lolo, my grandpa, I couldn't forget you," he clarifies.

My chest pinches painfully. I'm in trouble.

sixteen
Nessa

MATEO IS TIED up in meetings with investors this week, so I take advantage of the alone time and use the spare key to pick up the binder.

I swear that's the only reason I'm here. Okay, I also want to see how he's changed the place. I've refrained from snooping when I visit, but I have no shame now that I'm here alone.

The baby blue plaid couch, blessedly, has not been replaced. It's a close copy of the one from *Full House*, and Stef loves to make a never-ending stream of jokes about her proximity to becoming a Tanner. I'm just shocked she hasn't also added a bear in a trench coat to it.

With a sigh, I drop onto the cushions and open the binder. I knew he'd emailed everyone, but from the look of things, he's done so much more than that.

Color me impressed.

He followed up in person with each local vendor, even taking notes about the visits that include a typed checklist of next steps with tick boxes beside each line. And, damn, he's created a detailed map of the stalls with information on their preferences. Holy shit—this level of organization is sexy.

Though the last thing I want is to fall for this man, it's hard to remember why when, as I snoop, all I find are spotless, sparsely decorated spaces. Even the bedroom is relatively unchanged other than the crisp white bedding and a tan throw blanket. There's a masculine catchall on the dresser with a watch, a key fob, a few random buttons, and coins.

Lee's art studio has been turned into a home office. This room is filled with more personal items than any of the others. Mostly sports memorabilia. A shrine to Jordan Clarkson, a replica pair of Robert Stephenson's cleats from 2023, and some other items reflecting Filipino Americans in pro sports. Just about every item is accompanied by a plaque from one charity auction or another. Wow.

Dammit. None of this is helping me quell the attraction I feel for him. If I can't be turned off, then I guess it's time to make myself look a little less ideal. Pulling out my phone, I place a call.

"Hey Bea, it's Nessa." I don't bother to fight my smile. "I wanted to confirm that we're set for the overflow housing. I'm here now. Let me give you the address. I'll have space cleared for everyone."

———

AN HOUR LATER, a large passenger van is parked on the curb, and Bea and Jim, as well as a few high school volunteers, haul items into the house.

"Shua!" I call out.

He comes my way, holding a soft carrier with a mesh front.

"Who is this?" I coo at the creature peering up at me.

"They don't have names yet." Shrugging, he walks past me.

"Aw, bubbale! We need to name these babies." I baby talk to him and the animal in question as I follow him into the office space.

Jim and a few of the other teen boys have constructed a large closet-type thing, with silver dish pans at the bottom for litter and clear plexiglass fronts, creating three apartments for the cats.

Shua carefully hands the soft carrier to Jim, who puts the animal in its temporary home.

On the other wall, a second slightly larger structure is coming together, this one with five enclosures.

Jim sidles up beside me. "We've got five rabbits looking for homes too, so we'll set them up here. That okay?"

"Totally. What do we need to know to care for them?"

I'm beyond excited for Mateo to return and meet his new housemates. By the time the festival begins, he'll know for certain he isn't *that* interested in me. He's just killing time, and I won't be someone's second choice, waiting at home again.

"They need clean water and food daily; I'll leave instructions for each species. You can decide how often you want to change the litter. But either way, it's not going to smell like rainbows and unicorns."

Aw, he tried to make a joke.

When the group is finished, they've housed three kittens. One is a short-haired black cat with piercing yellow eyes. The other two are orange and cream colored with spots and stripes.

"These two look so similar. Are they from the same litter?" Shua asks, wide-eyed.

"They're sisters," Jim says. "We can actually remove the wall between them if you'd like. That way they can hang out together. It will be good to give them time to socialize each day."

"They can socialize?" I ask, imagining the snuggles I'm about to get.

"In this case, yes. The kittens are young and docile. But be vigilant. Without proper supervision, the cats could attack the rabbits like prey. But when raised together, they are capable of being friends. In fact..." Jim leans in, his lips turning up in an oily smile. "You deal with Dominants and subordinates at work, right?"

"Sure, sometimes." I steel myself to maintain indifference.

"And how do you identify who is who?"

Jim is really testing my patience here.

"Excuse me?"

"They're humans. I assume the answer is they'd tell you. Correct?"

Oh, maybe this is less gross than I feared.

"Yes. There are contracts and long conversations and ethics that are determined between the consenting parties." Where the hell is he going with this?

"Right. In this situation, the cat believes the Dom needs to groom the sub, but from the rabbits' perspective, the Dom receives the grooming. So if you have two of them out together, and the cat start to clean the bunny's fur, just know you're watching two stupid Doms who think they're both in charge."

Strangely curious now, I tilt my head. "So who is actually dominant?"

Jim only shrugs. "Depends on who you ask." With that, he strides from the room.

Shua grins at me. "You're up to something, aren't you?"

I give him a sly smile and put an arm around him, steering him toward the doorway. "No. No. No. I'm just doing my part for the fine people of Peacock Springs. Let's get you home, baby brother."

———

I'M WAITING on the blue plaid couch, fighting a shit-eating grin and watching the clock. It's almost seven p.m. Where is this man?

I need to fill this time, and as I sit here, I realize that I can continue my subtle sabotage by messing with his streaming algorithm. I navigate to a rerun of one of my comfort shows, one of the few he didn't introduce me to. Only to find that he's in the middle of my favorite season. Huh. That makes stirring shit up even more fun for me. If I'm lucky, he won't notice right away, and he'll end up confused about pieces of the plot he's missed. I press Play and continue to wait.

The sound of the door shutting startles me, and I realize I've drifted off. The screen has gone black, with a message that asks if I'd like to continue watching.

At the door, Mateo removes his shoes and coat, then puts them in the closet. As he turns, he runs a hand through his floppy black hair. He looks weary from the day, his eyes droopy and tired. His usually pressed dress shirt is rumpled and the top two buttons are undone.

He's starting to undo his belt when I let out a wolf whistle.

"Holy shit, Ivy," he nearly shouts, clasping his chest. The surprise only lasts a heartbeat before he gets back to undressing. Quickly, he shucks his pants and slips his dress shirt from his shoulders. Now in a pair of boxers in some sort of neon print reminiscent of the 1990s and a white undershirt, he walks in and rubs the top of my head like I'm the family dog.

The hell?

He shuffles to the bedroom and pulls open a drawer, then another, by the sound of it. When he returns, he's wearing a pair of low slung gray sweatpants. He drops down next to me, hitting Play on the remote, and stretches his arm around me.

"What are you doing?" I frown in annoyance.

"I came home and found my girl waiting for me on the couch. My show is ready to go... well, your show. I figured I'd check it out. I'm getting comfortable. Tell me about your day."

His lack of concern is unnerving, to say the least.

But that doesn't negate my excitement. "I finished the next step in the pet adoption portion of the festival process. Want to see?" It takes everything in me not to bounce on the couch cushion. I'm so excited to show him the new members of his staff in the office.

Instead of agreeing, he wraps his arm tighter and pulls me into his side.

"Nah, not yet. I spent the day talking to the folks at the bank, then a construction crew and current management. I need to zone out."

As the theme song begins to play, he relaxes into the couch.

"You'll miss the opening," I protest, trying to pull away.

"Nah." He holds me tighter so I can't escape. "This is when the cats come to visit and she screams about having viable eggs."

Warmth spreads from his touch. My muscles loosen one by one, beginning with the bicep he's squeezing, then moving on to my shoulders and chest. The hazy sleep I was taken from creeps back in. There's no harm in a little cuddling. Right?

I've almost surrendered to the thought when the dialogue on becoming a cat lady shakes me from the mist.

"Speaking of cats," I say. "You know how Harebrained needed help with fostering until the event? I helped Jim and a crew of volunteers get set up today."

"Cool," he says, barely moving at all as he speaks.

"They're here," I respond, going with the same flat tone he used.

Then I wait. And wait a little more. At least five minutes have passed before it clicks.

"Wait, who's here?" He straightens, eyes wide, and scans the living room, then turns to look at the kitchen. "Was I pants-less while there are other people in my house? How come they didn't say hi?" He's now twisting and jumping like a puppy who can't find his tail.

"No, no." I stand and tug on his arm, forcing him off the couch. "Here. Walk with me." I lead him down the hall to the office and open the door, where the animal condos are softly illuminated. "They need names. Want to do the honors?"

He scrubs a hand down his face and sighs.

Thank god. He's finally bothered by something. I've been wanting to get out of here, but I couldn't miss this look. Is he angry? Frustrated?

I'm ready to needle him, to push him over the edge, when he drops his hand and hits me with a massive grin.

"Yo, this is adorable. They have their own *houses*? I love it. This is exactly what I needed today, and how cute are these guys? They need names, you say?"

My stomach lurches as he bounces around the room, his grin splitting his face.

Shit.

This was an epic fail.

seventeen
Mateo

I WORK from home the next day, spending more time watching the cats napping and bunnies chewing their hay than I should, considering how I can get these furry dudes into forever homes.

"Time to exercise," I say to the fuzzballs.

It's too quiet, so I connect my phone to a speaker and pull up Nessa's latest podcast episode. The sound of her voice makes me feel like we're together.

"Welcome to Flicking the Bean with Rabin," she says after the intro music, *"where we dive into the relationships women have with sex and themselves. I'm Doctor Nessa Rabin, and as always, this podcast contains explicit content not intended for anyone under eighteen. So, if you're listening to this and not a legal adult, please hit Pause and come back in the future. Thanks!*

"Now that we've gotten that part out of the way, today's topic was sent in by listener 'Diamonds and Dildos.' Awesome. Let's dive in!"

While she talks, I grab the little mouse toys and the laser pointer off my desk and open the cat apartments. The kittens tentatively step onto the tower I've added for them to climb and scratch, then one by one, they leap down and explore. In the background, Nessa continues to speak to her listeners.

"Hey Dr. Nessa! Thanks for taking the time to read my note."

"Aw, of course, dear."

"I'm a longtime listener and a first-time writer. I'm recently engaged to the love of my life, and a few weeks ago, we moved in together.

"I was unpacking and he opened the box I'd packed my toy collection in, thinking it was something else. He'd never seen them before. I should probably mention we come from pretty conservative families, so some in our circle consider this a taboo subject. One thing led to another, and we had a huge fight where he insisted I throw them all away. If you ask me, he just feels threatened."

"What do you think, kitten? I can guarantee Nessa's got great advice for her," I say, scratching the soft fur of the orange and cream cat who's rubbing against my thigh.

Her reader continues. *"When I refused, he argued that I now have 'unlimited access' to him. I hoped to defuse with humor, joking about his inability to vibrate, but all that did was make things worse. I want to have a mature conversation about this. Help!"*

"Aw, D&D, I'm sorry. This sounds like a terrible way to spend your first night cohabitating. Fortunately, you aren't the first to go through this.

"Also, let me say—congratulations. I'm so glad you've found someone you'd like to spend your life with. Moving in together is a big step.

"Before we try to decode someone else's feelings, let's dig into your own. Is there a reason you kept your solo session supports from your partner? Can you examine that to start?"

Gently, I lift the kittens one at a time, nuzzling little kisses to their heads, then return them to their homes.

"Fresh water and kibble coming up," I say.

They meow in understanding.

"Perhaps you were aware he'd react this way," Nessa says, *"given your background. Perhaps you were afraid for another reason. Either way, it seems like explaining your reasoning could help you meet your fiancé with vulnerability instead of combativeness."*

I bark out a laugh. Nessa, queen of combative, is doling out advice on vulnerability? *Okay.*

"Next, while it doesn't mean you have to accept them, I suggest providing him with the courtesy of discussing his boundaries. But as a reminder, his boundaries aren't allowed to include shame or restriction on your alone time.

"As for fights—nobody likes to fight with their partner. That's obvious. But it's important to discuss how we 'fight' or disagree. How we handle difficult conversations. They're an inevitable part of life. It sounds like while you wanted to defuse with humor, he was prepared to be direct, and potentially even combative. Have you had big fights before this? How did each of your families handle disagreements when you were children? Like it or not, that is the style of conflict management you are potentially still the most comfortable with."

That shuts down my laughter. There was little fighting within our house, but now I'm combing my memories to reflect on how each of my family members behaved.

"Deflection with jokes, dismissing the other person's feelings, or neglecting to meet their needs and our own can all create a recipe for a person to be left feeling unhappy in the relationship. To have a successful partnership, you must work together to foster safety. Don't worry if you're imperfect at it now. The goal is to learn and grow together. Let's get you prepared to be a Dutchess of Dialogue—"

I tap the pause button on my phone screen. Dutchess of Dialogue? That would be a hilarious contact card change, but Ivy is personal. So instead, I push Play.

"—in your own life. I want you to do a little exercise. Grab a pen and paper now, and when this episode is over, leave all your devices in another room. Then take a few minutes to yourself—maybe outside if the weather is nice—and free write answers to these questions."

I lower the volume as she moves into specifics for the letter writer and lift the first bunny from its crate. "Seriously, this chick," I murmur. "She's saying this all with a straight face when she's just as bad."

Stroking the little critter's long, soft ears, I reflect on these last few months. Have I been honest with everyone? What do I need to ask for? What do I want?

I'm certain about one thing I want—I want to impress Nessa. But none of my usual tactics are working. I pause the podcast again, then send a FaceTime request to my sister. Propping the phone against the wall, I sit back down to supervise the bunnies while they hop around.

"Hey, Matty. What's up?" she says, the screen dark like she tapped *Audio Only*.

"Stef! Look at these cotton balls. I need to make sure they all find a home."

"Um, okay?" Her voice is raspy, like maybe I woke her up.

"Look at the bunnies, Stefanie Santos-Manolo!" I reprimand her.

In the background, Lee shouts, "You mean Stefanie Carter."

"Do you guys want to help me? I'm trying to make this something Nessa will..." I trail off. What do I want to do?

"Do something with her psych stuff," Lee says, being an absolute bro.

Meanwhile, my sister grumbles, "No. Good night," and disconnects the call.

As I hit the button on the side of my phone, I come face to face with a photo of the two of us looking like a couple. If anyone asked, setting this image as my lock screen is something I did *after* the town hall meeting. But the truth is it's been like this since the summer.

In the image, Nessa's arm is looped through mine as we walk up the aisle during the recessional at the wedding. The photographer caught us in motion, with Nessa's skirt flowing like she's floating on air. Her wide smile and rosy cheeks suggest she's happy. One might even say she looks angelic. But I can still feel how her nails dug into my arm. I can still hear her teasing words. No, this was all for me.

My mind flashes from one memory to another, every one making my cock twitch. A deep groan rumbles from my chest. She needs to see me, the real me. The man who works hard and still plays hard. I send up a prayer to any deity who might be listening. "Please, please do not let me fuck this up."

Nessa is sassy and challenging and out of my league, but I still want a chance. She's loud and takes no shit one moment. Then, in the next, she quietly observes while pretending to be on her phone. She's always aware of what's going on, no matter what kind of chaos is swirling. She's quick to defend the ones she loves, but who is looking out for her?

Stef told me that Nessa was different after she left Boston, but it wasn't until I saw it with my own eyes at the joint bachelor-bachelorette party that I truly understood. She spent most of the evening on her phone, not participating, her snark almost nonexistent. Now that I've had the displeasure of spending time around Satan—a truly fitting nickname if I've ever heard one—one thing is certain. That asshole dimmed her glow. Thankfully, I'm just the man to polish her back to her former sparkle.

With my thoughts still on the wedding weekend, I turn to the gang of bunnies and ask, "Truth or drink?" It's hard not to remember the game that led to our intimate night.

As I run through more conversations I've had with Nessa over the last few weeks, I grab my phone and navigate to a search engine to find the "horny" psychologist she told me about.

I'm pacing the hallways, trying to make a plan that will get Nessa's attention when I find her. "Karen Horney—with an E. Boom. Nailed it," I shout. It was a chore distinguishing the woman from the other *horny therapists* that populated in the results.

Laughing to myself, I snag a box of condoms from the bathroom. Then I find a fuzzy blanket and head back to my office. I set one bunny on the blanket, then scatter the foil packets around it and check my camera lighting. I grab a lamp to adjust the shadows and tell "Horney" to make a cute face. She nails it, seeing as she's a bunny and all.

I swipe through the images and tap the little heart beneath the one I like best, then do a quick edit. Once the updated version is saved, I pull up my messages app.

MATEO:

<photo>

Meet Horney. She's the runt of the litter, but what she lacks in size, she makes up for with attitude.

IVY:

What are you doing? <eyes emoji>

MATEO:

Bonding with my new housemates.

Returning Horney to her home, I search the internet for more inspiration. I've sent over one I named Gotti because there's both John Gottman, a therapist, and John Gotti, the mob boss.

MATEO:

Meet Gotti. Is he John Gottman? John Gotti? It's New Jersey; it could be either.

IVY:

Very Tony and Dr. Melfi of you.

You're acting loopy tonight. Maybe you should see Dr. Melfi next.

MATEO:

<bunny photo>

Please help name us. We're scared.

IVY:

Carl & Alice.

MATEO:

Those are just names.

IVY:

Carl Jung wrote about dreams and the invisible
string.

MATEO:

Like Taylor Swift?

IVY:

Like the story about yourself that you build on
your whole life.

MATEO:

Cool, can I have one?

IVY:

<blond facepalm emoji>

MATEO:

Okay, and Alice?

IVY:

<link: Alice Miller >

MATEO:

So she, like, stood up for kids who were abused?

IVY:

More or less.

MATEO:

That's dope.

This is when it hits me: I should be sending cute animal thirst
traps.

I toss my shirt across the room, then prop the phone up and
put the timer on.

———

A FEW MINUTES LATER, like déjà vu, she blows into my home

like a tiny tornado, her ample chest heaving with her rapid breaths. In a trench coat that's come loose and—

I swallow thickly, taking her in. Is that a hint of something sheer and lacy?

eighteen
Mateo

I RUB my eyes to keep them from bugging out of my head.

In my stunned silence, Nessa stalks toward me like a huntress. I am her prey, frozen in place.

With narrow eyes and hands waving wildly, she shouts words my brain can't process.

All I can do is watch her pretty pink lips move and grin so wide my face hurts. Fuck, I love getting her worked up, but this is next level.

When she doesn't pause to remove her shoes, I look down and my jaw drops. Those aren't shoes. They're over-the-knee stiletto leather boots.

"Holy. Shit," I say with an exhale.

My heart races, my cock thickening as my mind screams *do not come from the sight of her alone.*

A foot in front of me, Nessa drops the coat to a puddle on the floor and lunges for me, wrapping her legs around my waist. I catch her under the skirt, the smooth skin of her ass instantly registering under my palms.

No panties under this babydoll?

"Fuck me," I groan, gazing down to take in the full view of

her in the tiniest slip of material that does nothing to hide what lies beneath. I carry her out of the entryway, my heartbeat skipping as I come eye to eye with the pendant around her neck.

With her hands on my cheeks, she slams her lips to mine, stealing my breath. The kiss is hurried, all crashing lips, tongues, and teeth.

"I hate you." Her eyes ignite, the flames as intense as the heat from her core pressed to my middle. The sensations are overwhelming. Nessa is all-consuming.

I'm afraid to speak, worried I'll fuck things up again. Instead, I return her kiss and hope we're done talking.

To my dismay, she pulls back again.

"Nothing bothers you," she laments between each taste. "Do you know how hard I tried to get you back with that surprise?"

Unable to think of a reply, I simply resume savoring her mouth. My tongue parts her lips, and the sensual tussle continues.

She pulls back and forces me to make direct eye contact. "Worse, I hate every time you prove to be the opposite of what I believed. You're meticulous. Hardworking."

Goose bumps erupt on my skin at her admission.

"You've noticed?" My breath is barely a whisper.

Vigorously, she shakes her head, forcing me to grasp tighter so she doesn't fall. "The flirting. Oh my god, I hate the fucking flirting. It's like you know that I can't stop thinking about that night."

I'm stunned, smiling at these admissions.

When she puts her lips on my neck, every part of me is consumed with her.

My throbbing cock begins to leak precum. I need to free it, to feel her touch, to come *with* her instead of to the memory of her.

She pulls back, brow furrowed, and studies my face.

Dammit. I swear if she changes her mind again, I'm going to punch myself in the balls.

"Can I touch you?" I whisper, desperate to feel every inch of her.

She rakes her fingers through my hair and tugs. "God, yes."

I carry her into the living room and ease her onto the arm of the couch. When I pull back a fraction, I'm met with the most wonderful view of those luscious, perky tits.

Stepping back, I take her in fully with reverence. "Holy shit."

These are the only words I know now. "Holy shit." That's it. And longing stares. I've got those down.

I kneel before her and run my hands along the soft leather of her boots.

Before I can yank the zipper open, she scoffs and parts her legs wider. "If you're just going to stare..." She props her heel on my shoulder, letting her knee fall wide to expose her trimmed dark blond curls.

Letting out a long exhale, I place my trembling hands on her knees.

"So wet for me," I murmur, dragging my thumbs along the soft skin of her thighs.

All that separates us now is the most insignificant fragment of space. Despite my longing to dive in, I use every bit of my willpower I possess to hold back. One word from her, and I'll touch her where she's dripping for me.

The longer I wait, the deeper her heel digs into my muscles, causing me to moan.

"You like that?" she asks, pressing harder.

I let another soft sound of appreciation escape my lips and am rewarded with her confident, throaty laugh.

"Are you going to tell me that you're waiting for me to touch, lick, and kiss this beautiful pink pussy?" I grit out, still gently caressing her legs. "Are you going to demand I make you come, twice, before even thinking of myself? I bet you'll go with three times once you find out that pendant around your neck is more than a—"

117

"Oh, I know," she interjects with a bit of mischief in her eyes.

"Tell me what you want. I don't like watching you deny yourself." I slide closer to her heat, teasing her but waiting for her command.

I kiss the inside of her left knee and drag my lips up, up, up. But before I give her what she wants, I pull back and do the same on the other side. I repeat this, getting a bit closer each time.

Eventually, I straighten and smirk down at her.

"If you can't tell me what you want, then I guess I'll just head to bed. Good night, Nessa." With a wink, I release her, then stroll toward my bedroom.

I'm going to ensure that she's clear and direct with her desires.

Stopping, I turn and repeat her words from the podcast episode. "Are you embarrassed to discuss your needs with your partner, Dr. Rabin?"

She leans forward until her breasts nearly spill out of the cups, unzips the boots, and pads after me, her feet bare.

"Not in the slightest," she says casually as she passes me.

I give her a moment before following her into my bedroom.

Nessa is a vision in pink. The bedside lamp is on, emitting a soft glow, but otherwise, the room is dark. She's in the center of my bed—on my new mattress and sheets—sitting on her knees. Her long, shiny blond hair flows over her shoulders and curls around her breasts, and her kiss-swollen lips shimmer.

Nessa is sultry, powerful, and confident. All of my favorite things.

Resting a forearm on the doorframe, I wait for her command. My gray sweats leave nothing to hide, so she knows how badly I want her too.

Heart squeezing, I ask, "Who's calling the shots, Ivy? I can take the lead or follow yours. But if you don't pick soon, then I'll choose for you, and you'll be forced to listen to me begging you to ride my face until you're screaming my name."

She swallows audibly, her throat bobbing, then croaks, "Beg me."

Growing bolder, she traces her hands up and down her thighs, her long, thin fingers leaving goose bumps in their wake.

I want to beg, but I'm frozen, watching her lithe movements. I want to watch her. I want to interrupt and give her all she could ever need.

In my stillness, she's reached the hem of her skirt, lifting it to tease her clit with one hand while she massages her barely contained breast with the other. She sways in rhythm with a song only she hears. "Beg for permission to eat this magnificent pussy."

These words do me in, and the memory of our night together —and her admission that nobody had focused on her pleasure— crashes into me.

"Fucking hell." I blow out a breath and enter the room.

In her pink lingerie, centered on the mattress and writhing, she reminds me of a delicate jewelry box ballerina. Moving but going nowhere. I want to help her reach her bliss, and I don't want to interrupt the soft murmurs and sighs that create a soundtrack to this moment.

I prowl to the foot of the bed, doing my best to not blink for fear I could miss a millisecond of her softness and strength on display. I'm mesmerized by the cycle she's created. She winds herself up, hums in pleasure, and closes her eyes briefly. Each time she opens them again, our gazes lock and she starts again until finally, she slides her fingers effortlessly through her own slick.

Mindlessly, my own hands drift to my pants, and I stroke the erection I'm dying to release from its cloth cage.

"Who said you could touch yourself?" Her reprimand is in direct contrast to the gentle way she's handling herself.

It shakes me momentarily from how she has me clitmatized.

I place my hands on the edge of the mattress so she can see them, and when I sink to my knees, she rewards me with a smile. I'm playing my part, but I really wish I could pause to praise her for finding this voice in herself. When she purrs out her next statement, though, all of those thoughts are forgotten.

"Good boy. If you want me to sit on your face, then beg for it."

"Nessa," I exhale her name reverently. "Gorgeous, I need to taste you. Soak my fucking face. Ride me until we find out just how wet you can get. Take what you need. I just need to hear you scream my name."

She rewards me by spreading her thighs wide and uncovering her pussy again.

"Lay down. Right there," she instructs me.

I'm more than happy to comply. Fuck, I'm so taken with her.

She tries not to giggle as she hovers above me. It reminds me briefly how new this is for her.

Looking up her skirt causes my cock to thicken further. I lightly skim her calves and resume my plea as arousal drips from her swollen core.

"Please smother me with that pretty little cunt of yours. I haven't stopped thinking about it in months."

All at once, her skirt covers my face and her knees rest by my ears. This is all the invitation I need to flatten my tongue and lick her from her entrance to her clit and back.

Her approval comes in her touch. She rakes her fingers through my hair, making tingles erupt across my scalp and down my spine.

I make a meal of her, licking and sucking and nipping, relishing the way her core flutters around my tongue when I plunge it into her.

Grasping harder at my hair, she grinds herself against my mouth, chasing friction. I reward her with the smallest bite on the nub, then soothe the prick of pain with a soft kiss.

Hands on her hips, I dig my fingers into her flesh, causing her to gasp.

"Hold me tighter," she cries when I loosen my grip. Her voice raspy with need.

I ignore any concerns about leaving bruises and press harder.

The moans grow louder with each roll of her hips until her legs shake, making it hard for her to hold herself upright. She slumps forward, laying her head on the carpet, her core spasming as I lap up every drop of her release. With a long exhale, she goes limp, and I ease away so she's lying on her belly, sated.

When I stand, the sight before me forces a groan from my chest. Nessa, her skirt riding high, revealing the tiniest view of the curve beneath her ass cheeks. She's so magnificently beautiful.

The word *fuck* rolls off those pretty pink lips on an exhale.

I crave closeness, desperate to maintain the connection we've built. "Can I hold you?" I ask while gathering her in my arms. Her head lolls against my chest as I scoop her up. We ease onto the bed together, spooning.

"Fuck," she says a moment later, flopping onto her stomach. "That was..." She peers back at me, wearing a small grin.

"As you wish, princess." I drape myself over her so that my length drags along her tiny ass. As I pull away, she rolls onto her back, popping up on an elbow.

"Nuh-uh." She wags a single finger at me. "I'm calling the shots here, mister."

Nodding, I rest on my haunches and wait. She scoots back toward the headboard and lounges, arms wide against the pillows, then beckons me with the crook of a finger. I shuck off my pants and boxers in a single move, then line my body up with hers and press my lips to her ear.

"As you wish," I whisper.

In response, goose bumps erupt along her skin.

"What if I want to use you for my own gains and deny you the ability to finish with me?"

Mischievous little pixie. I let my grin bloom into a megawatt smile as I continue to kiss up and down her neck.

"Then I focus on what you enjoy, and the minute you go home, I'll replay every second of tonight while I stroke my cock."

I nip her earlobe, and her breath hitches.

Clearly surprised by the variety of options, she switches gears. Twisting the bullet vibrator pendant between her fingers, she asks, "So I could just rub myself with this, and you'd watch without complaint? You wouldn't get jealous?"

"Why would I be jealous? I got it for you. Toys are teammates, doll."

"I could ride your cock while I did it?" Her brows pull low, like she's not sure of how I'll respond.

"Real men are in it for more than just getting off. We're in it to win the *how many orgasms can I give her* contest in our heads."

Laughing, she shakes her head. "You wouldn't be tempted to say something like..." She drops her voice an octave. *"You don't need that; you have me?* Or *I'm more than enough man for women who aren't..."* she drifts off, shutting down the memory it raised.

I brush back the soft golden strands that have fallen in her face, yearning to show her the reverence she deserves, but somehow doesn't expect, with every touch.

"Listen to me, Ivy. I'm a thirty-three-year-old man. You'll get one, maybe two, goes out of me in a short window. But with enough hydration, the sky is the limit for you. Forget orgasms being reciprocal. I'm in it to win."

That admission breaks any returning anxiety, and her laugh brings our bodies closer together.

"So just to confirm, if what I wanted was to..." she drifts off, averting her gaze.

With a finger under her chin, I turn her head so she's forced to look at me. "Be the one on top and stimulate yourself using the gift I gave you? Yes. You should do that. Fucking hell, please do that. Take what you want from me, Nessa." It comes out husky, because is she kidding me?

"What if I never give you a blow job, but I expect you to let me ride your face anytime I want, day or night?" She worries her bottom lip, her lashes fluttering.

"Then that's what we'll do." I shrug.

There is no denying she's *very* comfortable in her skin when alone. It's a lack of trust in a partner she's hinting at. I won't be like the men who couldn't be trusted with her body, her pleasure.

I'll be happy to show her it's possible. That she deserves that and more.

"You want me to be your on-demand orgasm delivery service in addition to driver? You want me at your beck and call, available any time so you can ride my face and cock, but I don't get blow jobs? That's it? Those are all your terms?" I tick this list off without much thought. *Works for me.*

She's chewing on a finger and nodding along, a smirk creeping up her face. "And a reminder: nobody but me. Until he's gone and we end this fake relationship."

My heart stutters. Game on.

"I'm surprised," I admit. "You're always talking to other people about sex, and you read all those romance books, yet you've hinted time and again that you haven't actually *had* that sort of mind-blowing sex."

"Mateo, it may come as a shock to you, but reading about sex and *having* wild sex are not the same."

With that, I roll over, snag a box of condoms from the nightstand, and toss them to her. "Well, you deserve to *have it.* What's next?" I ask.

She deftly tears into the box and pulls out a foil packet while I get situated with my back against the headboard.

With the square pinched between her teeth, she crawls up my body and lines her center up with my erection. She grinds against my shaft but she doesn't let me in.

She straightens, balancing on her knees, and removes her bracelets. One, then the other, is secured around my wrists overhead. Then she guides my hands down.

I lace my finger behind my head, elbows out, smile wide. She opens the condom with her teeth while grinding her slick pussy against my length, teasing the fuck out of me. Then she sheaths me inside the protective cover with her warmth still lubricating me and raises her hips and grinds over me hard and fast a few times.

My smiles fade to breathy requests, my focus locked on the necklace still resting between her tits. "Show me how you'd play with yourself while you ride me, sweetheart," I bite out.

Filling herself with my swollen cock, she pauses and narrows her eyes. "Sweetheart, doll, princess... you throw all these names around because you never know who you're with. I am not just some random fuckkk."

I buck my hips, pulling that last syllable from her on a long groan.

"Fuck me, Ivy. You're not a random fuck. You are Doctor—" I inhale sharply but force my hips to still. "Nessa. Fucking Rabin. There's nobody like you out here."

She continues to look at me pointedly, still not moving, torturing us both.

"Please, Nessa, please. I need to move. I need you to move. Please," I beg. My smiles are gone, my desire taking over. My spine is tingling, and my balls are drawn tight, my cock painfully hard.

"Good boy." She pats my chest. "You can move with me." She rolls her hips, and I thrust up into her, keeping time until we're a mess of grunts and moans and sighs.

"Holy shit. Fuck, Ivy. I'm close..." I stammer.

She tugs the necklace over her head and taps the button, then holds it against her clit. As the light vibrations cause her muscles to clench around me, spasming rhythmically, I lose all sense of control. The world around me falls away, and I spill into the condom. When my ears stop ringing, she's still moaning, although the sounds quiet little by little. I don't move. She's still in charge. Eventually, she lifts, and I slip out of her. When we're lying side by side, I turn and kiss her temple.

"These cuffs didn't do much in the way of keeping me secured." Grinning, I hold up my free hand.

With a huff, she shoves my chest.

"Take them back." I release the one bracelet still circling my other wrist and hand it to her. "I'll go toss this and bring you a towel."

She must be sated because instead of arguing with me, she hums in agreement and buries her face in her pillow.

When I step back into the room a few minutes later, warm wet washcloth and a hand towel with me, she's asleep, her blond hair fanned around her like a halo. I slide in and drape my arm over her, taking a full hand of her lace-covered tit. Without opening her eyes, she turns and nuzzles against my chest.

She whispers, "Oh, fuck. I forgot how much I enjoy that."

Her breathing evens out quickly from there, but I lie awake for a long time, my nose buried in her golden hair, and inhale her sweet citrus scent—vanilla orange perfume; bright and tangy, just like her—mixed with the sweat and smell of sex that clings to the air.

I fall asleep hoping this is what we need to turn a corner.

nineteen
Nessa

I WAKE to an unfamiliar glow and a shockingly loud snore.

It takes a moment for my eyes to adjust, and when they do, I find the digital clock.

His digital clock. I fell asleep at Mateo's. Fuck. I don't do this. I don't do sleepovers. I need to go home.

I slide out of bed and tiptoe to the living room to pull on my coat and boots. I make it to the front door without stirring him from sleep, but the moment I turn the deadbolt, I've been caught.

My morning has officially gone to shit when a siren, loud enough to wake the dead, wails.

"Stef never had a security system," I say and shut the door.

Heart thrashing, I turn and come face to face with Mateo and his smug fucking smirk.

He shuffles to the keypad I hadn't noticed, and the second the blaring stops, his phone rings. He brings it to his ear, gives them a password, then ends the call, his eyes locked on me the whole time.

Unfortunately, in a town this size, there isn't exactly a lot of overnight excitement for any of the first responders, and a moment later, there's a loud knock. Mateo opens the door and shakes hands with Liam.

"My man. I heard a rumor about this." He points from me to Mateo and back again. He's dressed in a navy T-shirt with the PSFD logo over one pec and a pair of navy pants. Thankfully, the crew didn't show up in their turnout gear. That would have only made this moment more humiliating.

He keeps glancing at me, then looking away quickly, and that's when I remember that all I'm wearing is lingerie and a trench coat. I pull the jacket tighter.

"William." I nod.

"Ma'am." His tone is serious, but within seconds, he and Mateo burst into laughter.

"Bro, you gotta give *Not-Vanessa* here the code if you're going to have middle-of-the-night rendezvous. Or at least don't set the alarm. Prudence and I are the only ones on duty tonight—"

As if on cue, Prudence Cleary comes flying into the room with her usual tote on one shoulder and a large EMS supply bag on the other.

"Liam, you were supposed to wait for me," she huffs out, forcing herself to sound winded when she's holding these parcels like they're weightless.

She's diabolical and I love it.

"False alarm. You can head back to the rig. I'll be happy to carry the gear."

Waving him off, Pru grasps my wrist and pulls me over to the fireplace. A chill is coming in from the door and the opening of the hearth, so I grab hold of my coat and tie it tighter still.

"I'm so glad I bumped into you."

Bumped into me? That's one way to put it.

"That boy Caleb was sniffing around, trying to confirm whether you're really spoken for. Finding you here is good. Good. Very good." She's chattering so quickly I can't follow the words, but her anxiety is palpable.

Placing a hand on her bicep to get her attention, I meet her eyes. The fear reflected back is familiar. She reminds me of the women in the ER reporting attacks.

She reminds you of yourself around him, a suppressed inner voice shouts.

"Can I walk you out? Or do you want to sit and visit for a bit?" With a gentle arm at her back, I lead her toward the door.

The sight of Liam and Mateo still chatting there warms me. Mateo has always been surrounded by people. It's been odd to see him on his own so often lately.

Shit, I'm doing it already without even trying. I'm adding him to my list of responsibilities. Ugh.

As we approach, Pru reaches into her tote and pulls out an oversized magician card. Only it's not a card. It's actually a cell phone case. She taps at the screen, and then three phones around the room vibrate, light up, and ding.

"Prudence, what did you do?" I grumble as I read the message on my home screen.

PEACOCK SPRINGER:

First responders were called in for a five-alarm fire at the residence of Mateo Santos-Manolo. No property damage, but looks like things are heating up between our Sunflower Fest co-chairs.

Mateo and Liam bite back laughs. I narrow my eyes, glaring at them one at a time.

"Get back to bed. I'll text you tomorrow." Liam tips his ballcap at me. "Vanessa," he quips.

"Not my name, Billiam, but nice try," I retort, though my tone lacks venom.

This is an old game of ours. Liam was one of the few guys on Mateo's team who didn't buy the bad-girl façade, hence the faux formality.

I have to talk myself through this internally. Being caught and having my business shared to the town is so uncomfortable. Caleb's venomous jabs that my field of study, my desires, made me... *words I won't let myself think* cause ringing in my ears.

I'm not a "bad girl" for being here, whether Mateo is my boyfriend or not. I'm thirty years old. There's nothing wrong with owning lingerie or hooking up with a hot guy.

The logical and rational self-talk helps, and I barely register Mateo closing the door and lowering the lights.

twenty
Texting Break One

Group Chat: Bad Bitches
[Stef Carter, Lily Long, Delia Shane, Nessa Rabin]

STEF:

What happened at my house last night?

LILY:

<smirk emoji> Someone who isn't me is causing a scene in town.

DELIA:

<high five emoji>

STEF:

The Springer alert says something happened there last night.

NESSA:

<shrug emoji>

LILY:

Oh man, the town gossip is so much more fun when it isn't about me!

NESSA:

Those are inside thoughts, Lil… and yes, it is…
<blond facepalm emoji>

———

STEF:

What the fuck?

MATEO:

New phone, who dis?

STEF:

Hilarious. What did you do?

MATEO:

Nessa tried to sneak out in the middle of the
night and set off an alarm.

STEF:

When did I get an alarm?

MATEO:

You're welcome?

STEF:

Okay, so what else?

MATEO:

I need an epic date to win her over. Any ideas?

STEF:

<link>

MATEO:

Genius. This is why you're the one getting a
PhD… Thank you. Best sister ever.

STEF:

Why did I just get a $500 cash transfer?

MATEO:

Because dinner is on me. Grab your husband
and go out to dinner. Pick someplace nice.

———

STEF:

Nessssssssss, what's wrong with my brother? WE
COULD BE SISTERS!!!

NESSA:

It's almost midnight. Are you delirious from
studying?

STEF:

Mateo sent us out to dinner and asked me to
help him. Is this working?

NESSA:

Where did you go?

STEF:

We went to the East Village. We ate too much
and wandered. Got some drinks. Got more
drinks. They were yummy. Now Lee's sitting with
the tattoo artist, discussing drawing techniques.

NESSA:

Tattoo artist? LEE IS GETTING A TATTOO?

STEF:

No. Well, yes. But he wants to get an
apprenticeship.

PARENT SHIP

PIRATE SHIP

NESSA:

Apprenticeship?

STEF:

<face palm emoji> That.

Drink some water and take Advil before bed. Go enjoy your date with your husband.

STEF:

Hey, wait... you distracted me. You didn't answer me...

———

MATEO:

What are you doing tomorrow?

NESSA:

Trying to prep for Rosh Hashanah. That's Jewish New Year.

MATEO:

That's the apples one, right?

NESSA:

Apples and honey, yeah.

MATEO:

Perfect. Get dressed. Wear something comfortable and cute and be ready to go around 11. We're taking your car. It's good top-down weather.

NESSA:

Perv

MATEO:

I meant the car, but if you want to hang out with me with your top down again, I'm not going to argue.

twenty-one
Nessa

AT ELEVEN A.M. SHARP, Mateo saunters up in light wash jeans paired with a fitted henley that emphasizes the muscles rippling down his shoulders and biceps, covering the tattoo sleeve he has down his right arm that stops just above the elbow. It may be hidden but it's burned into my memory.

The fabric stretches perfectly across what I now intimately know are a defined chest and a full six-pack. He even has that stupid hip bone V-thing guys who work out too much get. I can't stop my mind from drifting. *Shit.*

I try to fix my red lipstick subtly but find myself forced to wipe a little drool from the side of my mouth.

"Give me a twirl, gorgeous," he shouts with a spin of his finger.

"Who, me?" I press a hand to my cheek and toss my hair, feigning shyness, though I quickly erupt into a giggle.

Have fun today, I repeat to myself. I don't want to admit it, but spending time with Mateo is fun. *Don't be afraid. He is his own person.* These are the kinds of phrases my therapist and I work on when the negative thoughts creep in.

I hop down the porch steps and give a little pirouette.

He scans me up and down, eyes lazily lingering, causing heat to rise into my cheeks. *Since when do I blush?*

My hair is pulled back from my face with a bright red claw clip, showing off three gold hoops—one in each ear and the third in my left nostril. I typically wear a simple clear stopper that prevents the piercing from closing, but fun Nessa is here today, and she's bringing it back.

"Whoa, rockstar. Look at you..." His words trail off, but the warm appreciation is there.

My reaction—the skin tingles and a longing to hug him—feels foreign. I open my mouth to reply, but my throat is dry and my voice is scratchy. Has all the moisture in my body rerouted to my panties?

I clear my throat and try again.

"You told me to wear sturdy footwear but to dress up. Does this work?" I ask.

I worry my lip, noting his casual outfit. I'm about to head in and change when he steps forward and grasps my wrist.

"Don't go. If you change, I'll cry."

The tone brings memories of him begging in the bedroom flashing back, and I nod.

"Can I take the wheel?" he asks, lazily pointing at the green sports car.

"Can you drive *your* car? Um, yeah. That's fine." I scoff, trying to keep my lips from twitching.

He guides me to the passenger side with a hand low on my back. Always showing off his chivalrous side, he opens the door and waits for me to be seated before softly closing it.

———

MATEO IS RELAXED behind the wheel. I've come to cherish these moments because he's stopped poking me for information and is now focused on playing deejay. Today, we sing along—loudly—to his eclectic playlist.

When it switches to a hip-hop song about "stoners," I retrieve my vape pen from my bag and wiggle it in his line of sight.

"This okay?" I ask tentatively. *Stop testing him,* a voice argues back.

Mateo nods nonchalantly before making a very *chalant* face. "You smoke around me more than I expected is all," he says, his eyes quickly darting to me. "Not like it's a problem. Just, surprising? You've always seemed so... put together..."

"I'm not put together?" I push back, my tone biting, betraying the mental claw sharpening. Is this a *here is the history of how racist that is* moment or a *medical education* one?

I swallow down some of the hostility, but not enough, to disguise my tone as I say, "I see some shit at work. Then, I'm everyone's emergency contact."

Fuck, that sounded like a complaint.

Lifting my chin, I infuse an unnatural level of confidence directed toward myself and say, "Not that I don't love what I do. And I'm really fucking good at it."

Yeah, as long as it's about someone else. That damn annoying voice is back, and the more time I spend with Mateo, looking for Caleb over my shoulder, the louder it gets.

Inhaling, I take in that unique mix of damp peat and spicy smoke that comes from heavy clouds and bonfires this time of year.

"I wouldn't expect someone like you to care," I admit sheepishly while playing with the edge of my chipped nail polish.

He grasps the knob on the radio and turns the volume down.

"Someone like me, huh? What am I like?" His voice wavers as he asks, betraying insecurity behind the playful façade.

He's been nothing short of vulnerable and kind, while I hide behind a wall. The wall he laid bricks in when we were teens, but that Caleb topped with barbed wire.

136

I gasp, taking in the rolling orchards and vineyards on each side of the road. Sometimes it's easy to forget we're so close to these farms. I shove the vape back in my bag, unused, and exhale.

Ready to move on, I turn the volume up again. "Oh, wait. Good song."

In the back of my head, I add to the list of ways he's responded any time there's mention of him being less serious or intelligent. I don't particularly want to care, but it's starting to weigh on me.

The air between us remains charged, grinding my frayed nerves.

"We still need to name the kittens. Want to figure that out as we go on this mystery drive?" I ask, hoping he can read the gesture.

"Dope, let's do it." He shoots me a grin.

"Should we give them witchy names? The black cat could be Salem—like the show? Maybe the orange ones can be, um…" I'm trying, but this TV thing is really his domain.

"Nah, that kitten is no warlock," he says. "He's more of an artist. He's a little trouble, a little snuggle. Sort of like you."

Finally, he turns the car from the paved roadway onto a winding dirt path.

We're volleying names and reasons for our choices when a Fugees' song comes on.

Cocking a brow, I suggest, "Wyclef, Lauryn, and Pras Michel?"

"Yes. Wyclef is a perfect name for the black cat." He grins, though the expression quickly fades. "Aw man." He scrubs a hand over his face.

"We named the bunnies for the psychologists and cats for The Fugees."

I frown, confused. "Okay, and?"

"The Fugees are a hip-hop group. Bunnies *hop*," he says, his tone genuinely disappointed by this revelation.

With a laugh at his ridiculousness, I pat his shoulder. "There, there, Matty. It'll be okay."

THE CAR slowly creeps down the dusty roadway as he follows the signs telling us to *park here*. In the distance sits the Kelly Orchards. Yet instead of the usual crowds, the lot is empty, and rather than pull into the gravel lot, Mateo rolls toward the family home.

I aimlessly reach for him, my hands tracing the lines up and down his arm. I'm drawing invisible swirls over the hidden intricate black ink design encircling a sun with eight rays.

What is happening with me lately?

It's completely inappropriate timing, which only encourages me to tease him further. Ghosting my hand from his knee up his thigh, I watch as he thickens against the fitted denim, relishing the way his breath hitches.

He quickly schools his expression and clears his throat. "Trouble maker."

I hum, tapping my lips and feigning innocence. "I'm not doing anything."

He unbuckles his seat belt and turns to face me. "Nessa, what are we doing?"

He exhales and rubs at his forehead. "First you can't stand me, then we have sex. You barely speak to me the rest of the weekend, but then, for months, text me randomly. You hate me. You swear we'll never fake date." He licks his lips. "Next thing I know, I'm coming to your rescue and we're together every day. Suddenly, we're making out, then you storm off. Now there are foster pets in my house." His lips twitch a little there but quickly fall into a flat line again. "Then, you arrive in lingerie and we have an amazing night together, only for you to try to sneak out."

Fuck, when he puts it that way, it's hard to deny I'm playing games.

"This is what I know: we both have reputations that don't quite fit who we really are. I haven't been with anyone but you since May, and I don't want to be with anyone else, even if you can't see what I see."

"What don't I see?" I whisper, sliding my hand again. Oops.

"Insufferable, woman," he grits out between clenched teeth. He swings open the car door and heaves a deep breath. He stomps around the car and pulls open my door. "Let's go," he says, hand held out. "Folks are waiting for us."

With one more huff, he yanks me toward the front door of the farmhouse.

Instinctively, we lace our fingers.

He brings his lips to the shell of my ear, his breath lightly tickling me as he whispers, "This is a date and a mission to get information."

He presses a kiss to my pulse point, and in response, blood whooshes in my ears. It's so loud and all-consuming that I lose touch with reality for a moment. I'm jolted back when he knocks loudly on the wooden door.

The door swings open, and Liam appears, wearing a grin. "Nice to see you during daylight hours." He winks at me before exchanging a single-armed hug with Mateo.

Confused, I shuffle into the house. This is the start of a horror movie, or a porn, or both. A horror porn. Is that a thing? It's probably a thing. I should look it up.

"Gran was so excited to hear that you're visiting *and* bringing a dose of estrogen with you," Liam says as he closes the door behind us.

The home is decorated in a country style, from the giant rusty milk pail filled with umbrellas and canes to walls covered in family-photos.

The most heavenly scent filters through the house, with hints of cinnamon spice, vanilla, and something fruity. If I could morph into a cartoon character, I would float my way toward the steaming scent trails.

I no longer care about whether I've found myself in a horror film, porn or not. I want to know what Liam's Irish grandmother is cooking.

Inside the kitchen, we find Gran and his dad, James, who greets Mateo with a bear hug and a genuine smile.

"It's great to see you, son."

twenty-two
Mateo

"THANKS, COACH."

Liam's dad was my high school basketball coach, and he's also the mayor emeritus.

"Seriously," I say, turning back to Liam. "Thank you for setting up today. And thanks, Gran"—I give her a nod—"for helping me."

In the warm kitchen lighting, Coach looks relaxed. He's gregarious and fatherly, like the man I've always known, dressed like he always is, in a polo emblazoned with the school logo and pleated-front khakis.

"You kidding?" James says. "This is a favor to me. Ma has been excited about this for days." He leans in, his hands in his pockets. "But I have a bone to pick with you. Why is it that I have to hear about this development"—he nods at Nessa—"from the Springer?"

Nessa's expression morphs from confusion to hesitant courteousness. I bask in the way she's so easily brought into the circle, despite the ongoing banter at my expense.

Maybe that's why I'm a bit too earnest when I say, "Let's not scare her off yet, please?"

"Yeah, Dad. Come on. Let Mateo scare her off on his own," Liam teases, his eyes dancing.

I blow into my fist and lift my middle finger, causing the room to fill with laughter.

Even Nessa is hiding her own smirk behind her hand.

"Okay, enough already. My turn," Gran says and she envelopes me in a hug. She rests a tiny hand on my arm, eyes twinkling. "It's good you're home, Matty. We missed you."

Turning toward Nessa, she puts on a lilting brogue and teases, "Is a real banger fest here, you agree, lass?"

Looping an arm through Nessa's, she leads her to the table in the breakfast nook.

She lifts the cloche off a cake stand, then slices and plates two pieces of apple cake. "We're going to have some tea and talk, then we'll get to cooking. You boys want to collect more apples?"

Nessa brightens. "Oh! Is the plan to pick apples and bake?"

Yes! Add one point for Mateo.

"Actually, I wanted to have Gran teach you to make her famous apple cake so you can bring it to the family holiday," I say, scratching the back of my head.

"We can all go. No problem," Liam says. "But give us a moment with Mateo first, Ness."

"Go have your man chat, Mateo. But don't take too long, or I might convince this pretty lass to jump ship for my Liam." She smiles at her own wisecrack.

"Gran," Liam groans.

As we cross the kitchen to the back door, I catch Nessa's eye and give her a wink.

———

THE STONE PATIO hasn't changed in the years I've been gone. The unlit firepit sits in the center, surrounded by weathered wooden Adirondack chairs.

Once we're out of earshot of the women, I turn to Liam. "Does Gran not know?"

He shakes his head with a laugh, puffing out his chest. "Oh, she knows. Won't stop her from trying to steal your girl and set her up with me. I am, after all, a strapping fireman, as well as her favorite grandson."

"William," James says in that sort of tone parents give in warning.

"It's not my fault that I have more common sense than—"

"Actually, sir," I interrupt, eager to get to the reason I'm here. "I wanted to ask you about Jim and those Reynolds folks. He seems pretty taken by their false promises, so I need every advantage I can get to stage an upset." My stomach twists with a mixture of anticipation and fear, but I power through. "Got any information that would help me?"

"Of course he's impressed by the interloper." Liam throws his head back and barks out a laugh.

Mostly because of my nerves, I find myself joining in.

"Be nice," James chides, though his lips twitch a little, like he's resisting the urge to chuckle. "That's your brother." Turning to face me, he says, "Who cashes the checks each month isn't what's important here. It's who holds the deed."

I frown as I decipher the comment. "The deed isn't in Grant's name?" Grant, who thinks he's selling an entire block on main street, has been courting my rival and the mayor, who may have no power in the sale whatsoever. This is exactly what I came to James for. I tuck this information away for later.

"It's the kind of information I would want before investing too much time courting someone for a sale, that's for sure." He nods. "Glenn Morgan is a good friend of mine. If you need help getting a meeting on the books, give me a call. However…" He stretches his legs out. "Why are you wasting your time with us? Didn't you bring your girlfriend out to do something else?"

"Like impress her with his hometown hero best friend," Liam says, giving a wide smile.

Rising, James gives us a stern look. "No doing donuts in my fields in the carts, gentleman. Understood?"

"That happened one time, and we were *sixteen*," Liam protests.

I clear my throat to camouflage a chuckle. "Yes, sir. Let's go grab the apples for your Gran," I tell Liam.

As if on cue, Nessa appears, all bouncing curls and wide eyes.

twenty-three
Nessa

"LEARN ANYTHING INTERESTING IN THERE?" Liam asks with a smirk as he and I stand. Together, we head toward the pair of golf carts parked behind the house.

"Yeah, Bill-I-am. I learned that you are 'woefully' single." I lower my voice. "Hasn't Gran met Christian? Like, many times?"

Liam rolls his eyes. "My 'roommate' who shares a bedroom with me? Of course she's met him. She loves him. She seems to think being bisexual means it should be easy to move on from this phase and 'find a nice girl and settle down like a good Catholic.' After going to Confession, of course."

I exhale and keep my expression open, holding space for him.

He grunts. "Don't be a therapist right now, Nessa."

I shake my head and say, "Shit, sorry. That sucks."

Because I work in human sexuality, people assume I'll always know what to say in moments like this. But I typically steer clear of inserting myself into queer issues. When the victim assistance intake work at the hospital indicates a patient may need support in that area, I pass the forms along to therapists with specialties that will be more helpful. I end up with a caseload full of women in their teens and twenties, generally from the colleges in the area, before they transition to private practices.

Liam makes his way into the driver's seat. Before I can climb in next to him, Mateo grabs my hand, and in one move, he slides into the passenger seat and pulls me onto his lap. Wrapping his arm around my middle, he whisper-begs, "You have to say something nice about me in public or act like you like me. Your rules, gorgeous."

I slide off his lap, squeezing between him and the safety bar. Mateo and I are so close I can feel the heat from his thigh against my own. I lace my fingers with his and turn to take in his face. Our eyes lock and hold long enough for a flicker of warmth to take hold.

"Maybe," I say.

His focus drifts to my mouth, and on instinct, my tongue slides over my bottom lip. I think he's thinking of kissing me—

"Time to go, lovebirds," Liam calls from behind the wheel.

Then he does just that, jostling me to the side toward the safety bar. Mateo recovers quickly, pulling me back into his arms. The thick, corded muscles beneath the soft cotton of his waffle-knit shirt press into my side, causing goosebumps to erupt on my skin.

"Easy does it, Ness. Let's not toss you from the cart just yet," Liam says.

With a huff, I steady myself. Then, determined to ignore the heat emanating from Mateo, I force my attention fully to the scenery.

Liam provides us a tour so polished it must be part of his routine here. While holding the steering wheel with one hand, he waves toward a tiny cluster of trees mixed with beautiful yellow and blue-violet bell flowers that seem out of place.

"What's the tiny grove with flowers?"

Mateo relaxes, holding my waist and brushing his lips to my temple. This is just for us. Like so much of the actual intimacy we've shared, it's blurring the lines I'm trying to draw for myself.

Rich with emotion, Liam says, "Those are the original apple trees. When Grandpa took over the property, they didn't even bear enough fruit to sell at the market. He reached out to other local farms and started a seed-swap network. That's how we became connected to the Morgan and Hendrix families." Liam beams a megawatt smile.

"What did they add?" Mateo pulls me closer, one arm banded around my midsection. He's like my own personal seat belt, but warmer.

"Was it the flowers?" I wonder audibly.

That brings an appreciative laugh from Liam's lips. "Dude, she's good," he says to his friend.

"That's my Ivy Monster," Mateo says, watching me with a sparkle in his eye.

Liam laughs. "They wanted to use plants that would serve as additional food sources. They tried mint, basil, chamomile, and chives that first year. No new trees—those cost a ton. Still do."

"Smart business sense," Mateo chirps.

"Would have been if it worked." Liam shakes his head. "To answer your question, Nessa, those flowers are nonedible. Some are even poisonous to humans. It's tansy and Comfrey. They're pretty, but you have to know how to handle them properly."

Mateo tickles my side, though he keeps his face neutral as he says, "Ironic that *poison* fixed the problem."

I give him a side-long glance. *Poison ivy—professional fixer.*

"The goal was to fight off apple scab and pests, and they succeeded. Even if it wasn't how they originally imagined doing it." I swear if a voice could wink, that's what Liam's did. Like the guys are in on this together.

As I lean into Matty and listen, *really, truly*, listen even if the metaphor is frustratingly pronounced, something starts to shake loose in my chest.

"All that hard work by more than a few generations, and your brother is willing to sell your family history to the highest bidder? Even if it means destroying your legacy?" His lip curls in disgust, though his tone more questioning than declarative.

I let the words sit. I want to say so much. I want to scream about the injustice. I want to call his brother a massive douche canoe. I want to let my anger at the Calebs and the Jims of the world lead this moment. But I'm grounded in the present by the man beside me. The one who shows a deep love and respect for his family and their sacrifice—and surrounds himself with like-minded men. A tingling sensation erupts throughout me as the hairs along my arms and the base of my neck rise. That voice that has been trying to warn me to run even jumps in, taking me in a new direction. She says, *Nessa, these men are more like Aba than your ex or your clients' partners.*

A few rows of bushes and trees farther, the cart slows to a stop.

"All right, this is your stop," Liam says, giving Mateo a look I can't quite read.

The silent conversation that passes between them is ended by the golf cart's engine turning over noisily.

"I've got one more item to grab while I'm out this way. Be back in a bit." Liam winks, then he speeds away.

———

SILENTLY, I stare down at where my hand is engulfed in Matteo's and decide not to pull away.

We amble down the row of trees until we find a large empty basket waiting at the aisle cap.

"While we're alone, can you please tell me why you've been playing hot and cold with me?" Mateo exhales, then pulls his shoulders back, resolute.

As we walk, I focus on my breathing, fidgeting with the ring on my free hand.

"Nessa." It comes out like a whisper. Concern and confusion lace the soft tones. "What happened between us?"

My heartbeat ticks up a notch, and I can feel his scrutiny as he takes in every slight twitch I try to suppress.

I'm too warm, so I tug on my sweater, desperate to feel the early fall breeze. I kick at a fallen apple, then finally force myself to look at him.

"Well," I start, nerves skittering through me. What do I want him to know? Heart pounding a little too hard, I say, "Do you remember the joke you made the summer before we started high school?"

"I made a lot of jokes," he says, brows furrowed.

With a groan, I say, "The joke was 'do you know why Jewish girls give the best head?' but it has a bunch of different punchlines. I can't tell you which one you used, but I can tell you about the summer leading up to it and what happened after you said it."

I drop my shoulders, detangling our hands, and step to the side so I can take him in fully as I unload this story.

"You probably don't remember, but that year, when I went to camp, I left without..." I look down and wave a hand in front of my chest. "These."

His dark eyes are intense and full of curiosity and confusion.

I try to push forward verbally and physically by strolling down the next row of trees, kicking apples on the ground as I go.

"So..." he says, leading me to continue.

"So... that summer, I kind of... ballooned? I wasn't prepared to jump up two cup sizes in, like, a month. All those new, cute bathing suits Ema bought for me? They couldn't contain me. In a blink, I jumped from girlhood to womanhood. And ..." I breathe out, reminding myself that the man I've spent time with over the last few weeks is no longer the teenage boy who said those things. I know that. Rationally.

That doesn't quell the anger I've held on to for so long, though.

"I suddenly became the butt of every joke everywhere I went. Everything about me was suddenly sexualized, and I wasn't anywhere close to being ready for that kind of maturity. It went on the whole time, so I just, I just wanted to come home. I wanted it all to stop."

He swallows audibly, his expression full of apprehension.

"It wasn't just you. I mean... fuck. The 'adults' at camp were just as bad as the kids. Most of them were young. College age. This was the era of paparazzi up-skirt shots and tearing down Jessica Simpson's body. The world didn't care about 'body positivity' or slut-shaming, or the hyper-sexualization of teens. I think I kind of knew that, but I was fourteen. I didn't fully understand." I stomp on an apple and am rewarded with a satisfying crunch.

Not realizing I've walked ahead until the echo of a loud snap echoes behind me, I spin to see Mateo kicking apples into tree trunks.

We move this way for another moment. Thwack. Stomp. Crunch. I'm getting mad, but I'm taking it out on the rotting fruit, so it's fine. "Feelings are all good, Nessa, even the negative ones," my own therapist's voice repeats in my brain.

With shaking legs, I pause to inhale deeply and force the words out. "All summer, I was teased. Called a slut because my shirts were too tight. I've reflected on this a lot, and I think it was also because I was still a loud and silly little girl in many ways, but my body had decided it was time to grow up."

I was trapped somewhere between the little girl I'd been and the woman I'd eventually become.

"What does that have to do with us?" Jaw ticking, he sends another apple hurtling toward the tree. His fists are balled at his sides like he's concentrating on not touching me or hitting something.

With a deep breath, I focus on the toes of my combat boots.

"The Jewish community is small but visible, so this feels a bit like betraying family, but okay." I exhale another shaky breath.

"The type of summer camp I attended was pretty secular, but the leaders still initiated lots of intense conversations with us about culture. Or, I guess, in America it's seen as religion. Anyhow, the biggest talking points were that we should date, marry, and someday have babies with a Jewish partner. There was so much pressure around dating, and we were American teens. So, all the typical 'he's a stud, she's a slut' things were there too."

My shoulders droop. I don't think I'm explaining this well.

"Do you watch documentaries at all?"

"Sure. I watch ones like *The Industries that Built this Nation.* That kind of thing. They're pretty dope." He rubs at the back of his neck. "Did you know that ketchup exists because people used to eat meat that was practically rancid?"

"Gross. Also gross: purity culture. Your mom took you and Stef to church, so you know what I'm talking about, right? Where we're taught that girls have to be virgins until they get married and then they have to magically be sexually liberated performance artists for their one true love?"

His eyes widen. "Well, yeah. But that's, like, the church. This was different. You said it was a Jewish camp."

"It was inescapable in America. Didn't matter whether it was from a church or not. Like, obviously, as a Catholic, you've heard stories about priests who did terrible things. But other groups had horrible leaders too." I swallow thickly, feeling the heat pricking behind my eyes.

"My camp was one of them." I shake but press forward. "The little brother of my good friend is my hero. He's a rabbi; their older brother is a lawyer.

"The younger brother, the one who's now a rabbi, was a victim as a teen, and lawyer brother was, as you can probably guess, his lawyer. He was one of multiple John Does in an FBI case. He was brave as hell.

They went public in an op-ed to encourage others to speak up before the clock ran out on the statute of limitations. There have been other articles about our camp too, but this was the closest to me personally."

I throw my head back and let out a sardonic laugh. I swallow thickly and prick at the backs of my eyes as I recall the day my phone blew up with the link over and over.

"The thing is, everyone wants to have former-slut and current Doctor Masturbate help them process *their* emotions. They forget that I chose to call my podcast *Flicking the Bean with Rabin* to take back another shitty joke from that era." The words come faster now, and I just let it all fly.

Despite the tears, my chest fills with pride at all I've built. I continue to stare at the ground, but I can feel Mateo's eyes on me. I let it all spill out. Every story I've been holding in. Story after story people have brought to me. The weight I've been carrying laid before his strong arms; I give every friend, acquaintance, and patient my full undivided attention. Every. Time.

He lets me monologue through this.

"Back to where you and I are concerned," I eventually say. "I was miserable by the time I came home. My time at camp had always been the best part of the year. That year, though, it was not fun like it was supposed to be. And Shae heard whispers of it all. That fucking destroyed me. I was supposed to be looking out for her and Tal. Instead, I was setting them up to be considered trouble because their sister was."

He laughs. He fucking *laughs*. "You are trouble, but it's not like I'm one to talk. And so what? Don't you have fun when you let that side out?"

I ignore the comment. I need to get the rest of this out. "So here I am, fourteen years old, excited to be out of this pressure cooker summer. I'm so happy to be home. I'm in your yard, where your folks are hosting a cookout like they always did. We'd been singing karaoke."

"Classic Santos-Manolo event activity," he adds.

I laugh, and the tension eases. Yeah, every party there included an impromptu talent show.

"This year, the entire basketball team was there with you. I brought my copy of *Eclipse*, excited to compare notes with Stef and Lily—"

He grins. "Is this when the Team Jacob obsession began?"

I give a sly smile. "After that summer, it became impossible to not see the good in an underdog." I blow out a breath. "Anyway, here I am. I'm home. I'm with my people, and all I want is to leave that undeserved reputation behind me."

Deep breath, I coach myself.

"It wasn't just your joke. It was that my whole summer had been one bad joke. During our teenage years, girls are either virgins or whores. That's it. And your joke spiraled out of control. Somehow after those jabs, a rumor began. I've heard all the versions. The most extreme included giving four basketball players blowjobs in a line. I was called a chicken head for my entire high school career. I was a slut. I was a bad girl even though, at that point, I had only kissed one boy." Moisture pools in my eyes again. I hate this contradiction.

I hate that I speak about being empowered but am still restrained by judgment I received a lifetime ago. *Not only a lifetime ago*, the little voice digs.

"It never mattered what I did or didn't do, or with whom. I'm loud and willing to say outlandish things, which must mean I do them too. Right?" My voice cracks. "I don't judge what other people do. Consenting adults should be free to do what they want. But they're also entitled to privacy, and given that I've only been with two—excuse me, three—men in my life, I don't like being seen as some wild thing. It makes me angry. Virginity is a myth. Whores were powerful women, so we took away their power, and... I did what I do when something is hard for me to understand. I studied it. I dove into understanding it all from every angle."

My anger mixes with all the other big feelings swirling, causing tears to flow hot and quiet down my face. In that moment, the restraint he's been holding on to breaks, and he moves to me.

Between one breath and the next, I'm pressed against the rough bark of a tree, my fingers tracing knots in the wood to steady myself.

His large, soft, manicured hands reach my face with superhuman speed, his thumbs swiping away tears that refuse to recede.

His lips quirk up on one side. "That's my Ivy Monster."

I peer through my wet lashes, finding Mateo wearing a reverent expression, lips parted and breathing slow and steady. He's my anchor in this storm.

"What happened next, gorgeous girl?"

"Boston," I croak.

He wraps his arms around me, and I allow my body to go slack, supported by his warm strength.

"I went from being the inexperienced troublemaker to the good girl who was 'wife material.' My sorority and Satan's fraternity kept us in each other's orbit, and it just sort of happened from there. I don't know. It was awful to feel like I had to make myself smaller for him. That I had to hide myself."

I look down, scoffing at my bust because it could never be considered small.

"I fit his image of the perfect WASP wife—despite being Jewish and my German and Middle Eastern backgrounds. Oh, and I did not come from the kind of money he did. The more I had to repress myself, the more I hated being with him. But I didn't know how to move on. I was stuck in a cycle. Even when things became toxic between us, I couldn't walk away."

I force myself to breathe evenly. I can't believe I am telling him all this. Even Delia hasn't gotten this out of me.

"Like I said, I studied these things, yet I couldn't prevent them in my own life. Satan really believed the hype around my identity and oral sex skills too. Some of my Jewish clients have told me the same. Everyone has a different punch line. The punch isn't what's significant, but being punched in the back of the throat when you're teary eyed and trying to say to slow down is."

There. I said it all. I exhale deeply, desperate to end the conversation.

His eyes meet mine, the dark brown molten with anger. "Excuse me?"

His hands make their way from my face to my shoulders as he hunches like he could take off and run or maybe throw a punch. I don't know. I just know he's not mad at me. This is sheer protectiveness.

"I need to know right now," he says, his voice shaky. "Is this something that happened to you or a patient?"

I can only nod. The answer is both.

He steps back, as if checking to see if I need space. His gaze is intense, making it hard to look at him.

As I lower my focus to our feet, he gives a loose strand of hair a twirl, then brushes it behind my ear.

The distance between us is too much. I need to be back in the comfort of his arms. I wind my arms around his middle and pull him back to me. As we melt into one another, the weight of it all pushes me against the rough bark of the tree behind me.

"I'm so honored you told me all of this," he murmurs softly at my ear. "My side of the story is not going to measure up, but if you want to know, I will tell you."

twenty-four
Mateo

FUCK. I'm such an asshole. I have to make this right.

Do I comfort her? Apologize to her? Tell her I can't believe I didn't know even a little of this?

When her tears have slowed and she gives me permission, I lean back to look her in the eye. "Of course you hated me. I was a jerk. Of course that 'joke' isn't funny. I should never have said it."

Her lips twitch, like she's fighting the urge to say "no shit."

I lightly stroke at the curl that keeps springing back in front of her face as we talk.

"There's something more important that I need to check on, though." My hands shake as I lower them, feeling like I should move away, give her space.

But she grasps my hands and laces her fingers with mine.

"The first time we were together..." My voice quivers as I ask a question that could change everything. "You'd been drinking. I didn't think you were too drunk to consent, but... You did want to be with me, right?"

My heart lurches. I need her to respond, even if it's to tell me how badly I fucked up.

I loosen my grip. This way, if she wants to take her hands back, she can. Instead, she squeezes tighter and meets my eyes. Our height difference is her advantage right now.

"You mean the wedding weekend? Where I went to your hotel room and took off my own dress? That was my choice. It was a choice that tequila may have helped make, but it was mine."

Her answer eases only a little of my tension.

"From now on, I won't touch you unless you're sober. Or unless you storm into my house wearing something like you did the other night." I crack a smile, hoping to settle my anxiety and hers.

"I knew the improv king would appreciate a movie moment," she teases.

My chest lightens. "Life with you has been a bit of a rom-com, if you think about it."

"You know the way those go, right?" she says. "Every one of the heroines I looked up to when I was a teen started out nerdy. The story is always the same. The nerdy girl gets a makeover, and then bam! She gets a boyfriend."[1]

"Not all of them," I argue, guiding her along the aisle of trees again. It's easier to talk while I'm moving. "Take basically all of Lindsay Lohan's movies," I counter. "In *Freaky Friday* a wild child learns that she's perfect as she is. In *Mean Girls* the new kid at school learns that popularity and boys aren't worth the price."

"Okay," she relents. "I'll give you those, I guess—".

"You're Olive from *Easy-A*! I know that's Emma Stone, but listen to me: she lies, she fakes a reputation because she wants to *help people*, even if it means she gets hurt. Oh. My. God. You're Olive." I release her hand to pump my fist and jog backward so she can't look away.

"Excuse me?"

"You let some guys talk a big game. Say things about you that weren't true. You didn't fight for your reputation. You—"

"I used it to my advantage and disappeared behind it," she says, with a beleaguered sigh.

I turn back to walk in step with her, worrying my lip. I mentioned that my side of the story looked different. It's probably time to put it out there.

"While you were dealing with those rumors," I say, my chest tightening. "I was battling my own fallout from our verbal sparring."

This drains the levity from our conversation, pulling us up short. As I catalog her eyes, the way her lips turn down, I worry this isn't the right moment. She's still so defeated. But if I don't get it out, then I'll never clear the air.

I swallow past the lump in my throat. "That night, in my parents' backyard, the guys had just finished another round of hilarious jokes about my grades when you arrived. Always the optimist who wanted to help, my dad said, 'You know what they call the guy who graduates last in his class from medical school? Doctor. They call him doctor.' That had the guys hooting and hollering about how I couldn't possibly get into medical school.

"They were doubling down on jokes about how I was a dumb jock and the token Asian. They concluded all the brains in the family had gone to Stef." I lift a shoulder and let it fall. "We both know that's probably true; she's fucking brilliant. But I was a kid, and I was embarrassed."

"You're smart too, just in a different way. I see it." Nessa presses a palm to my pec. Can she feel how fast my heart's beating? How stupid I feel admitting to the lame reason I said what I did?

"Regardless, what I did was wrong. I was young and stupid. So stupid. You walked in, looking so grown up. Truly, you didn't look like a little girl anymore. You did look like... well, you looked as gorgeous as you do now, Ivy." My chest tightens at the memory. "You caught my eye, and somehow, the hormones and the jabs between the boys turned my brain to mush. So I opened my mouth to make a joke, thinking I'd keep the same energy. Instead, I bombed. Hard."

Blowing out a breath, I duck my head, letting the shame engulf me.

"Can I?" I swallow past the lump in my throat. "Can I just make a joke of this all right now so I can say it?"

"Sure." She presses a little harder, like she can slow my racing heart.

"Then the vicious girl, Poison Ivy, clapped back. She shouted, 'You can't suck a dick you can't find, Mr. Chow,' referencing *The Hangover*. Then she stormed off."

I hang my head, knowing there is no comparing the two, wincing at the thought of meeting her gaze. *I really am a fucking idiot.* The silence stretches on, but neither of us moves. The only sounds are the leaves of the trees rustling in the wind and the periodic exhales we take.

Breaking the silence, Nessa croaks, "Did I really say that?"

"In front of the whole team, and all your friends. You didn't let me get away with shit. How the guys turned that into a story about anything other than how you handed me my ass is insane. They called me Chow for months after that."

I chance a look at her. Her lips quirk, and then a giggle slips free. That laugh causes all the tension to evaporate.

I lean in closer, wrapping an arm around her waist. "Let it out. Can we laugh at how horrible teens are?"

That earns me a full smile and a chuckle.

Laughing together feels good.

Leaning closer, I whisper, "I am truly sorry, and you'll never have to do anything you don't want to. You're in charge. You'll always call the shots."

Her laughter dying, she slides her hand to the back of my neck and guides me down until our noses touch.

Eyes glimmering with mischief, she says, "You started it, but I guess this will finish it." With a whimper, she crushes her lips to mine.

All at once, it's frantic. Like we can wipe the slate clean. Start fresh and be free of those memories. A real chance. I part my lips and lick into her mouth lightly. The air around us grows warmer, my skin flushes, my muscles tense. My cock stirs to life as our kiss deepens, but we're yanked from the frenzy when a heavy cough cuts in.

"Sorry to interrupt, but since you were busy, I got these." Liam points at the large crate of apples on the front seat of the golf cart.

Heaving a few breaths, we turn to him. If I look anything like Nessa, we're both flushed and glassy-eyed.

twenty-five
Nessa

ONCE WE'VE RETURNED to the main farmhouse, Liam hauls the apple crate, shepherding us in through the kitchen door. While I'm at the sink washing my hands, I catch him discreetly pass something to Mateo.

Mateo steps behind me at the sink, caging me into his arms. I'm pressed between his body and the basin so firmly I can't even turn. With a weighty clink, he pops a mason jar on the counter next to me.

"Liam grabbed you some fresh honey to bring to your folks too. There's even a piece of the comb inside. Look," he whispers.

My face heats from the thoughtful gesture, and I'm glad I can't turn to see him just now. The earlier stomach flutters return and I feel almost hazy, forgetting where we are or who else is around.

The spell is broken when Liam boyishly shoves Mateo over and says to me, "excuse me, not-Vanessa," as he scoots me to the side. He fills a glass with water from the tap and chugs it, giving an exaggerated, "ah."

"Back to work with you." Gran swats the air while giving Liam a firm stare. Looking around, I see that she's laid everything out in premeasured cups and created a workstation on the butcher block island for us.

"Mrs. Kelly, you didn't have to go to this much trouble for us," I say while struggling with the apron neck loop.

"Here, let me," Mateo says, then gently places the neck strap over my head and tenderly sweeps my long hair out from underneath. His touch skims the back of my neck, then traces down my spine, leaving a buzz of electricity in its wake.

Grasping the waist ties, he pulls them taught. "This okay?" he quietly asks, loosening his hold before making a bow. He lets his hands graze and linger on my lower back.

Overwhelmed by the emotion such simple gestures elicit, all I can do is nod.

In a low voice just for my ears, he says, "Looking good, Chef."

When he steps back, I feel light enough to do a silly twirl like I did in the front yard this morning. Was that only a handful of hours ago? It feels like a lifetime since then.

Once we're both standing at the station, Gran explains the basic construction of the Irish apple cake's layers. "The foundation is a cinnamon spice cake. You'll need to peel and thinly slice apples for the middle layer, then a crumb topping will finish it before baking. Some folks make a vanilla crème anglaise to drizzle, while others prefer good old-fashioned vanilla ice cream. Either way, you can't go wrong."

Giving a conspiratorial wink, she adds, "It's even better with a tea and whiskey."

As Mateo peels apples over the sink, Gran explains the steps for sifting, mixing, and combining the dry and wet ingredients to me. Mateo returns to my side with the apples in a large bowl of water for us to slice. My first few cuts are a bit messy, and he reaches around from behind me to lay a hand over mine, guiding the process.

I blush when Gran and I make eye contact, but she simply

sighs, her eyes going unfocused. "Seeing you two makes me miss my JP."

"Would you tell us about him?" Mateo asks, his hand on mine as he guides me to slice the apples. His hold is secure, as if he's sure of himself despite the prying eyes.

"Ah, James Patrick was a good man. His family connected us to the Morgan and Hendrix clans—way back in the days when those know-nothings were trying to stop us Irish Catholics from moving. The three families built their enterprise hoping that having a corner of property between us would allow our extended families to move across the pond. It was safer over here. The Hendrix farmhouse became The Featherweight. Our town history was written within those walls regularly. These men have been leading this town around in circles for a good hundred and fifty years, you know."

I'm desperately trying to focus on her words, but every time Mateo breathes, his front presses a little closer to my back, distracting me again.

"And now it's River, Grant, and Jimmy. So those are pretty dizzying circles," Mateo says.

"Grant and Jimmy?" Gran laughs so hard she breaks into a coughing fit.

Mateo steps away, and the air around me cools. He sweeps over to her with a glass of water and a stool, easing her to sit and helping her catch her breath. The gentle kindness he shows her does something to my already overactive lady parts.

After several small sips of water, Gran clears her throat and straightens. "All right, I'll get on with it. No, dear children, Grant and Jimmy do not have any sort of say in anything. River? I think Betty did sign her votes over to him when he officially bought the business after John got sick."

"What do you mean? And honestly, I need to know. Why was Lily treated worse than Grant when *he* blew up their marriage?" I bite my lip, worried the question was too aggressive, but Gran's eyes twinkle.

"Oh, yes. You're one of that crew. Well, I have good news and bad news for your friend. She was definitely given a raw deal, but some of that was in her head. Grant, however, has *still* not earned Glenn's trust, and a little birdie suggested he's not as in charge as he pretends."

Heart stuttering, I dart a look at Mateo, who's zeroed in on the tiny informant.

Brow furrowed, I ask about my friend again. "But what about the whole 'she's going to sit in the stocks' thing? They even made her do it last spring, and it had been ten years!"

Setting her glass of water down with a clank against the island, Gran laughs so hard she needs to wrap her arms around her middle. "Is that what you all thought happened?" She's wheezing, and pauses to sip some more water, nearly spewing.

"All right. Lily, first of all, was supposed to volunteer for the stock photos at the next festival because some team made it to finals. After all that time, there was no way we'd let them hold her to this. But then she and River were dancing around each other. When he told Betty he was going to do this 'for her,' we couldn't get past the grand gesture of it all. Then she went to Jimmy, and we realized that the boy was never going to tell her all the things he needed to unless we locked them in a room together—or, I guess, that bench. Anyhow, I'm pretty sure that all happened to amuse Nicole, Betty, Pru, and me more than anything. Those two kids have been in love since they met."

My heart rate is erratic. This is all hilarious and a little horrible. I could easily see Delia and myself being these kinds of old ladies. Oh, I cannot wait to tell her and Lily.

As I start to imagine the schemes we could concoct once we're the elders, I realize the conversation has continued between Mateo and Gran. I missed what Mateo asked, but I catch up with her reply.

"The Hendrix, Kelly, and Morgan clans all hold seats on a board created long ago. They must vote together about any major changes to the partnership, including letting the Morgans out of it. While Grant and Jimmy like to think they're the voting parties, the leadership team will not approve them."

"Gran, who votes from your two families?" Mateo asks tentatively.

She barks out a laugh. "Well, as the first woman to be the voting party..." She does the sign of the cross and whispers, "Thanks to my love trusting me to be our decision-maker, I've said without a daughter or granddaughter, I will die before giving my vote to a man."

The room erupts with laughter, and Mateo and I make eye contact, realizing that Satan is being played.

We return to our baking station, and she instructs us on how to set the layers up to bake, then drops the dish into the preheated oven. I should be happy right now. I have good news for Lily, good news for the town, and good news for me—I don't have to pretend to like Mateo. Although, I don't know if I'm pretending anymore. I'm just so nervous that I can't trust my own eyes and ears again.

When I moved home from Boston, I made myself a promise. The idea of love blinded me once before, so I was going to be wiser. Focus on my clients, my family, and myself. I don't need a partner. I'm fine on my own. *Right?* I want that confident inner voice to agree, but she's quiet.

With our lesson wrapped up, Gran washes up. While she's humming and rinsing the items we dirtied, the back door opens with a creak of the hinges and Liam returns.

"All right, my favorite grandson," Gran says, drying her hands. "I'm going to take my afternoon nap. You enjoy your visit with your friends." She pats his cheek and takes off toward the stairs. In the doorway, she turns back. "Was lovely spending time with you two."

With a sparkle of mischief in her eyes, she disappears.

twenty-six
Nessa

A FEW DAYS LATER, I pull up to the curb in front of my parents' house. As I approach, I take in the structure, noting the ways in which it has aged alongside us. The white exterior could use a fresh coat of paint, and some of the shutters are more faded than others due to their sun exposure.

We really should collect estimates and schedule painters to give it a fresh coat. I pull out my phone and add this to my ongoing to-do list called "bio family," then slip the device back into my pocket.

I step inside just as Tal pads down the stairs dressed in jeans and a short sleeve button-down. They look fantastic and perfectly androgynous. Knowing that the conversation tonight could turn to grammar or their sudden lack of femininity, I take a moment to pump them up before things can get moving.

"Sib, that is majorly passing the vibe check. You ate this glow-up," I say giving them a gigantic goofy smile.

"Too extra. Dial it back, sis." They roll their eyes hard.

"It's my job as your sister *and* a millennial to be cringe," I shout to Tal's retreating form.

My skin prickles with irritation, but I swallow it down and

take deep breaths, then continue to the dining room. I drop the apple cake with the desserts on the sideboard and head to the kitchen where I find Shae. She's still in an oversized T-shirt and basketball shorts, with her hair a mess, as though she's forgotten about tonight.

"Glad to see everyone is ready for dinner." My words are a hair too sharp, causing Shae to drop the knife on the cutting board with a huff.

"Great, reinforcements are here to continue the prep. I'm going to finally shower and change." She storms upstairs. Halfway up, she turns and shouts, "And you're welcome for getting things started." Then she gives me the finger.

Returning the gesture I reply, "Love you!"

The bathroom door closes with a thud, then opens again for Shae to scream, "Love you more, you pain in the—"

"Shae Eliana Rabin!" Dad booms.

The door shuts again, louder this time, then the rush of water through the pipes sounds above me.

While Shae showers, Tal and I finish organizing the tray of veggies to roast. Dad enters the kitchen, his tall, broad frame and olive complexion as handsome as ever. And I swear there's a bit more salt in his salt-and-pepper hair than there was the last time I saw him.

Mom enters, reading as she moves.

"Don't you love the new series?" I ask her with a huge grin. "I just had to recommend it when I saw there was a Jewish historical romance that was set right here in Philly."

"Kiss-ass," Tal says under their breath as they pull down a cutting board.

Whatever, needy middle child, I scoff internally, then bask in the glowing review my mom has for the first in the duology.

As I gaze off just above her head at the variety of plants in the window, our smiles are mirrors—me because helping someone else makes me happy, hers because she's back to reading.

Watching this fills my lungs deeper than usual, and I relax into my role at home.

―――

A SHORT WHILE LATER, as we're readying to eat together, I stand back and watch, overcome by the mood tonight. Our house feels exactly like home should. It's noisy, chaotic, a little disorganized. There's gentle ribbing and frustrated outbursts; but there's so much love.

Moving through the holiday meal preparation feels like a well-choreographed ballet—we ebb and flow between the kitchen to the dining room taking turns bringing dishes, silverware, and cups to seats.

Across the way, Shae lifts a few bottles of wine from the fridge and I attempt to watch without staring.

"We have company tonight, stop looking at me like that." She scoffs as she moves out of my line of sight.

A few feet away, Dad wraps an arm around Mom's shoulders and kisses her on the temple. The easy look that they share causes my palms to sweat and my lips to loosen.

"You're both so easy-going. You make your relationship look seamless, how are we supposed to find partners who'll help us create a family that lives up to your standard when you make it look so...so..." I wave a hand wildly, my cheeks heating.

Mom's brow furrows, and Dad leans in to whisper something for her only. He shimmies out from around her and enters the dining room. I hear him herd my siblings away. Fuck, my throat has gone dry, and I reach to get a glass of water.

"All right, my little miracle, what's eating you?" Mom asks.

I shake my head, not sure what to say exactly.

Crossing her arms over her chest, she gives me a pointed stare. "Not nothing. Not you're 'fine.' What's going on with Mateo?"

I groan. "Mateo? Have you been reading The Springer? You should know better than to trust a gossip chain..."

Mom pokes her tongue into her cheek, inhaling, then shows me where I inherited my strong will from. "I have other sources."

Voice dipping fully into an adolescent cadence, I grumble, "Shae Eliana, I'm going to strangle you in your sleep, I swear to..."

"Not during the holiest days of the year," Mom says. "I know I can't say a whole lot about the religion since I left the orthodox world and we chose to teach you that this is our cultural identity, but please. Be respectful, a little kavod. No need to sign yourself up for a bad year to come."

She goes on to say something to ward off the evil eye, because you can take the girl out of Lakewood, but you can't always take the Lakewood out of the girl it seems.

"Sorry, Ema," I say, hoping to placate her by saying the words meant to prevent the evil eye.

"From your lips to Hashem's ears, now, what is wrong with things with the young man? Betty said you were with him at the Kelly Orchards and that Gran taught you to make her famous cake."

"Yes, it's in the dining room with the desserts—"

"He took you to the farm to bake. He's given you that gorgeous car to drive while you are getting yours fixed, although, mamale, it is okay to say goodbye to the old clunker. You held on to her for a long time. He's defended your education when folks try to call you Miss instead of Doctor, you worked hard for that honor. You work hard all the time. You are allowed to rest."

"I rest," I protest.

She waves a hand. "No, sweetheart, you do not rest. You take short breaks to switch gears, but you aren't taking time for yourself. Or you weren't. It seems like he's helped you to get out of your own head, and to do the things you enjoy. How often do you add to that never-ending to-do list in your phone? How often are you letting your brain take a break from thinking about everything and everyone around you in an effort to just be in the moment?"

Eyes averted, I pick at my nails, a habit I've never been able to break.

"You don't like that I'm correct, I can tell," she gently places her hand over mine and softens her tone. "Mamale, you do not have to do everything for everyone. It's okay to be selfish every so often. It's all about balance."

She pulls down the challah bread board, the honey and salt. She grabs a kiddush cup—a ritual wine goblet—with a beautiful stem full of shards of colorful glass and turns it, looking at the colored bits. Those are from the broken glass at their wedding.

"I wish your Zaydie could hear this. He'd never believe it, but let me put this the way my dad would. Take a look at this here: the challah is round because things continue to move: seasons, life. Time passes with or without our consent, so it's best to keep that impermanence in mind. It's dipped in both sweet honey and tart salt, we think of these in a number of ways because—"

"Two Jews, three opinions?" I smirk, and she nods affirming the old adage.

"The table is a replica of the altar in the mishkan, the wandering tabernacle, and the temple in Jerusalem. Salt is for perseverance and honey to appreciate the goodness before us. To remind us that, as the fields are picked clean and the cold sets in this time of year, goodness is to come in its own time."

Piling the items onto the wooden tray for me to carry, she pauses and takes my hand. "Good things take time, and you've put a lot of time toward goodness. You are allowed to receive goodness too. Even when it comes from the last place you'd expect," she says, her gaze drifting.

I was so lost in her speech I didn't see my dad join us back in the room. The look they share is intimate.

"Sometimes, your bashert, your soul's destiny, isn't packaged the way you think it will be. That doesn't mean it isn't a gift." She cups my cheek and looks at me sincerely. "Do not fight falling in love, my beautiful daughter. You deserve as much good as you put into the world."

The pressure building behind my eyes is unbearable. I drag in a long breath, swallow hard, and hug her. "I love you, Ema," I croak. "You really would have made your dad proud with that one."

She drops a kiss on the crown of my head. As she pulls away, a commotion pulls our attention.

"Why didn't we know you were coming home! Mrs. Carter! Mr. Carter!" Shua says from the entryway.

My heart thumps against my breastbone. "Ema, you didn't."

With a shrug, she strolls out of the room and an instant later, she greets the full Santos-Manolo/Carter family: Susan, Eddie, Stef, Lee, and Mateo.

Sighing, I straighten my sweater. Then I set the bread, salt, honey, and wine goblet on the table and greet our guests.

———

AFTER DINNER, Lee insists we light the firepit, so the four of us make our way to the back patio. Stef and I carry twin glasses of white wine and large slices of apple cake topped with vanilla ice cream to seats close together.

As I look around at the group, Stef's inebriated text comes to mind. The *we could be sisters*.

I drift closer and whisper so the men can't hear. "You know you drunk texted me about being sisters?"

Her eyes dance in the firelight.

"No, silly, this is about *us*—you are my sister already. No matter what happens with him," I say and glance toward Matty.

Stef leans closer and we give an awkward side hug, and affectionate exchanges of praise snowball.

"Oh no. Emotional wives at twelve o'clock," Lee teases.

172

"Ignore my husband. He just likes to say *my wife* because he read that book you recommended to me," Stef says, causing us to giggle.

"Lee, tell me about the tattooing you're doing." Mateo breaks into a wide smile. His request catches my attention, and we watch their interaction.

"Not much tattooing yet, honestly. They've got me working the front desk, cleaning, setting up workstations, prep work. Nothing exciting. My mentor gives me artwork assignments, and we go over them together. I do a lot of flash tattoo sheets based on things happening in the city for the shop to use for marketing. Creating those has been fun. Promise me that when you outbid them for the north side of town, I get dibs on a shop of my own."

"Are you coming back?" I ask, my words more slurred than I expected.

Damn. Have I been comfortable enough to have a few more glasses of wine than usual? Maybe I have.

"I miss you, but also... this is the opportunity of a lifetime—I want to see Stef achieve everything she's setting out to." I have fully crossed into emotional-wine-drunk territory.

Before Stef can answer, the gate creaks open and Delia, Seth, River, and Lily appear.

"I hope you don't mind that we opened the gathering up to others," Lee says.

Mateo scans the group, and I swear disappointment flashes across his face.

Loud and proud, Shae steps into the yard. "Look who I found at the market when I was picking up supplies." She holds up a twenty-four pack of alcoholic seltzers and a twelve pack of non-alcoholic ones.

As I'm considering telling Mateo to text Liam and invite him, he appears behind my sister.

"I figured there's never enough ice at these sorts of things," Liam says, looking charmingly rustic in his flannel and ball cap.

With one hand he holds up a large plastic bag of ice, the other is clasped with Christian Cleary's. He is so similar to his Aunt Pru, with their rich brown skin and catlike eyes. It's why he can pull off the lime green athletic set and white sneakers in complementary neon accents.

"I heard there was a fire code violation that needed attention," Christian teases, looking Lily's way.

"Sorry, Chief. I had nothing to do with it," Lily quips with a grin.

My heart squeezes. I swear if it were any fuller, it would burst.

There's a loud metallic pop and fizz, drawing my eyes across the circle to Shae. I try to focus on the can. Shae notices and waves a non-alcoholic cranberry lime seltzer for me to see, giving me a sour face. "Bitch, I told you that is all work stuff online. Stop being judgy."

I ignore her and pour the final drops of the wine from the bottle I brought out into my glass and eye Lily. "Oh. My. God. Lil," I mouth. "You will not believe what we learned from Gran Kelly." Though my words are quiet, the hiccup that follows them is anything but.

The whole circle looks at me, and Mateo and Liam exchange a knowing look.

Ignoring them, I straighten and clear my throat. "That motherfucker has been parading around like a peacock, all proud of his supposed wealth and respectability in the community." Eyes narrowed, I look at my friends one by one to make sure they're listening. "He isn't the deed-holder or even a voting party. So he tormented you and brought Satan back into my life because he's a raging asshat who thinks his shit doesn't stink. But his farts give him away."

By using our grandma's favorite insult, I break the tension with Shae, and our laughter is so vigorous she snorts. Her cheeks flush red, and she slaps a hand over her mouth. "Well, cheers to

Grandma for that phrase," she says, holding her can in the air in a mock toast.

Everyone dissolves into laughter. The conversation moves easily through our grandparents' funny sayings and drifts in and out of new topics.

Just as we question the contagiousness of yawns, one seems to pass its way around the circle. That starts the trickle home. As the circle thins, Mateo moves closer, until we are left alone with the dying fire.

twenty-seven
Mateo

WHEN DID someone turn on twinkle lights and music?

"Which movie is this from?" I ask Nessa as the opening of a slow song plays. She looks my direction, bringing us close enough for me to lean in. I brush my lips to hers, a soft kiss. This is different from the heated and hurried ones we've previously shared. It's languid and paced.

This is another shift. Hopeful adoration drips over me like honey. A budding belief that *maybe* this is not about optics anymore.

I bury my face in her neck and inhale her citrus and vanilla scent. "Dance with me," I say pulling us to stand and sway.

I don't think I've ever shared this kind of intimacy with another person before. *Shouldn't I be afraid of this sort of relationship?* The question pokes holes in the moment. But I don't think it's about whether I want it. It's whether she finally sees that I'm worthy of it.

Before Nessa, it held no appeal. There was always someone who might be better, hotter, more spontaneous or special. It is impossible to imagine someone who is *more* anything than her.

She wants this as much as I do, right?

I'm startled from my spiraling thoughts when a cool drop of water hits my face. Then another. We pull apart and, in unison, ask, "Is it raining?"

Only then do I notice the distinct chirp and whoosh noises of the inground sprinklers.

Nessa's eyes narrow, her expression calculated, and in one quick move, she darts away.

But she's too slow. I grasp her arm, then pick her up and swing her directly into the spray. Like the music was made for us, the tempo matches the movement, so I take the opportunity to pull her through the water and sway to the rhythm again.

"You love your movie moments. Is this supposed to be a downpour declaration of love?"

Love. Mouth agape, I'm searching for the words when the song switches to something upbeat. The music video choreography is so set in my muscles that I break out into the band's moves on instinct.

Looking over to ensure she isn't waiting for an answer, I see an even better sight. She's joined me in hopping and spinning, laughing and singing along.

The grass quickly gets slick, and on the next jump, her heeled boots squish in the puddle, and she wobbles. I reach out to stabilize her, but the momentum is too much, and we both tumble to the now muddy lawn.

Laughing as we slide, my hand falls to the grass and comes up covered in earth. Unable to resist, I raise it in front of her.

She shakes her head as I nod. *Game on.*

I lunge forward as she shrieks, "Don't you dare."

Still on her back, she scrambles away, dragging herself through the muck.

"Brains. Need brains. Big, beautiful brains," I tease. I clamber after her, low and stiff like a zombie, groaning. The raucous mix is cut with howled laughter. When her back reaches the stone retaining wall, I prowl forward, closing the gap. Breathless we hover there suspended in time and space, lips a whisper from touching. Her legs part ever so slightly, causing my pelvis to fall snugly into hers. This wakes my dick up, and she gives a soft, appreciative moan in response.

"If I were a human, I could reach into your panties and I bet they would be absolutely soaked for me," I whisper. This elicits another breathy, wordless reply.

As our mouths join, my hands rove on instinct into her hair, around her face and down her neck. The cold dirt is a jolt to her warm skin, drawing another gleeful shriek, as she leans forward to paint my brow with a matching strip of mud.

I want to keep kissing her, build a home of arguments—real and playful. I want to strip her bare and sink deep inside her. So delirious with lust and affection I nearly forget where we are.

I'm rudely brought back to reality by the boom of a deep voice and floodlights that evaporate our cloak of darkness.

"Is someone there?" Gabe calls out. "Everyone all right? I thought I heard a scream. Hello?"

We quickly scramble apart and rush to stand. "It's me, Aba," Nessa calls with a laugh. "Sorry, the sprinklers caused me to slip, and Mateo tried to catch me, which caused…" She waves a hand at our soiled attire.

"I'll be back with towels. Give me a moment." He nods and steps back inside.

Maybe it's my imagination, but I swear he winks at Nessa before retreating.

"You little minx. Did you know this would happen?" I push.

She's trying to withhold her smile, but the mask cracks quickly. "I had no idea, I swear. This was completely an accident." She holds her hands out in front of her.

I throw back my head and laugh, then rest my muddy hand on the back of her neck and pull her in for another kiss.

Towels land on the steps behind us with the soft thunk, and her dad yells, "Don't make me hose you two down!"

Heart lurching, I scramble away from Nessa. I dip my head respectfully. "Sorry, sir. I'll wash these and return them to you, if that's all right."

"Bring them back on Sukkot. We'll camp out in the yard," Gabe orders before heading back inside.

"Soo-coat?" I say, eyeing Nessa.

She nods. "Never in my life has he built one of these traditional temporary structures in the yard. Let alone slept in one."

Nodding, I have to hand it to him. Game respects game.

twenty-eight
Mateo

"HEY, GOOD TO SEE YOU, SIR," I say as I shake hands with Gabe.

I slide the reusable grocery bag off my shoulder and hold it out to him with a bright smile. He peeks inside and places his free hand over his heart.

"I was not expecting to see these again," he says, light dancing in his eyes.

"Ah, I see where Nessa gets her sense of humor from," I say with a grin.

The dinner between our families was the start of a strong few weeks together. With how well we're getting along—in and out of the bedroom—I'm fairly sure that we've crossed over into real relationship territory.

After shaking hands with a number of local business owners I've rekindled my relationship with, I grab a chair. I'm sitting in 'our seats' at Lily's studio, arm stretched across the chair next to me, swiveling periodically to check for Nessa. Where is my ever-punctual girl?

She should be here.

Fuck. She's been cornered by that walking Brooks Brothers ad she used to date.

She fidgets with the bracelet I gave her, then crosses her arms. The action causes her breasts to move, and a heartbeat later, the fucker leers, and an oily smile spreads across his smarmy face.

My fists clench reflexively. I know she can handle herself, but I'm two seconds from jumping out of my seat to intervene.

Delia plops herself down on the chair I was holding for Nessa and says tersely, "Matty."

"Cordi." I mirror her tone but swerve to continue watching over her shoulder.

"Can you please, for the love of cheese and crackers, tell me what is going on with you two? She keeps shutting me down. She evades questions, changes the subject. Is this bullshit, or are you two... you know?"

"Fucking?" I tease, figuring go big or go home.

Delia sighs, her face flickering from irritation to acceptance. She follows my gaze, and that changes the conversation topic quickly.

She drops her voice low and says, "Shit, got to get that man away from her. Quickly."

Nessa has played things about this man close to the vest. "How much do you know about him?" I ask with a raised brow.

"Not much, but just enough, you?" Delia asks, shrinking in the seat.

"About that much. Potentially a little more, but it seems it was shared accidentally," I say, raising my hands in surrender.

"I'm sure she'll tell you when she's ready," I say when I catch Delia's sour expression. "Let me move her away. Can you hold the row?"

Appearing at Nessa's side, I drape an arm over her and tug her into my embrace. I fully intend to ignore Caleb, but when he clears his throat, I'm forced to acknowledge him.

"Reynolds." I nod, then return my full attention to Nessa. I've softly guided her to move away, angling to force him to watch the soft, chaste kiss we exchange. I do everything I can to sell the ease, the sweetness, the comfort between us, and she matches my energy perfectly. *Because it isn't fake*, I reassure myself despite the niggling doubt that pops up like a rodent in a game of Whac-A-Mole.

I lean in to whisper in her ear, my lips skimming the thin skin of her neck, pointing out that Delia is holding seats and we can get away.

Her amber eyes lock with mine and she says a husky "yes please." The words are a plea. Nessa doesn't beg. What the hell did this fucker do to dim the fire in my woman so intensely?

———

JIM KNOCKS the gavel against the wooden podium, calling the room to attention. "Nice to see everyone here. I'm going to open the meeting by having Grant Morgan provide an update on his family's prospective sale."

"Thanks, Jimmy." Grant and Jim shake hands and smile at the room, looking like dupes of the buyer they're courting. If Caleb is a walking Brooks Brothers catalog, they're Banana Republic Outlet.

I lean over to Nessa, smirking. "It's like when Joey and Chandler try to be Richard but decide to flip a coin for who can have a mustache. It isn't working, but it is damn funny."

She bumps my arm with one shoulder, her body shaking with suppressed laughter, then tilts away from me. She repeats the comment to Delia, who looks at me with chipmunk cheeks full of air as she tries to not laugh.

Liam eyes me, so I mouth "knock-offs" in explanation and wags a finger, indicating the three men at the front.

"Upper. Hand," he hisses.

With a huff, I settle back in my seat and force myself to listen to the bluster and self-aggrandizing going on up front.

When Jim returns to the podium, he begins a rundown of the

upcoming community events. Albert, the town librarian, is a sweet old Dutch man in his seventies. He's been a staple when it comes to literacy programs for as long as I can remember, always creating inventive ways to keep all ages engaged with reading.

"For the next twenty-one days, anyone who borrows twenty-one books, reads them, and fills out a review card for each will be entered into a contest generously sponsored by the Reynolds Group. We'll be hosting..."

He tosses out the names of a Nobel Prize–winning author duo who will be visiting us to close the Sunflower Fest.

My muscles go rigid. *Please don't be impressed*, I silently plead with the townsfolk in attendance. These are totally empty promises.

Unfortunately, a cursory glance shows I'm one of few people not believing this bullshit.

Nessa gently draws a finger up and down the veins bulging out of my fisted hand until I force myself to relax. When my fingers unfurl, she flips my palm upright and continues to draw lightly on the sensitive skin. It takes a few minutes to notice, but she's spelling something over and over.

A curved line.

The letter *U*.

Quick loops and a line.

Okay.

Biting back a laugh, I grab her hand to make the tickling sensation stop, then lean in and whisper, "I'm okay."

Caleb steps up to the podium and gives Bertie a double-handed shake, then takes over the microphone. "Good evening, everyone. Thank you for having me," he says like the snake oil salesman he is.

I squeeze Nessa's hand, watching as beads of sweat develop across her hairline.

twenty-nine
Nessa

CALEB IS HERE, lying through his teeth and staring at me. As he speaks, he radiates superiority, his posture at the podium too casual and friendly.

He doesn't even know these people. My blood boils as I'm forced to endure this farce. I'm cold yet sweating as his speech goes on for an eternity. .

The more Caleb pontificates on half-truths that will coerce the people I love to join him, the heavier the lead in my stomach becomes.

Knowing there are clauses to trap and bankrupt these good, hardworking, well-meaning people causes me to double over in pain.

I hiss out a breath during one particularly violent roll of my stomach, and Jim chides me. His use of the word *miss* drips with derision and disrespect.

Leaning toward Delia, I whisper, "I need to get out of here."

Mateo tries to stop us, but I tell him to stay. This is information he needs.

Liam repeats his comment about keeping the upper hand, and Mateo promises to come see me as soon as the meeting is over.

I shrug, and we slink out of the room.

———

DELIA HOLDS my hand and rubs my back soothingly for the duration of our walk. Once we're inside, she insists I change into pajamas while she does the same. I'm already lying in bed when she knocks on the open doorframe.

"Duh, I left it open for you," I say with half the sass I normally would. This is really taking it out of me.

She sits beside me with her laptop open, but instead of the movie I expect her to have cued up, I'm met with the faces of Stef and Lily. I groan, rolling over to pick up a pillow to hug, and hide behind.

"That's okay, Nessa. We don't need to see you as long as we can all hear each other," Stef says.

"You're getting good at the school counseling portion of the degree," I say, hoping to deflect the conversation.

"Thank you. You're very skilled yourself. I think that's how we ended up here." She doesn't hesitate to keep to the night's topic. *Me.*

Pulling my knees up toward my chin, I bunch into a tiny ball.

"Remember when you had me put up those signs in the women's bathroom for angel shots?" Delia asks, starting the next round of interrogation. "And told me about some of the signs to look for when someone was in distress?"

"Yes," I say, trying to keep my voice even while my stomach continues to roll. "It gives someone in distress the ability to ask you for help without telling everyone in the bar, and it allows you to get the police to them discreetly. It's been life-saving for some of the women I've worked with." I pull the pillow tighter.

"Ness, your work sounds scary," Lily says with her usual low filter this late in the day. "Are you scared?" The question is innocent and soft. She's not judging me.

"I don't want to talk about it," I say, hoping to avoid triggering Lily's sensitive soul or disclosing more than I can handle tonight.

"Okay." Delia wraps an arm around my shoulders, causing the computer to wobble in her lap.

While I can't say for sure, because video calls are *weird*, it sure feels like I have all eyes on me.

I take a deep inhale and let out a noisy exhale.

Lily uses her yoga class inflection when she says, "That was really good. I think a cleansing breath together could be a nice next step."

"Sure, Lil," I croak, sadness seeping out of my pores.

"Okay, let's all take a moment to send Nessa our healing energy and the strength to share in her own time. Good. Now, take an inhale for four, five, six, seven. Now exhale loudly," Lily says sweetly. "That was beautiful."

"Ness." Stef's tone is direct. "Does my brother know what's going on? Or is this about him? Because—"

"No," I interject. "Matty's been a sweetheart. We're... whatever. I don't know. I'm not supposed to get tangled up with men again." That kernel of truth slips out.

Three sets of eyes remain locked on me, unblinking, waiting for what I'll say or do next.

"Caleb is toxic. You know that. Yet, somehow, even as a doctoral candidate graduating summa cum laude in psychology, I missed all the signs in my own life." I scoff, still bitter that I could be so smart and yet... "I was *so very* stupid at the same time."

"You aren't stupid." Delia shrugs, her expression soft. "You were thinking out loud, honey."

"Not everyone you meet will be like that," Lily promises. She's been through her own challenges with men and women, so she's speaking from first-hand experience.

I sniffle. "Or I'm meant to be the love doctor and everyone's cheerleader. I'll keep you safe and you'll keep me loved."

"I'll accept that offer, but only if you promise not to lead Matty

186

on. He really has high hopes for you two—" Stef's words are interrupted by our doorbell.

Glancing at my phone, I see I have multiple calls and texts from him. "Speak of the devil."

"It's okay to be scared," Stef says.

Lily hums. "I'm pretty sure you guys were the ones who told me I could only be brave if I did the scary thing. You can be scared *and* brave, Nessa."

Heat and pressure build behind my eyes.

Delia squeezes me once more before sliding off the bed.

"I'm going to let him in before he calls the PSPD to do a welfare check," she teases as she exits my room with her computer in hand.

thirty
Nessa

DESPITE NOT WANTING TO TALK, the call did ease some of the tension in my muscles. The knots in my stomach have loosened, even if they are not completely gone.

Scared but brave.

Getting up to meet Mateo in the kitchen, I pause to give myself a quick assessment in the mirror. I'm in my oversized crewneck that says *Read More Smut* and is styled like the vintage *Everyone Loves an Irish Girl* shirts. I'm wearing soft sleep shorts, too, and a pair of fuzzy kitten-covered socks.

I leave my hair in its high pony, then sweep a little bit of ChapStick on.

Good enough.

I tiptoe into the kitchen and see Mateo standing at the sink, dish towel slung over one shoulder, washing the dinner plates we left behind. His deep teal joggers are tight around his strong thighs. The matching zip-up is hung on a kitchen chair, leaving him in a fitted white tank top. With every swipe of the sponge, his corded muscles flex.

"Hi," I say. My voice comes out quiet, my breaths shallow.

"Hi, gorgeous. Can I make you tea?" He asks sweetly.

That's all it takes to make me crumble. Acts of service are my move, and being the one who needed the chat, being cared for. *Who am I anymore?*

He sets down a steaming mug alongside the jar of honey and a teaspoon.

"Hey," I repeat, out of words. The light tinkling of the spoon on ceramic complements the sound of the trickling water from the slowed faucet.

He turns the water off completely, then turns around to look at me while he dries a plate.

"Hey, yourself," he echoes.

In this moment, with those dark eyes locked on me, I experience a moment of true calm like I've never known.

"Did you bring your own tea?" I inhale the unfamiliar but wonderful scent.

A chuckle rumbles out of him. "Pru…" He shakes his head and brings a small canister to the table. "She stopped me on my way here and said I was supposed to share this with you." He smiles, drawing me in. It really is a beautiful smile.

I eye the container and erupt in hysterics. "Did she happen to say why?"

Lips pressed together, he hums. "All she did was instruct me to pour the tincture into hot water and mix with honey. It smells amazing, but I haven't tried it yet. I wanted to wait for you." He lifts a second mug and holds it out in a little toast-like gesture.

My life has always been noisy, teasing, and chaotic. With a family so large, there's no way it could be anything else. But this moment reminds me of those quiet interactions between my parents, the looks passed in the thick of it all.

A little voice needles me though. Haven't you tricked yourself into seeing this when it wasn't there before?

I shake the thought from my head.

I read the note she taped to the jar to him "*Salabat calamansi.*

Brewed with Hendrix Farms Ginger and a potted calamansi lovingly tended to by Eddie Santos-Manolo."

He lowers his face, inhaling the citrus and ginger vapors, the move causing his soft black strands to fall over his forehead. "I want to say you learned this all from Stef and are messing with me."

"Look!" I push the canister across the table, and as he examines it, I take the quiet moment to go back to my stream of mixed thoughts and feelings.

"What's that highly educated brain of yours thinking about right now?" He stalks around the table, moving closer, slow and soft, like a jungle cat. He's trying not to spook me.

"A lot of things. I'm trying to figure out why you are doing this for me." I sigh. "Wondering if maybe it's just for your own financial gain. I'm thinking about how relationships are complicated and I understand them better than most people. How, because of my work, I've seen some of the most dark and depressing moments of many, many people's lives, yet I can't recall ever seeing a man other than Aba washing dishes by hand. I am thinking that you don't seem real, and that if you are real and I get it wrong, then I'm going to be furious with myself for missing out on more."

As I fight back tears, he bops my nose and winks.

That's pretty much all I need to pick a side in this internal war I've been fighting. I stand and fist his shirt at the collar, then pull him in for a kiss.

With his arms wrapped around me, he lifts me, abandoning our half-empty mugs on the table. He carries me back to my room and places me on the bed gently. Straightening, he scans the space, and when he spots my water cup, he snatches it and motions one finger for me to stay put, then steps out of the room.

Soft clinks and tinkling noises drift to me, the padded bop of the dishwasher closing.

Then I find myself accidentally eavesdropping. "Thanks for coming," Delia says. "Your sister text you too?"

"Yeah. Everything okay?" Mateo asks, his tone soft and full of concern.

"I think it will be, but the way she ran out when Caleb got up to speak, flushed and ill, has me worried. She's dancing around it, but—"

"But she's allowed to have things that are only hers," he says. "We just need to keep her away from that asshole."

My chest swells with each word. The two of them are practically fighting over me.

My mom's words echo in my ears. "You deserve the goodness you put out in the world."

This is good—my friends, *him.*

When Mateo returns, he has a glass of ice water in each hand. With an impish grin, he kicks the door shut behind him. He sets the cups on my side table, then joins me in bed, sitting with his back propped up against the headboard and his legs stretched long. With a fake yawn, he drapes his arm around my shoulders and rests a hand on my breast.

The move is so silly it pulls a giggle from me.

"I want to show you something," he says, snatching the remote from the comforter.

My body goes slack against his, and I turn his way, finding him already studying me. He leans forward and presses his lips to my forehead.

"Mmm, that feels nice." Eyes closed, I sigh and drop my head back to his chest.

He pulls a soft blanket over us, tucking us in tight, holding me in a way that suggests no expectations. No performance in lace required to be close—a kind of loving touch no man has ever shown me before.

"Good," he says, pressing Play. "This is all supposed to feel nice." With a sigh, he pulls me in tighter still.

I don't even know what he wanted me to see, because within minutes, I drift off to sleep in his arms.

I dream of letting myself fall in love with this man, the one who's working so hard to prove he won't hurt me. We walk along the beach, hand in hand, with a tiny dark-haired toddler wearing nothing but a diaper ambling ahead. The child has dark hair, like Mateo, and my complexion.

A black cat appears magically, then a couple of bunnies.

Without notice, dark gray storm clouds blow in off the shore. The sea turns rough and choppy as the bunnies combine into a super-sized rabbit. The creature then tackles the black cat, and they wrestle for dominance before a wave sweeps in and washes them all away.

When I wake the next morning, all I find beside me is a note on the pillow.

Getting an early start and didn't want to wake you. See you tonight

−M

thirty-one
Mateo

BY FIVE A.M., I've polished off a pre-workout shake and I'm headed out for a run. I hit every corner of this town. The day is perfect; it's chilly, but the air is clean and clear. The weekend should be sunny, meaning the days won't be too cold.

The leaves are a mix of red, yellow, and brown. They fall to the ground, and as I run over them, they make a satisfying crunch. This is fucking picturesque. This is movie shit. This is it. I just need to get to the part where I show up, defeat that dipshit, and prove to Nessa this was never fake for me. I've seen more than my fair share of romcoms. I can be the hero in this story.

Clearly my endorphins have kicked in, washing away last Sunday's fears.

Nessa is okay. We've spent every night this week together, and I've even managed to keep my hands to myself. Mostly. I want her to know I'm here for more than just her amazing tits or the way she sasses me.

I'm here to show her the same kind of compassion and care she shows others.

Mom promised to light a candle for me at church, and I'm trusting that everything will work out. This morning routine feels like that pump-up scene in *Rocky*. Maybe I should have added "Eye of the Tiger" to my workout playlist.

This is my time to shine, in the movie of life, I'm about to be the down-on-his-luck hometown jock who returns and shows them all.

I'm more than they believe I am.

I am going to defeat this nepo-baby, save the town, and win the heart of the woman I love.

This is going to be an epic weekend.

I repeat these phrases throughout the run, throughout my post-workout shake, during my shower, and as I get dressed.

I return to the town center—making it here before Nessa for our seven-a.m. pre-kick off meeting; *score*—and stroll all four sides of the square, assessing the work.

The town business owners have outdone themselves. Every lamp post is decorated with a scarecrow or corn stalks. The doors are flanked by flowers or pumpkins, some even have both. There are even mini apple trees in pots lining the path to The Featherweight. I pull my phone from my pocket, set on texting River a compliment, but stop mid-message when he and Lily step outside.

The front lawn has the usual eclectic mix of seating arrangements. Each is decorated by lanterns with flameless candles, fall flowers, and mini pumpkins. We wave, then they return to unloading fall-themed pillows and throw blankets onto the porch rockers and swing.

"This is making me wish there was a prize for the most festive business," I call.

They high-five, though when River lowers his arm, his hand goes straight to her butt and his mouth goes to hers.

I turn, giving them privacy, and continue on. I'm pumped. This festival is going to be my legacy, and that legacy is entwined with that of my girl.

At Curl Up & Dye, the young Salvatore ladies add large faux

scissors to their planters. In the window, there's even a pair of gold skeletons in chairs wearing wigs. The first has its hair rollers in, and the other is wearing some sort of glittery spider clip updo.

"Amazing work, ladies!" I call out.

"Better than River?" Chiara teases me.

Inside Pages, Pippa is behind the counter. I stride up to the door and knock.

She jumps, but when she catches sight of me, she breaks into a smile and scurries over and unlocks the door.

We hug and catch up briefly. She mentions that they plan to bring out a few carts of books, which is why their portion of the sidewalk is sparse for now. While I'm here, I offer to help haul boxes out front, since Seth has yet to appear. While we work, she tells me about how she's hoping to step back from the store, but mentions that Seth is trying to convince her not to.

I agree with her. He's ready to take over. He just needs to have more faith in himself. *Maybe Liam and I should include him in a guys night soon.*

Next door, outside Rosie's, a series of baskets creates a wraparound fixture to the window. They are stuffed full of fall blooms the colors of a vibrant sunrise like the one I saw during my run: wine red, fuchsia, bright red-orange, and saffron yellow. Each basket has its own big bush of blooms that doesn't move despite the topsy-turvy design. They all lead to an enormous silk sunflower, like the sun within the sky of color.

"Whoa." I say, letting the final sound linger.

"Right? It's a masterpiece," the rockabilly woman covered in patchwork tattoos says, holding a hand toward me. "Millie."

"Mateo." I accept the greeting. "You the new florist?"

At the scuff of the wheels from a library cart along the sidewalk, Millie beams. "Good morning, sugar."

"Good morning, Mildred." Seth grunts in return.

With a laugh, I shake my head.

"I'm Rosie's great-niece. I just moved in. Is everybody in town this friendly? I met a few women last night at The Featherweight. Damn, I haven't been this hungover in a while," she says with a light laugh.

I grin. "So you met my—"

"Nessa," she chirps waving past me.

And there she is. Long golden curls flowing and a surprising look of exhaustion behind her eyes.

"What did your roommate put in those drinks last night?" Millie asks.

"Hey, gorgeous," I say, leaning down to kiss her.

When Nessa turns her head, the first thing I notice are her puffy eyes. She looks like she hasn't slept, and she's nursing a sports drink.

"Ah, so you're *that* Mateo," Millie says, eyes twinkling. "Also, ow. My head."

"Everything looks great. Should we introduce her to Goldie?" I ask Nessa.

Turning back to Millie I say, "she's the barista at the Coffee Crumb."

Nessa's weird and distant this morning, but I'm going to chalk it up to the hangover. There's nothing else that would make sense.

Eyes narrowed, she gives me a once-over. "Maybe you've already had too much coffee. You seem really fucking chipper." She sighs and sidesteps me, lowering her sunglasses.

What the fuck?

———

FROM THE MOMENT we stepped into the coffee shop, everything went sideways. First, I spilled an entire container of milk from the coffee fixings bar. Then, in the middle of our introductions and dividing up the day's work, Nessa disappeared. When she came back, I didn't have the heart to tell her she still smelled like the contents of her stomach. I offered her a stick of gum, which earned a glare. Though the expression faded quickly, and she turned green again.

Watching Nessa nurse a water bottle while picking her nails clued me in that something more than a hangover was happening, I just wasn't sure what. Not knowing what else to do, I texted Liam to come take a look at her. She was angry when he arrived, and even more so when he instructed her to go home, but she gave in quickly in the end.

Once she left, the tides turned, and the day went well. Everyone I encountered greeted me with a smile. They talked about their crafts and goods with potential clients and passed out samples.

I don't mean to brag, but it was a well-oiled machine made up of townies and visitors eating, mingling, and shopping.

They say when a black cat crosses your path it's bad luck, but what if it's a woman with black cat attitude?

When Nessa returned later in the afternoon, freshly showered and stunning, it felt like she knocked the wind right out of me. That tiny butterfly effect was enough to shift everything—and the literal winds picked up.

Now, tent flaps blow around like crazy. Vendors close down booths quickly and abandon their tables.

I'm surveying the street, working on where to go from here, when the first thin gray-blue clouds roll in fast and heavy.

What starts as a fine mist turns dark as night. The rain picks up, and the wind swirls as I help person after person pack up. Volunteers abandon their posts and before long, seek shelter, making me wish I was an octopus so I'd have more arms.

When we get to a place where we can stop, we leave empty tables and heavier equipment that won't be ruined if left out and lead our remaining volunteers into Lily's studio. I send Nessa back home, hoping some more rest will revive her spirits both mentally and physically.

Lily and I do our best to account for everyone, but the chaos makes it hard to know who's missing. Over and over, we ask that volunteers check in with their shift partners so we can ensure everyone is safe.

After several minutes, one of the members of the volleyball team yells, "Who was getting the key to let the athletes out of the stocks?"

My heart plummets and Lily's face goes white. Shit. There are two teenagers still locked in the stocks. Our town loves to use the stocks for sports fundraisers during the festival. I yank the radio Liam supplied from my belt and ask him to help locate Prudence, who should have the keys.

He and the other guys on shift arrive in minutes, sirens blaring, since the station is just down the street. They're dressed in their turnout gear, and Liam carries an axe.

In a matter of seconds, he knocks the lock from the stock, freeing the kids.

Around us, the teens are laughing and recording the commotion as their teammates are rescued.

Lily waves at Liam, and when he lowers his axe, she approaches and asks for a turn. After a quick lesson from him, she chops off a piece of the old stockade and raises it above her head triumphantly. "As a council member, I hereby promise we will never rebuild these things!"

A few folks cheer, though far more wear confused looks, and many dash to their cars to head home. Once everyone is cleared out, I do the same.

———

I POPPED INTO MY PARENTS' house and bummed a container of homemade soup my mom had stored in the freezer.

She also let me raid her pantry, so I stocked up on all the comfort foods I like when I don't feel well, then I headed to Nessa's place.

I knocked and rang the bell, but nobody answered, so I left the food on the covered front stoop and sent her and Delia each a text about it.

Now, I'm sitting on the ridiculous blue plaid couch at Stef's, flipping channels. Every time I come to a family sitcom from my childhood I see some version of this damn couch.

"Stef, tomorrow I am throwing out this fucking couch. It looks like it belongs in one of these reruns."

Across the room Lee gives me a worried look. She doesn't speak or even look up.

"What's with her?" I mouth to my brother-in-law.

"Midterms," he says like it explains it all.

"How are your studies going?" I ask him.

"I'm almost ready for skin. Just need a volunteer."

A volunteer, huh? Hmm. "I might be able to help," I say.

thirty-two
Nessa

BAD IDEA:

I'm headed to the square to move hay from the maze to soak up the mud before today's events.

NESSA:

I'll meet you there.

———

I'M MAKING my way into one end of the maze, map in hand, when footsteps sound behind me.

"I can start here, you start on the other side, we'll cover more ground," I grumble.

A weird discomfort has pressed on my chest all morning. Blowing out a noisy breath I accept that yesterday was pretty uncomfortable too, and I was taking it out on almost anyone who I saw. I should try to tamp that down better today.

Caleb is around today. Nothing good happens when he's around.

"What if you fall? What if there's quicksand? Or a secret Bermuda triangle?" Mateo teases.

"If I fall, I'll stand up. If there's quicksand or a Bermuda

Triangle... I will call for a cartoon character." I pinch my lips together, tamping down the desire to throttle Mateo.

"Nessa," he says, his brows pulled down. "It's going to be fine. I promise." He reaches out in an attempt to soothe me but stops inches from my arm and drops his hand.

My heart pinches painfully. What the hell is wrong with me?

I want him to hug me. I step into his personal space inviting his touch.

"Sorry, I'm just tired." I deflect, trying to hide the tears blurring my vision. I know he's trying, I'm trying too. *Scared but brave?* How about *braving it solo.*

We've wound to the middle of the maze already, and he's so close I can smell the aftershave he used on his smooth jawline. His eyes are a rich brown, swirled with lighter streaks. When he looms over me like this, I feel small. My breath comes heavy as my pulse picks up. It is hard to stay coherent when he infiltrates all my senses like this.

Traitorously, my mind runs through memory after memory of the last few weeks. Laughing. Touching. Playing. I had fun.

Damn it, I don't want Mom to be correct. I want to scream. I want to run. I want him to hold me.

Before I can make up my mind, a mewing noise and a streak of blue darts by.

Startled, I bring a hand to my chest. "What the fuck?"

Turning so I'm safely tucked between him and the wall, he says, "Wait here. Let me get the little dude back to his home."

It's ridiculous, how much I like when he gets overprotective. The intruder is a damn bird, yet he acts as though he's shielding me from a dragon. Heat pools in my belly, adding to my mixed emotions. Looks like horny Nessa has entered the chat. Great, just great.

I meander out of the maze, finding Millie with a large coffee, watching as Mateo reaches the kiddie section. From here, we can see his head bobbing over the wall of hay. He zig-zags all over, losing sight of the bird at different turns.

Mid-giggle fit, I point at the peacock flapping over the top of the hay. "Town tradition. Peacocks escaping from the pen at the most inconvenient times. What are you doing out so early?"

"I could hear the commotion from my apartment," she says and points to the window over her storefront.

"Ah, yeah. Sorry about that," I shrug sheepishly.

The bird perches on the top of the hay-bale wall, then runs from there. Mateo continues the chase, and a moment later, the bird hops down into the grass beyond the maze. He's followed by my too-good-looking man, who rushes the wall and bursts through it like he's the damn Kool-Aid Man. Bales topple over, thudding to the ground and drawing more attention from people wandering about.

Millie and I clap and cheer and whistle for him, and he takes a bow.

"What the hell are you doing?" Jim appears, face red, stomping over from his vet office with a tech on his heels. "You're destroying the maze the folks of this town set up for the festival and being far too loud this early. This is ridiculous. And what the hell are you doing letting the birds out?"

He's having a meltdown of epic proportions. His beard has grown out significantly since the last time I saw him. The dark circles and bags under his eyes are so large, TSA would require them to be checked. There's a sour tinge of man-sweat in the air around him, too. He appears completely strung out.

Does he know that his plan isn't going to work? Is that why he's so out of sorts? Or is this something else? Fuck, I don't even like this man, yet I can't help but pity him, maybe even feel drawn to help.

Behind him, the tech has successfully lured the peacock back to his pen. Once the door is secure, she retreats into the office.

Jim snarls, "I'm going back to fucking sleep. This chaotic town would fall apart without me. I am going to win, and Peacock Springs will become a highly sought-after home for the wealthy. You'll see."

"Who. Was. That?" Millie asks, wide-eyed.

"That," Mateo says, "was our esteemed mayor. The douche canoe James Kelly Junior, himself."

Scrubbing a hand through my hair, I roll my eyes. "Sorry for the wake up, Millie. Mateo," I turn to face him, looking at the mess before us, "let's get a move on with the hay so we can change before volunteers arrive."

Now that I've mentally prepared the day's to-do list, my shoulders relax. Having tasks to focus on, then checking them off, is how I am going to survive this day.

thirty-three
Nessa

THE WORLD TAKES on a peachy glow as the sun dips lower in the sky and the event wraps up. I meander the aisles, relishing the scents of hay and popcorn in the air. Between the hay and sunshine, the morning's mud is now caked earth.

Families linger at the tall wooden photobooths, taking pictures of their children's faces centered in oversized painted sunflowers. A few feet from there, Shua is inside a pen with a litter of golden retriever puppies.

I step inside and sit next to him, bumping his shoulder. "How's your volunteer experience, mister?"

The puppies climb all over him, licking and nipping, making us laugh. He passes one of the dogs to me, and I cuddle and coo as I stroke the golden fur.

"Amazing. Today was *a-may-zing*. These are the last puppies available." He puffs out his chest, making direct eye contact, looking so much wiser than his sixteen years. "I made a decision too." He peers around, then ducks his head, and in a low voice says, "I'm going to become a vet."

Mirroring his tone, I ask, "Why are we whispering?"

"Because I'm going to be way better than Dr. Kelly," he says.

I give him a knowing grin and bump his shoulder with mine one more time. "I have no doubt you will."

We continue to play fetch and tug-of-war with the little guys until they flop over with exhaustion.

"Time to pack up, kids. Town meeting is starting soon" the elderly tech calls to us.

Shua and I carry the last few pups into the vet building and get them settled. In their crate, they pile on top of one another, snuggling up.

"Reminds me of when you'd insist we have slumber parties during family vacations. Climbing into bed and making up stories about adventures with your imaginary friend. What was his name?" I ask.

"Harley," Shua says with a smirk. "Because I wanted us to have motorcycles."

"Yeah, Harley. You'd pretend to ride all over the world. And look at you, about to plan an even bigger adventure." He's growing up so quickly. Tears start to form, and I press the corner of my eyes, hoping to prevent them from falling.

"Stop it," he says with a soft shove. "I have a whole year of high school left."

Then why do I feel like my job as mom is done if they're all adults? Do I want to be a mom-mom?

"Hello?" the tech calls back to us. "I need to lock up before town hall. Rabin kids, you coming?"

Looping his arm with mine, my brother steers me away from the puppies, not knowing he just stirred a big question in me.

Am I going to let one bad relationship dictate the kind of family I want to build?

―――

JIM KNOCKS the gavel against the wooden podium, calling the room to attention. "Nice to see everyone here. I'm going to keep this evening short since it's been a long weekend. I'd like to take a minute to thank all of the businesses, volunteers, and of course, the co-chairs for making this festival such a wonderful experience."

The responding applause is tepid due to a mix of low attendance and volunteers moving larger items indoors until they can be returned to storage for next year. Shua and I weave our way around the obstacles until he sees a group of his friends. He gives me a high five, then takes off toward them.

Delia and River stand together, locked in a conversation about the breakdown crew and what will happen to turnover The Featherweight tomorrow for the week ahead.

I linger, trying to figure out where I want to be, when someone steps up from behind me. I tense momentarily, but when I discover it's Mateo, I immediately sink into his warmth.

"I need to go home," I admit.

"Let's go." With his arms slung low around my waist and his front pressed to my back, he attempts to turn us.

"Won't they notice?" I ask, glancing around.

"Out of respect for everyone's time, we're going to postpone any further business until next week," Jim says.

The crowd erupts into cheers.

"Run," Mateo says, a playful grin splitting his face.

He speeds toward the exit, turning to check for me over his shoulder.

I take off after him, and we cut across the square and zigzag to my street. Mateo jogs slow enough to hold a normal conversation, while my muscles are burning.

As we hit a small hill, my panting becomes full-on gasps for air. Damn, I'm out of shape.

"Hop on," Mateo calls, tapping his shoulders.

"What?"

"Come on, I'll give you a piggyback ride. We'll still get back twice as fast."

Laughing, I jump onto his back. He holds my legs tight under the knees and speeds past the final few houses. Once we're on the front porch, he eases me to my feet and breathlessly captures my mouth with his.

"I'm feeling pretty gnarly after running around in the sun all day." He gives me an exaggerated sniff. "And phew! You are ripe."

"Shut up." I give him a playful shove.

"I thought we were at the point where we could be honest." His mouth splits into that stupid dimply grin that is my undoing.

"Good thing I have a solution. " Smirking, I drag him toward the bathroom.

As we stumble in, I shush him. The house isn't very large, and Delia could be home any minute now. The moment the door clicks shut, he has my back against the smooth surface. Pressing his hips harder into me, the strain of his cock against the fabric of his pants sends a shiver up my spine. Our mouths reconnect, his tongue parting my lips to deepen the kiss.

My fingers ache with the need to touch him, so I slip my hand beneath his shirt. His body is smooth and rippled, and I relish in the heat emanating from it. He's been so patient with me. Even when he's been able to chase his own release, his whole focus has been on me. *My wants, my needs, my desire.*

That desire is growing as the swarm of emotions from today leaves behind the urge to build. To connect. To try.

Stepping back, he removes his shirt in one swift motion, and I feel the cold air briefly before he's returned. A dizzying speed takes hold, his lips on mine while his hands skim under my layers.

Pulling apart, he removes my top gently, leaving me in a sturdy beige bra. This is nothing like the sexy items I've come prepared with in the past. Pausing, he asks me gently, "Is everything okay?"

I nod, but the way my teeth worry my lip betrays my thoughts.

He licks a line up the column of my throat to my ear and says, "If I'm being honest, I like this better than the fancy sets."

Pressing a hand into his powerful broad chest, I pull back and survey him. I look deep into his eyes and assess the lines that crinkle around them. The wide smile that causes that fucking dimple to pop. The soft and boyish way his face comes together around his smile.

"I don't get you," I admit, my throat tightening.

"I like that you're being the real you," he says so casually it takes me a moment to process his words. *Real.*

Zeroed in on my cleavage, he works the five-hook clasp of my least sexy bra.

When the clasp is undone and the support of the bra is removed, my breasts drop against the upper part of my ribs.

He tosses the bra behind him, then dives back in to continue his exploration of my naked body. We break apart here and there to wrestle free of our remaining clothing, leaving each piece in a pile on the floor.

I double- and triple-check that the door is locked as Mateo turns the knobs. The old pipes groan and clang, but the spray warms quickly. The steam begins to rise, but the mirror is not yet fogged as I catch sight of us, my head barely skimming his shoulders. Fully exposed and on bare feet, I take in how tiny my five-foot frame is next to his six-foot-two. I wrap my arms around him from behind and run my hands along every inch of his torso, diving into the details of the tattoo sleeve at my eye level.

He opens the curtain and steps in, then extends a hand to me. Taking it, I follow him into the warm spray. I continue to trace around the ink and examine with delicate touches as he tosses his head back, allowing the water to run through his silky strands.

"Can you tell me about this?" I ask, my tone sweet and sincere, the usual banter and agitation all but a distant memory. I've landed someplace curious and demure. I'm usually anything but demure—I'm far more demonic when it comes to him.

"That," he points to the circular center, "is an eight-rayed sun. It's a symbol from the Philippine flag and represents the original eight provinces that fought for freedom. The Spanish arrived and called us the painted ones because of the number of tattoos the indigenous people had. I don't know as much about the history of my culture as I probably should, but my grandparents, who lived on the islands, passed stories down to my parents, who passed them on to me. I brought a bunch of old photos with me to the tattoo shop and asked the artist to design something that integrated several indigenous traditions. These lines look like the traditional patterns from far away, but if you look within, there are repeating courts and nets. The nets are my favorite because it ties basketball to the fishing history of the islands."

I follow around the lines and find myself giggling a little. "What's with the old-school S out of the '90s?"

"There are a few letters mixed in, actually. The S, an M, and an E. For the family, but I really don't want to think about my family when I have you naked like this." He levels me with a carnal look, then pulls me to him so that his hard cock is resting against my upper stomach.

I lower slightly to reach for the soap behind him, and the shift in position causes him to slide between my breasts. I tease him like this a few times, relishing the effect I have on him as his cock stiffens further.

The groan he releases creates a fire in my belly, and I'm confronted by the desire to slide a bit farther and capture his head between my lips.

Am I about to surprise him and initiate the one thing I said I would never do? Will I break my rule?

Rules? Where we're going, we don't need rules.

I lower onto my knees, my face centimeters from his veiny, thick shaft.

Looking up through my lashes and drops of shower water, I say, "Fuck it."

thirty-four
Mateo

"HOLY FUCK," I let slip as she kisses my crown. The touch of her soft lips sends tingles up my spine. She trails her hands over my thighs, then slips one between my legs and cradles my nuts.

This is unbelievable. There's no chance in hell this is happening. Right here. Right now.

Tensing to quell the need to thrust my hips, I press a palm against the wall and grasp the shower curtain rod. I'm trying my damndest to not rip the fucking thing down. If this isn't a hallucination, I don't want to have to fix it later.

I move my hand to the wall in front of me, my arms spread in an L shape. The pink tiles are cold against my hands, so maybe this is, in fact, actually happening.

She rolls her tongue over the ridge and under the head, then flattens it and licks up my length along the vein as she continues to massage my balls. There are so many sensations all at once, I'm weightless.

"Fuck," I grunt out as she teases me with her exploration.

With needy little hums, her long licks make it virtually impossible to think straight. But through the haze, I remember that I should check in.

"You good with this, gorgeous girl? I wasn't trying to…"

She pulls back, taking my breath with her.

Expecting this to be the end, I look down at her. I need her to know she doesn't have to do anything she doesn't want to. Ever.

Before I can continue, though, she gives me big doe eyes, though the expression quickly morphs into something far more playful and brattier.

She flutters her lashes as she works my length with one hand. Her strokes are slow and firm, keeping me on the edge.

"What?" I gasp out.

"Would you prefer something more like…" she says, then changes the direction her tongue swirls around the head of my cock. All while maintaining the pressure-filled strokes against my shaft. The hand that's been massaging the boys moves to my thigh. Her nails bite into the skin, the pin pricks causing the tension in my body to ramp up again.

Spine tingling, I focus on breathing. My balls tighten. My abs tighten. Hell, everything tightens. The tension coils and intensifies until I'm chasing the release she's promising me. Remembering her comment about choking and gagging, I keep from touching her, from grabbing her hair like my instincts beg me to do. As my vision goes spotty, I shudder out a breath.

"Move," I say. "I'm going to come on those perfect tits."

She pulls back with a pop, grinning up at me.

"I'm going to make you orgasm until you can't walk for a fucking week."

I don't have time to enjoy her surprised expression before the waves of my release paint her chest.

Heaving out harsh breaths, I pull her to her feet, kiss her hard, then massage her tits under the spray until I can't stand the wait anymore.

I tug on one nipple with my teeth, then do the same to the other. "I've been letting you call the shots. I knew you. Had to build trust. In me."

My sentences are choppy between kisses and nips at her ample curves.

"It's so fucking sexy, the way you know yourself. You make me wild. I'll give you anything. Whatever you want, it's yours."

I pause my rambling gratitude to furiously leave kisses all over her face.

"Shopping trips, vacations, a full ride for three more doctorate programs? Name it. It's yours, gorgeous."

The words escape in a rush, but also, I can't get them to her fast enough. She needs to know that I understand the gravity of what she just did, even if I don't understand why she did it.

"Slow down, mister. What did you say?"

I shake my head, nearly motorboating her.

With one more nip at her breast, I move so we're eye to eye and keep my expression serious. I have to prove I can pull this off, she has to believe me. I need her to continue to trust me, because I've been nothing but honest with her.

"I said that you can have anything you want. I want you to keep the car."

I wait and count to three. Then ten.

It's creeping up toward fifteen when she finally replies.

"Hand me my shampoo. You have something in your hair," she says, reaching upward attempting to touch my scalp.

The sweet citrus scent I associate with her overtakes me, but her balance is still shaky. Watching her stand on her toes is causing me to worry that maybe *she'll* be the one who slips.

"Let's switch. I don't think this is going to work otherwise," I instruct her while removing her hands from where they linger near my nape.

Tossing my head under the spray, I quickly rinse my hair. I squirt body wash onto a ballet pink loofa and lather it up, then start at her neck and shoulders. When they're thoroughly clean, I pull her to me and run the loofah over her back, guiding the suds along her spine and the dip of her hips and ass.

With a kiss to her neck, I spin her, pressing her back to my chest, and get to work on her front, beginning at the soft patch of trimmed dark blond curls.

She flinches, the move reminding me of Satan's full nickname. Satan's Bikini Waxer.

"Also, no man should have any opinion on how you maintain any of this. His only thought should be 'holy shit, she let me near those perfect pink lips and soft curls.'"

She relaxes instantly, her body sinking into mine, and I feel about ten feet tall. Fuck, yes. I love seeing her so at ease.

I return to my task, my hands roving up and down her body, washing over her stomach and chest with care.

Finally satisfied that I've cleaned any mess I made, I nibble at her neck making the most ridiculous noises, like she's my favorite dessert. The laugh that escapes her is a reward in itself, musical and sweet. This is a layer of Nessa I hadn't expected to be granted access to. This is the part of her I never want to lose.

I detach the removable shower head and move it in a circular motion, rinsing away the remaining suds. With each revolution, I bring the spray lower. Eventually, I get it where I want it, using the water to massage her clit, and she sighs, her knees wobbling. With my free hand, I massage her heavy breasts and pinch her nipples as the water pounds against her. I bring my lips to her neck, peppering kisses, adding in a nip of my teeth here and there.

Those sighs turn into moans, and as they grow louder, I tug on her earlobe.

"Please come for me, gorgeous," I beg, knowing she gets off on being in control. "I'll hold you up while you let go. Give me the sounds of your release. Then I'll carry you to your bed and give you as many orgasms as you can take. Hell, I'll watch you take them for yourself. I want to feel you go boneless."

At that, she gives in, head falling back onto my chest, her nails digging into my forearm as she grasps for dear life.

"Fuck, Mateo. Oh my god, hold me tighter," she cries.

I obey, palming her breast more firmly, keeping her body pressed to mine.

"Do you feel what you do to me?" I growl as I come alive, my erection thickening against her ass for a second time.

"Fuck, I'm going to..." she pants.

"Please, baby. Please," I encourage her.

She shakes against me, her legs are barely supporting her. When she slumps, spent, I sweep her into my arms and kiss her forehead. I turn off the water, wrap her in a towel, and place her gently on the counter next to the sink.

Once I've dried off and secured my towel at my waist, I pick her up again and stride to her bedroom. Inside, I kick the door shut quietly.

I lay her out in front of me and make a meal of her. I take my time bringing her to orgasm on my tongue, thrusting my fingers deep inside her warm, slick center and curling upward. "Can you give me one more, little monster?"

On a whimper she shakes her head, her hands clutching the sheets. "I need you inside me."

The world shifts. We're hanging on the edge of something completely new. I hear those three words in my head, but it's not the time for them, so I grab a condom from her drawer beside the bed.

"I don't think I can move my legs," she whines with the cutest little flush as I lie on my side.

"Are you all done for tonight?" I really hope she isn't, but I'll deal, if that's the case.

In answer, she parts her thighs. I don't know what to do with this sign of trust, but as I slide home, I let the words I was trying to control come out in a way she can't understand. Maybe saying it this way can quell the urge to admit that I am madly in love with this little spitfire.

"Mahal kita." I let the Tagalog words fall from my lips. It's strange to hear them in this moment, and yet exactly right.

Though she doesn't know the language, her core muscles tense in response, like she understands on some instinctual level.

Before long, I quicken my pace and angle my pelvis to rub against that bundle of nerves to increase her pleasure. We're sighing and breathing together through stifled screams until release hits us both.

Sleep hits hard and heavy. I'm surrounded by vanilla and citrus and something all Nessa.

Maybe this can actually work. And I can't help but hope that it'll be even better than I planned.

thirty-five
Nessa

WITH A GROAN, I turn, overtaken by the urge to stretch. But I'm met with resistance, like I'm trapped beneath a weighted blanket. I try again, this time with more force.

"Ugh," a deep, groggy voice says. "What the, ow."

"You're still here?" My voice is hoarse, a mix of surprise and annoyance.

He brushes the hair away from my face and kisses my mouth softly. "As long as you want me here, I'll stay."

My heart stutters. Shit. He's too heart-eyed; I can't handle this right now. I groan again, trying to stretch, and nearly throw myself off the mattress.

He keeps me from tumbling, and once I find my bearings, I scramble to my feet and pull on a robe.

I dig through my bag and find that my work phone is dead. Cursing myself for being so irresponsible, I plug it in on the nightstand. The instant it comes back to life, it lights up with one notification after another.

With shaking hands, I unlock the screen and scroll through the call notifications and texts. When I get to the voicemail transcripts, my heart plummets. Shit!

"It's work. I have to run." I dart to the closet and frantically search for hospital-appropriate attire.

With a quick sniff test, I determine a body shower is called for, so I jog down the hall, clothing clasped to my chest. As I approach the bathroom, Delia steps out into the hall, and we almost collide.

"Something happened to a patient last night," I say. "I'm in a rush. Mateo is in my room. We can discuss it later. I've got to go."

My heart races, causing blood to whoosh in my ears. I look at Delia, but my eyes lose focus, and the room fills with black specs floating. My mind races with all the possibilities.

The little voice that has been relentlessly poking me gets louder. This is what happens when you stop paying attention. Did not want to think about how Caleb makes you feel, as if you don't know that pushing feelings away just causes them to pop up somewhere else. You tried to copy Mateo's carefree ways, but you ignored the differences between you.

It takes victims seven tries, on average, to leave their abusive partner for good. All the while, the partner continues to escalate in their attempts at control. I knew this was going on.

Finally, the devil's advocate—truly the angel on my shoulder—shows up. We made a safety plan. I was one person in a series she was set to call. She should have been fine getting out of there.

My mind races with all the possibilities. I was too panicked to read through all the information on my phone before springing into action.

Delia, thank god, reads the room and pulls me into a tight hug.

"It's going to be okay," she says. "I'll make coffee and leave your travel mug and water on the counter, go get ready. If the patient is already at the emergency room, they are safe and they have someone on call to help," she says and rubs soothing circles on my back.

Tears threaten, but I swallow them back. "I am the one who knows the case history, though."

"And you will be there faster if you focus. Get in the shower and head out. I got the coffee; you get yourself together."

"And Mateo?" I squeak and slap a hand over my face.

"Tell him to grab his pants and be out by noon when I leave for work," she says with a shrug.

"Okay," I exhale. "Okay, I got this. Thank you."

I speed through my morning routine and pull on a simple pair of black trousers and a camel sweater. Shoes on, I grab my bag, coffee, and water, then dart out the door.

———

AS I HIT the open highway, my frustration with Mateo grates on my nerves. I keep replaying the events, searching for a different perspective. None comes.

Mateo lay in bed, watching me spinning out, half asleep and wearing a dumb relaxed smile. He didn't pick up on the shift in the energy or any of the *many* ways I put it out there.

This shouldn't have happened.

I have only let my phone die when I've been with you.

I knew she wanted to go this weekend.

The angel on my shoulder shows back up and asks how often has this client claimed it was the weekend she'd leave? It didn't happen then, you couldn't have known.

The pesky devil says, but you should have. You would have if you paid better attention.

Pressing the foot pedal to accelerate gives a satisfying rev to the engine, and I watch the digital speedometer tick up from forty-five to ninety-eight almost instantly. Trees and grass along the sides of the interstate blur.

"Fuck," I scream, I clench my fists and bang the steering wheel. I am so angry I am seeing red. Oh fuck. No, literally, I'm seeing red.

The red and blue lights of a police cruiser flash behind me, and a siren wails.

"Fuck," I silently scream as I slow. Once I've come to a stop on the shoulder, I dig into the glove box for my registration and my hospital ID, hoping that I don't get one of those assholes who doesn't consider my work essential and will dick around.

Please, I beg the universe, please let this be a decent person.

"Do you know how fast you were driving this morning, little miss? Where is the fire?" He asks, his face fixed in a smarmy smile.

Dammit. This is going to be awful.

"Good, morning officer. I prefer Doctor over little miss." I hand over the stack of items with my hospital badge on top.

He snorts, but I hold my poker face while thinking *fuck this, you're an asshole.*

"Oh, is there an emergency that required you to drive like a surgeon headed to rescue the president?" He scoffs. "Sit tight, Doctor Ray-bin. It'll be a moment while I check on this."

Fuck. Fuck, fuck, fuck.

As I wait for Officer Douchebag to return my documents, my phone rings. I silence it from the touchscreen.

Not today, Satan.

It rings again. Then again. Voicemails and text messages are rolling in one after another.

The officer returns holding my documents and a summons when my phone rings again. I touch the screen to silence it, and he places a hand on his service weapon.

Are you fucking serious, dude?

"Hands on the wheel, now," he barks out.

I move my hands back as requested and don't move while he peers into my vehicle, neck craning, then looks down at my ID again.

"New York plates, New Jersey resident, speeding in Pennsylvania, huh? In a vehicle this nice? This is the final roll-out of the Audi TT with all the bells and whistles. It isn't registered to you. It's made out to—holy shit. That real estate guy?"

Swallowing thickly, I nod. "Yes, he's my…" I trail off unsure what we are to each other right now. He's my friend's brother? My boyfriend? My ex-boyfriend? Can we be exes if we were never actually a thing?

I'm taking too long to answer, and the officer arches both brows. As if on cue, my phone rings again, and Satan's name flashes on the display. I lift my hand to silence it, breaking the final straw.

"All right, I'm going to need you to step out of the vehicle, now, miss." The last word is said with a sneer.

After a field sobriety test, a thorough search of the car, and a ride to the station in the back of Officer Douchebag's vehicle, I'm officially miserable.

———

THIS SMALL TOWN in Pennsylvania makes Peacock Springs look like a major city. The dark wood police precinct has faded yellow letters painted into grooves spelling out the town name. There is one cell holding a man sleeping off a bender along the sole bench, so Officer Douche Canoe let me sit in the visitors chair with my left wrist handcuffed to the plastic armrest.

I made my one call to my lawyer father and waited.

Finally, Aba arrives. Mateo waltzes in beside him, chatting like old friends.

I give a tiny smile and wave with the hand that is not attached to the chair as they approach. Aba steps in close and speaks Hebrew to make sure our conversation is private.

"You didn't say anything to them without me, correct?" His question is firm. This is my attorney, not my father.

I shake my head, sighing.

"You make any smart-ass comments?" he asks with narrowed eyes.

Another head shake, my gaze on my shoes.

Switching to English so Mateo understands, I say, "I just asked to be called Doctor instead of little miss."

Our eyes connect briefly, only for me to look away quickly. All of the rage I felt earlier is mixed with sadness.

I hear Mateo's loafers click against the tile floor, and a fluorescent light flickers and buzzes nearby. Placing a hand on my shoulder, my dad tries to reassure me.

"Mateo will clear up the matter with the car. That should be enough, but I'm here if not."

I raise my eyes, pressure from unshed tears building, and nod. I'm so lucky to have this man as my father. His footprints leave an impossible space to fill, and despite thinking that Mateo was able to come close, he was just a distraction. He led me astray, and when my focus dropped from the people I care for, we all suffered.

Trying to break the tension, Aba asks, "Is your client okay?"

"I don't know," I say as a sob breaks. An ache ripples across my shoulders and down the center of my chest, causing my shoulders to slump and my arms to fall.

"I had only gotten through the first voicemail when Satan started to call. I used to block his number, so he got a new one. After so many times I gave up. He won't go away. Then, when the officer brought me in, he confiscated my phone." The tears stream down my face hot and fast now.

My dad strokes a hand down my back and kisses the top of my head. I want to hug him, but I'm immobilized by emotion—and this stupid handcuff.

"Oh, sweetie. I am sure the doctors on call can use your notes to help until we get this cleared up," he murmurs.

That only causes the tears to come faster. "My notes are vague, and I use codes to protect the client because of the abuse involved.

I can't risk the abuser getting access to them, because. Because—"
I stammer and stop there. If I don't, I'll break confidentiality by
blurting out "because the abuser is a hospital board member with
major connections who could easily pull strings and manipulate
the situation." And not only would that put my patient's life at
risk, but also my job.

Officer Douchebag, whose nametag I can now see says Officer
Doughterberg—close enough—approaches Mateo.

Mateo's dimple and grin are on full display, but I'm in no
mood to be swayed by his pretty-boy antics right now. He's a big
part of the reason I am in this mess in the first place. I let him
distract me and took my eye off the ball.

"Doctor R, I apologize for the confusion this morning. I've
spoken to Mr. Santos-Manolo, and he'll be retrieving the vehicle
from the impound lot after it's been processed. We appreciate the
generous donation to the precinct, and I'll have Linda in finance
get you those tax forms today. However, Miss—"

Mateo clears his throat.

The officer side-eyes him and straightens. "Excuse me, Doctor.
You should consider taking your boyfriend up on the suggestion
to put both your names on the car's title to protect you moving
forward. It'll take a bit to process your possessions out, so just
hang tight."

At this, my father rises to his full five feet, eleven inches. He
may not be overly tall, but he's broad-shouldered and
intimidating, nonetheless. He extends a hand to the officer.

"Hello, I didn't get to introduce myself. I'm Attorney Gabriel
Rabin, her counsel and her father." He eyes me, then turns back,
giving that statement a moment to sink in. "Given my daughter
isn't being charged with any crimes, I'm not sure why her items
are being processed at all. Seems like it's a pretty quiet morning,
and given this misunderstanding has delayed her from handling a
safety emergency for her client, it would be prudent of you to
expedite her release. You have no reason to hold her."

The men engage in a staring contest, my gaze ping-ponging between the pair and Mateo.

"I just need my phone," I say quietly. *And my wrist.*

"I'm happy to sit and wait if I can have my work phone. I need to check in with the team in the ER and my client."

"Surely we can make that happen. Right, Officer?" Mateo breaks into his signature wide smile.

"We'll see what we can do." Officer Douchebag narrows his eyes, though they quickly drift lower, appraising my figure.

Gross. Today sucks, and it's not even ten.

thirty-six
Nessa

THE MINUTE my phone is in my hands, I pull up the remaining voicemails and skim the transcripts again. Inhaling deeply, I remind myself how inconsequential my problems are compared to my client's. It's my job to protect her so that the ongoing financial, emotional, and physical abuse is documented properly. I exhale and take another cleansing breath before pulling up my supervisor's contact information.

Our conversation is a blur. By the end of it, I am nodding in relief and wiping away additional tears. Into the phone, I say, "Thank you again, Ruth Anne. I will absolutely take the day."

According to my supervisor, my patient is okay. Her sister drove up from Delaware immediately and will stay with her.

Maybe it's naivety, classism, or colorism that makes the average person think abuse happens somewhere else. However, I have seen abuse victims from all walks of life.

My phone vibrates with a text message, because, somehow, Satan's mother fucking Bikini Waxer has not taken the hint in the last few hours.

SATAN'S BIKINI WAXER:

Cute picture <image of Nessa being brought into the police station>

NESSA:

Are you having me watched?

SATAN'S BIKINI WAXER:

The family keeps a close eye on a lot of things.
Got lucky.

NESSA:

Delete this number.

SATAN'S BIKINI WAXER:

Was good seeing you at the festival, princess.

I can barely keep my head above water to make sense of what has happened in the last seventy-two hours. All I know is somehow having money and a penis increases a person's credibility. The charges have been dropped, but the photo cannot end up in the hands of my licensing board. This is the exact type of power game I was sick of when we ended things.

The angel and devil are talking to me again. They've teamed up now. We're going to hold your hand while we tell you this: Caleb is an abuser. Those were signs of PTSD, and he's trying to control you again. Don't let him win.

I study Aba, then Mateo. I can't tell either of them about this.

How could I be so smart and yet so very stupid? This is all a big, bright spotlight on the sign from the universe: Nessa is not supposed to date. When I date, I get distracted. If I hadn't been distracted by Mateo, my phone would have been plugged in. I'd be the first to respond to my client. I'd keep everyone safe, and my girlfriends will keep me loved. Those who can't do, teach. I have to stay in my lane.

Time to reset this thing with Mateo—I knew all along I didn't have the time or energy for him. I knew he would cause me problems. I hate that I was right because it was fun while it lasted.

Handing over the keys to Mateo, I look at the ground and shake my head. "I'm sorry," is all I can get through my lips before my lungs constrict again.

Despite the heartbreak, I smile and ask, "Aba, will you take me to visit Shae?"

thirty-seven
Mateo

"YOU CAN'T FORCE it to ring by staring it at," Liam says, handing me a beer.

I haven't heard from Nessa since we parted ways at the small police station days ago. The last thing she said to me directly was "I'm sorry."

Christian joins us, sitting on the third chair we dragged from the fire station out to the garage parking lot. His large brown hand clasps around the cap of a water, twisting, his eyes roam across Liam. He cocks an eyebrow, watching as we mindlessly sip from our beers.

"Babe, I'm going to turn a blind eye here because you aren't on station property right now." He nods at the beer in Liam's hand. "But you are literally only over the line." His expression softens, and so does his tone, when he turns to me. "What has you all twisted, Matty?"

"Nothing," I answer, quickly shoving my phone into my pocket.

"It's the blonde," Liam says, pretending to hide his smirk behind the beer.

Christian and Liam exchange one of those knowing glances.

The kind Lee and Stef share. My parents too. Like they're all in on something I'm too stupid to see.

With a grunt, I take a long drink hoping to cool my nerves with the hoppy brew.

"Do you need me to get my aunt over here to lay into you?" Christian teases me.

All my life, Prudence has ambushed the folks of Peacock Springs with advice.

"Wouldn't she find me on her own if the spirit called her to? I thought she didn't need the guidance of a mere mortal." I tease with a quirk of my eyebrow.

"I'm her nephew, I'm no mortal," he counters—and honestly, I'm not sure if this is a joke or if they truly believe it.

Either way, it eases the tension building in my chest. We sit just beyond the main square, but from here, we can see all the businesses still decorated from the previous weekend's events.

It is as if autumn swept in and covered every inch of downtown. There are dried cornstalks tied to every other lamp post and scarecrows dot the street randomly, ready for the town-wide competition. Oversized planters with mums and dahlias greet patrons at the doorways of most businesses, while a few have opted for simple pumpkins.

I pull sips quietly from my bottle, absorbing the buzz of town life around me. I finish the beer, dropping it onto the blacktop driveway with a plink.

When I returned home, the city had my head swarming, but today the noise has dulled to a soft hum. I was desperately missing Nessa. Everything felt like the proportions were wrong. Like I was wearing clothes two sizes too small. Even through the silence, that feeling is gone.

I'm confident we'll find our way back to one another. *Eventually.*

"All right, lay it on me. What do you think I need to know?" I'm entertained, even if unconvinced.

Another wave of laughter rolls across the group when Prudence's gray cat pads our way.

"Looks like you've been made," Christian says as Zelda winds herself between Liam's legs.

Collecting my empty beer bottle from the ground, Liam rises. "On that note, I'm going to grab another round. Do you want one, Chief? Or are you going back on shift?"

"I'll take one. Why not," Christian says to Liam's retreating form.

Just as the heavy metal door on the side of the building closes with a thud, Pru herself materializes and drops into Liam's now empty chair.

"Are you doing my job now?" Pru gives her nephew a stern look.

"Never, Auntie, let me check on Liam." He rushes out before heading back to the fire station.

I wait, and wait, Pru is quiet and searching. She stares at me, as if trying to look deep into my soul. I squirm in my seat.

"Ready for your next client readings?" I ask, hoping I've mustered up enough enthusiasm to cover my abnormal mood.

Without answering my question, she pulls out her deck of cards, and hands me three of them. "The eight of wands, the Hanged Man, and the ten of cups," she says as she points to each one in my hand.

"This weekend is going to bring big changes, that's for sure," she says cryptically.

"Huh?"

"You've been good busy, Matty. And even if you are paused, you are avoiding seeing the way your relationship has evolved," Pru explains, pointing to the first two cards.

"But there may not be a relationship anymore." I say with shoulders drooping.

"All of your relationships, not just with Nessa," She corrects me.

"Plus, look closer at the last card."

"It has a rainbow covered in gold cups, a happy couple waving to a town, and dancing children."

"See, this here is a very good omen. There's a lot of good to come, a blissful community and family. Have a little faith in us, Mateo. We've seen you grow," Prudence says before looking past me. Both men have returned with beers in hand, waiting to take their seats.

She stands. "Well, I'm going to get myself a little afternoon sweet. See you boys for dinner, Christian?"

Once she's out of earshot, I lean closer. "Okay, tell the truth. She's a witch, isn't she? Zelda was doing her bidding so she could sit."

We laugh at the accusation, but I'm still not convinced.

thirty-eight
Nessa

BY THE TIME we arrive at Shae's Philadelphia townhouse, I've completely given up pretenses. I've gathered my hair in a messy knot and cried off all my makeup.

Aba rings the bell, and she greets us, her eyes wide with surprise, he scoops her into a bear hug.

I muster a passive wave, then walk straight to her bedroom and fling myself onto the bed.

"Nice to see you too, sissy," she calls.

As I'm willing sleep to take me, Dad guides Shae out of the room. They go out to lunch, leaving me to my fitful nap.

When I wake up, it's dark enough out to suggest I slept all day, and Shae's watching me from a colorful swivel chair.

"Where do you find these things?" I ask, pointing at the ridiculous piece of furniture.

"Dad had to get home, but he said you had a really bad day and asked for me. What is going on?" she asks. She's tense, no doubt because we haven't been close in a long time. And that's on me.

Before I can stop them, my eyes well and tears crest my lashes. Without a word, I wrap myself in her fleece throw and bury my face in her pillow.

The bed dips, and then she's at my side.

"You do *not* cry. What is happening?" she asks me, smoothing a hand over my hair.

"This goes back too long. To the summer before ninth grade…" I launch into the story I told Mateo months ago.

"I was so scared of forcing ten-year-old Shae to grow up, that somewhere along the way, I failed to notice you aging just like I was. And now you're a twenty-five-year-old woman with her own story," I say, dipping my chin.

I open up about everything, from how I found myself hiding the problems with Caleb for years, to landing in bed with Mateo.

"It's over," I admit. The tears come harder now.

"Was it good dick, at least?" She teases me, now knowing my full sexual history.

I laugh, but it's cut off by a sob.

"He's amazing. Huge, with thick, throbbing veins. The kind that rests heavy in your palm, like they describe in my favorite romance novels." I sigh through the mix of tears and laughter, adding on, "And he knew what to do with it."

She nudges my arm. "At least you have the memory for the spank bank?"

After a few moments of silence in our embrace, I feel myself drifting again.

"Can I sleep here? Everything at my place reminds me of him. It would only be one night," I say with a sniffle.

"Of course," she says, rubbing light circles on my back. "What flavor of ice cream should I pick up? And which movie?"

———

THREE DAYS and a few too many bickering sessions later, Shae comes back from work full of fury, looking at me in her clothing, burrito wrapped into a blanket, still wallowing.

She paces, pausing to rest her hands on her hips, before

unloading on me. "You are in love with him, and you don't want to admit it for some reason that may be 'logical,' but is completely cerebral and not human."

She flips the lights on and gives me a hard stare, her brows low and lips thin.

"The other night you were fresh off your broken heart, but now it's time for some hard truths," she says, dropping into her swivel chair.

I'm too empty to think. I'm unmoving and uncaring as she dumps fifteen years of anger on me like a bucket of ice water.

"You don't do all this because you want to be a good person. You do it because you need to feel important. You want to be needed. We get it. You are smart. You have an ivy league education. You climbed to the top of your field. Congrats. You have all the external trappings of a happy life, and you're still just a competitive, snarky bitch who keeps everyone at arm's length in hopes of maintaining control."

She jabs a finger at me.

"You know that we have a mom and a dad, right? You aren't in charge of us. I know you think being the oldest means we can't function without you, but that's bullshit. Your ex was toxic, and you tried to solve that issue alone—something you would never let a patient do. Then, when someone worth the risk of repeated heartbreak arrived, you did everything in your power to push him away."

When I finally push to my feet, I catch sight of myself in the vanity mirror. My eyes are bloodshot, and the bags beneath them are heavy and dark. Throat scratchy, I cough a few times, trying to find words. Any words. Despite how slow the world seems to be moving, it's like my thoughts and heartbeat are off to the races.

Her angry speech continues slicing through me.

"All anyone needs is your love and support. You work all the time, and then, during your time off, you take care of people who don't need it. Know what I saw at Jewish New Year's that I haven't seen since we were kids? I saw your fun side. I saw you look happy. Truly, undeniably happy. You made out with him in the mud, damn it."

The final few words are a cry for me to pay attention, and it works. They bring with them the memory of dancing with Mateo in the yard, falling over ourselves. Happy. That breaks the dam, and hot, salty streams of tears flow down my cheeks.

I'm not ready to have this conversation with her, so instead, I push back halfheartedly, having already hired a cab to take me home.

"Oh, fuck this," I haul myself up, blanket still draped over me, and shout, "And I'm taking the blanket!"

———

THE FIRST THING I see is the green sports car still parked in the driveway.

Instantly, fresh rage bubbles up. I stalk into the house and slam the front door, then stomp to my bedroom and slam that door too.

"Welcome home, I guess," Delia shouts from the hall. "Is there a reason you want to break the doors in my grandma's house?" She punctuates the question with a laugh, annoying me further.

"Why aren't you at work?" I ask, hoping to change the subject.

"Shift changes for vacations. But don't think you can change the subject on me, I know your ways," Delia says.

Whipping my bedroom door open, I wave her into the room. Then I skulk back to my bed and curl up in Shae's blanket.

She wrinkles her nose and sniffs at my disheveled appearance. "Decided on a new style? The Halloween blanket is a... choice."

"It's really soft, so I stole it from Shae."

"I bet she's so mad," Delia says with a light laugh.

The tension breaks, and the reason I call these girls *the framily*

—or my friends who are family—sends warmth rushing through me. I drop the blanket, trying to cool off.

"Not as mad as I am!" Okay, this may not be my finest, or most mature moment.

"Not as mad as you, because..." She raises both brows, waiting for me to continue.

I roll myself up in the blanket again so only my face pokes out.

She pokes the blanket a little again, prodding me to continue.

"First we bonded after my arrest," I say.

"I'm sorry, your what?" Delia exclaims.

"It was dropped. I was speeding in Matty's car. Speaking of, I thought I gave it back to him," I say, slouching forward and heaving out my breath.

"He parked it here. Said he wanted you to have the option if you need it," Delia softly replies.

"Can you put a tarp on it?"

"Do you have a tarp?" she quips.

I wiggle my arms free of the blanket and pop my head out, then snag my phone from the mattress beside me. "I will by tomorrow night, so yes?"

The annoyance in her expression morphs to amusement, and she lets out a laugh. The sound is infectious. I join in, and in seconds, the tension I brought home with me dissipates a fraction more.

"She tried to tell me that I was pushing him away because I'm scared. That I am punishing him for something he didn't do. Some kind of high horse babble like that. I'll give her credit for the effort she put into trying to psychoanalyze me." I huff. "Also, she said I think I'm better than her because of my education. As if I didn't work hard to get where I am."

"On days like this, I'm so thankful to be an only child. Damn. Must have been hard to hear that truth bomb."

Before the words can register, she snatches a pillow from the head of the bed and holds it up in front of her face.

235

My stomach drops. "Excuse you?"

She peeks around the pillow, cringing. "Babe, I've been too tired lately to be in your business as often as I used to be. But denial? River boat for one."

I take out an invisible nail file and pretend to sharpen my claws. "Yeah? Why is that?"

She clicks her tongue. "Because you did fall for him, and now you are treating him like he has the plague. But why? Because of your own mistakes? Because you discovered that, like the rest of the population, you're imperfect?"

"Because I'm scared," I shout. "I'm embarrassed. I'm an expert in my field, yet I missed the signs. It took Caleb showing back up and my public meltdown for me to realize he was *abusive*. That even if he didn't put his hands on me, that relationship was coercive and manipulative, and it broke me."

I retreat into the blanket, letting my shame wash over me.

Whispering, Delia asks, "So you pushed Matty away?"

My responding nod forces the blanket to shift, freeing my face. "I pushed him away."

The door opens a crack, and I jump sky high. The doorway is empty, but it continues to swing open. Then there's a tiny meow and a black cat jumps onto the bed.

Heart lifting a fraction, I scoop up the kitten. It's wearing a pink collar decorated with light pink bows. The tag around his neck says *Wyclef*. My eyes fill with tears again as I turn to Delia.

She's holding a piece of paper out to me, her lips tipped in a small smile.

With a shaky breath, I take it and wipe the moisture from my eyes with the back of one wrist.

Nessa, it says.

I hoped that during the festival, you'd see how great we are together, but I'm not sure how well we weathered the... um, weather? I couldn't let Wy-Guy go to anyone else. I hope we can talk when you're ready.

xo—M

Heart lurching, I hold the cat and note to me. "Wyclef?"

"He showed up in a little kennel, along with a basket of food, toys, and a litter box."

I nuzzle him, relishing the silkiness of his fur.

Delia stands and pads out of the room, flipping off the light, leaving me alone with my new kitten and an uncomfortable sinking feeling.

thirty-nine
Mateo

MY PHONE BUZZES, and I stupidly get my hopes up. Maybe she's had enough time to think. Or maybe she's had too much time and she has realized how right she was to call herself "out of my league."

"Hey, Stef. Hey, Lee," I say, picking up their video call.

They cautiously respond in unison.

I catch a glimpse of myself in the tiny box for my camera. The defeat coursing through me is obvious even in the thumb-size image. I rub my eyes, hoping to avoid crying in front of them.

"Okay." Stef gives a resigned sigh. "Time to rally the framily. You want to invite Liam and Christian?"

My heart squeezes. My sweet sister is coming home because, despite being older and wealthier, I'm still the fuck-up. At least I'm smart enough to know how to accept help.

————

"IT DOESN'T MATTER," I say as I tear off another piece of pandesal.

238

Mom places a cup of black coffee on the table and sits, then dunks the sugary bread into the rich black liquid. "What do you mean, *tisoy*?" She asks, calling me pale like she has since I was born.

"I mean, Jim got the entire town excited about this stupid country club that nobody will be able to use, and now they'll push the Hendrix and Kelly votes away from me."

Remembering where I am and who I need to be, I pivot to add a silver lining. "It's okay, though, I'll find a place on the break of a resurgence soon. I'll move there and start a new project. I'll let this one go. It's fine."

Before I can even fully wrap my head around what I'm suggesting for myself, she levels me with a stare. "And how does your girlfriend feel about this?"

My shoulders slump. "She isn't talking to me, and it wasn't real anyhow."

"Don't be a fool," she says and glares at me.

"I'm sorry?" I sit up straighter on instinct, her tone flashing me back to her scolds for slouching during church when I was a little kid.

Stef and Lee appear at the bottom of the stairs, clearly having come to town to participate in an intervention.

"You're as dumb as they say if you think it wasn't real, Matty." Lee plops into a chair and shoves a full roll into his mouth, grinning at Stef like a chipmunk.

"I have to agree with the room, sorry, *brosef*," my sister says.

Unease courses through me, making my muscles tense and my blood warm. I run my hands through my hair, at a loss for what to say. For what to do. I feel stretched too thin, everything I've worked for is a mess.

"Stef," Mom says, "can you and Lee step out please?"

I blow out a long breath. Time to face the executioner.

"Mateo, I did not raise you to give up on yourself so easily," she says, her tone firm, veering toward angry.

"We didn't raise you to give up on your community like this. Or the person you love."

More than anything, I want to slump to the floor and close my eyes.

"This is not how we do things. We take care of each other. Haven't I taught you that by now?"

"Huh?" I frown. "Are we having the why didn't you go into healthcare argument again?" I'm too tired for this.

"Do you need to use a stethoscope to help the people you love?" She hits the word love hard and heavy. That single syllable reverberates through my brain and across all my limbs. It pricks at my skin, makes my heart tick loud in my ears.

I sigh. Damn that word. I can't argue with her, because of course I love Nessa. She's brilliant, beautiful, strong, caring, hilarious, and so goddamn sexy. There will never be another woman like her.

"It doesn't matter," I say, roughing a hand over my face. "It's too late. I failed her, I was supposed to protect her from her ex, I was supposed to protect the town from the Reynolds Group. Protect the land. And now they'll develop it and destroy what generations have built here. I failed her, I failed us all."

Though I can't look at her, the heat of her glare incinerates me.

"You have done no such thing, *tisoy*, so pause and recall what you've already learned. Who votes?"

"One member of each clan: Kelly, Morgan, and Hendrix."

She arches a brow. "Which members?"

"Generally, Gran, Glenn because he doesn't trust Grant's judgment, and either Elizabeth or River."

"Which of those people do you think will be swayed by the fancy things Jim highlighted?"

Arms on the table, she angles forward, mischief dancing in her eyes.

"What things would make the community better, *tisoy*?" Mom asks, taking a pen and paper from the kitchen table. She writes

The Cathleen Kelly Community Center across the top, then makes a checklist.

Item number one: a pool.

I start to call out items, and she writes them down for me: childcare, senior care, healthcare, prevention, cooking classes, a fitness center, mental health programs.

With a hum, she jots down my ideas, then looks up at me, her face soft.

Sneaking in to grab more breakfast, Stef looks at the paper over Mom's shoulder.

"You know, Matty, one thing they focus on in education is the types of learners. There are at least four of them. Some people say eight." Stef pauses. "The point is, you are really good with seeing people, really seeing people. Tomorrow is the final conversation with the committee. I'll get her there. You got this."

"Looks like you better get to work, then," Mom says and drops the pen.

forty
Mateo

New Group text: Loch Ness Hunt <spy emoji>
[Mateo Santos-Manolo, Stef Carter, Lee Carter, Christian Cleary, Delia Shane, Liam Kelly]

MATEO:

I'm recruiting you all to help me pull off something big for Nessa, can I count on you?

DELIA:

WTAF is this group name?

Delia changed the group to: Matty Has it Baddy

STEF:

<rolling laughter emoji x3>

LIAM:

I'm in, whatever you need. Christian too.

MATEO:

Thanks guys.

DELIA:

You gotta include Lily.

Mateo added Lily Long

LILY:

Is it time for a grand gesture?

DELIA, STEF, LIAM LOVED LILY'S MESSAGE
LIAM:

When and where, brother?

MATEO:

> We got to figure out how to show her this was all
> real.

DELIA:

I'm pretty sure she knows. Next step is getting
her to open up to you.

Let's chat at The Featherweight. I'll reserve a
private room.

WE'VE JUST SETTLED when Prudence barrels in with Sofia
Salvatore. We all still, the room so quiet you can hear the blinking
of eyes.

"I thought I had this space for a reading," Pru says.

"We have a bit of a pressing matter. Can you use your shop?"
Delia asks, using her best customer-service voice.

"What sort of pressing matter?" Sofia asks, her cheeks pinking.

"Oh, is this about the boys who think they're men?" Prudence
asks with a knowing look.

Lily and Delia, along with my sister, who's patched in through
video call, fall into a fit of laughter.

"I'd swear you four are a coven if I didn't know better."
Prudence tuts as she pulls out a chair and sits.

Sofia glances around the room slowly, worrying her lip.

"Please, feel free to join us, ladies." I gesture to the table.

What the hell. Nothing happens around here without the
Salvatores and Pru finding out anyhow.

AS WE POLISH off bar pies, I call out, "Let's recap. Jim has been courting the Reynolds Group for a few months, hoping they'll purchase the land that Grant put up for sale. What he and Grant have conveniently ignored is that they have no voting rights. They cannot approve the sale.

"There's a mile-long list of reasons we should turn down the Reynolds Group offer. This includes their reputation for screwing over local companies they contract for work. Not to mention they will destroy anything in the historical preserve out on Kelly farms. And finally, they will run the current residents out of town using tax hikes and nefarious country club clauses."

I scan the assembled group, chest filling with pride, feeling like an even better version of myself as each person looks back at me, rapt.

"The people at this table make up the ground team. Your job is to spread the word about these bad business practices. But..." I drag the word out for emphasis. "But I need it to be authentic, and keep my name out of it. Avoiding any connection to me is extremely important."

"And you weren't going to have a Salvatore on the team?" Sofia scoffs. "Wow, you're lucky Pru and I showed up. Get me information on the lawsuits against the Reynolds Group. I'll tell Chiara I'm thinking of switching to prelaw and ask her to take a look at some of the documents 'my new class' is analyzing." She breaks into a devious grin. "She'll be excited I'm making decisions, and once she dives into the lawsuits, she'll get pissed off. Once she sees how they screw over contractors, she'll run to Tommy and warn him to not take any jobs with Reynolds. Tommy has connections to all the local suppliers and crews, he can tell them too. Nobody around here is going to risk losing the family business."

"Done. Stef, can you send the document called Adams vs. Reynolds to her?" I ask.

My sister nods and taps away at her laptop.

"We need to work on getting this to all the North Side business owners."

Liam points a finger around the table. "Nah, dude. You have all of us. Me for the vet clinic land. I'll talk to Gran tonight. And Lily's here. The property the library is on is owned by the town. You're set."

Nodding, I check an item off the list on my tablet.

"Okay, then we're set. Let's get the word out using the whisper network, not the Springer, to make sure people know what they're in for if they push for this country club."

Liam and Christian, both on duty, leave first, their matching navy cargo pants and PSFD shirts making a statement.

"Pru, why don't you take the room. I'll bring these two back to the office," Delia says.

"Thank you," Sofia says, again speaking softly and lowering her gaze.

———

SHOULD I have consulted the senior Salvatore women?

I run my hand through my hair, deciding a visit to the salon is necessary. Not only for my hair, but for intel. The bells chime overhead as I step inside, and every head snaps my way.

"Hey, Matty. Haven't seen you up close in forever. How are you?" Tina gives me a kiss on each cheek in greeting.

"It's been too long, for sure. I'm hoping to get in for a trim soon. Have any openings?" My smile is deep and charming. Flattery is the best way to handle Christina Salvatore.

"Let me take a look." She steps around the counter and peers at her computer screen. "It doesn't look like we have anything in the next month, and no offense, but that is too long given the hair growing in at the back of your neck."

The tone is light, teasing, perhaps even flirty. She rounds the counter again and runs her hands through my hair, her nails scratching my scalp lightly.

"I can squeeze you in tonight if you can come back after closing. How about nine?"

She preens and bats her glued-on lashes my way. They are so oversized she looks like a Muppet.

"Sure thing," I say as I extricate myself from her fingers. I'm playing with fire here.

forty-one
Nessa

DELIA CONVINCES me that I will feel better if I get some air, so I text Millie and we meet for dinner at The Featherweight. Dinner turns into a long conversation at the fire pit, which is equipped with a s'mores bar tonight. Before I know it, we're wandering back to Millie's place stuffed full of chocolate and marshmallows.

As we pass Curl Up & Dye, I'm knocked back like I've taken a physical blow.

In the dimly lit shop sits Mateo, wearing a cape, suggesting it is just a typical appointment. But that isn't what's taken me by surprise. No, what has my hackles rising is the sight of Christina Salvatore wearing a dress so tiny it might as well be lingerie.

"Guess he's moving on," I say, a chill running through me.

She's massaging his scalp, again not totally abnormal. But her low cut neckline and unconventional stance—she is standing in front of the chair instead of behind it—means her chest is inches from his face.

"Figures," I grumble to Millie. "He was always a man whore, and despite his pretty words, he moved on faster than FloJo."

Millie loops her arm through mine and tugs me along. Glancing back, a tiny fragment of light catches my eye and I stop.

"Wait, look," I say.

"Don't give him the satisfaction," she reprimands.

"I think she's wearing an engagement ring," I add.

"Intrigue," Millie coos, turning.

"I can't tell," I admit, slumping.

"Hmm, well, can I interest you in a distraction? Reruns? I find that TV shows I've seen before are always the best balm."

A FEW EPISODES into our rerun marathon, a heavy knock sounds on her apartment door. The deep banging is accompanied by angry demands for her to open up.

It startles me enough that I jump out of my skin, while Millie simply laughs and shouts, "If you asked nicely, maybe I'd get up faster," before moving toward the door.

"Should we be careful?" I ask, pulling my feet up onto the couch. "Is this man dangerous or deranged? Do you know who it is and what they want?"

It's then that the man shouts again, and I recognize the voice.

Instantly, my body sags in relief.

"Can you turn that down?" Seth asks as Millie swings the door open. "If I have to listen to you clap along to the theme song again, it's going to break me."

"Nice to see you too, Seth-ward." Millie pulls him into the apartment. "Come, join us."

Seth is looking past Millie, and we make eye contact. I give him a sheepish wave.

"Come on, we're about to watch the episode where Monica and Chandler's secret is revealed. And we have snacks. Help me eat my feelings." I wave a hand over the spread on the coffee table.

Sighing, he throws himself into the armchair to my left, sitting as far from Millie as possible and glaring at her.

There's a long sequence of characters saying "they know" back and forth, and when one of them is shocked about who is messing with whom, I bolt up.

"That's what I need to do!"

"Finally admit that you've fallen for Mateo and end the insanity?" Seth asks dryly.

"No. I need to make this into something academic. I've got to run. Millie, love that bookshelf. We need to discuss your taste in romance authors next time we hang out."

"This is a terrible idea," Seth groans.

Millie lights up. "I love terrible ideas. Count me in!"

DELIA KNOCKS on my open doorframe later the next evening after work. I've been slumped over the computer reading listener emails and research articles, and the motion causes my neck to crack. Leaning back, I press my chest forward and then roll my shoulders, turning to look at her once I feel a little less like the Tin Man.

Delia gapes, horrified. "You were in that exact position when I left at lunchtime. Please tell me you've moved since then."

Frowning, she surveys the space. There are multiple empty cans of diet cola, wrappers from snack bars, and a fork sitting in an empty pie tin. I cleaned that out first. There's also a half-drunk bottle of water.

"Um." I shrug and turn back to the notes scattered around me. "I've gotten up to pee a couple of times..."

"What is this?" She looks at me cautiously, like she's worried she'll spook me.

Wyclef uses this moment of distraction to walk across my keyboard and lay himself straight across my arms. He's become obsessed with getting head rubs, and I can't say no to those yellow eyes, so I pause my frantic scripting for him.

"Working on my final episode of the year, looking for articles and emails that can help," I say.

I puff my chest, raising my chin, and try to put as much confidence as possible behind my explanation.

"I'm going to analyze what happened like patient case notes. I have had some perfect emails come in for it. I'm going to figure out how to fix this by looking at it like it's someone else's problem." I pause my rushed explanation, blinking a few times.

The ache in my neck has set in, and I reach back to rub absently at the spot.

Delia nods and steps closer. "Can I see some of these listener questions?"

I gather the printouts I've highlighted and annotated and hand them over.

To my pleasant surprise, she smiles. "This is brilliant, Ness, I'm in. But only if you rest. I can help you with this tomorrow if you take a break now."

Cuddling Wyclef, I let out a large yawn. He swats at the curl that fell from my messy bun.

Rapping her knuckles against the frame, Delia gives me a soft smile. "Good night, get some sleep."

"Okay, Mom," I say, with an exaggerated whine.

forty-two
Nessa

Group Chat: Bad Bitches
[Stef Carter, Lily Long, Delia Shane, Nessa Rabin]
Nessa added Millie to the group chat

NESSA:

Ladies! Adding Millie. She's Seth's new neighbor and has the absolute coolest tattoos.

STEF:

Hi, Millie! I'll be home for Christmas. I can't wait to meet you -Stef

DELIA:

Hey there, I'm Delia, we've met

LILY:

omg. Hey girl hey!

NESSA:

and you are...?

LILY:

??

NESSA:

That's Lily

MILLIE:

So excited to be adopted by you all

NESSA:

Delia and I are working on a little project. Can I borrow everyone who isn't studying for finals?

STEF:

<prayer hand emoji> TY!! Going back on do not disturb & ignoring my phone now!

<moon> Stef has notifications silenced

NESSA:

Can you guys meet me at CCs?

MILLIE:

I have to prep some bouquets and arrangements. Can you bring coffees here?

NESSA:

Absolutely! Send over your orders <3

A FEW HOURS LATER, I'm sitting on the floor of Rosie's, wearing my *Read More Smut* sweatshirt and a giant burlap hair bow. I've scattered a mix of printed emails and the notes I typed up yesterday around my corner of the floor.

Delia and Lily take turns picking up random letters and reading me the bullet points I laid out. After the first hour, we have it narrowed down to our top picks.

Millie is unloading a series of dahlia blooms from specialty boxes. She trims the stems before placing them into old ten-gallon paint buckets. "Read us the list," she calls, grabbing sheers from her apron.

"Okay, Question 1: *Flicking the Bean* isn't cutting it." I read the title we scrawled on the page.

"Preach," Millie calls, and the room erupts in giggles.

"Don't think we won't get back to that, *Mildred*, my dear," I say.

"Ouch, who are you? Seth?" she replies then sticks her tongue out at me. There are more giggles throughout the shop.

"Okay, okay. So friends with benefits. Things ended. Now despite their status as 'president, captain, chairman of the self-love club,' this listener is struggling to enjoy their time *alone* the way they used to," I say, then place it in the keep pile.

"That tracks," Delia says, examining a few potted plants near her.

"Those are violets." Millie points her scissors at them.

Delia gently fingers the petals and murmurs "gorgeous" before turning back to the group.

"Lily, which did you have for her?" Delia asks.

"I've got the reformed playboy," Lily cries.

"Technically, you had the friends-to-lovers," I tease her, and her cheeks go pink.

Millie asks, "Are we talking romance book tropes or your life?"

"My life," Lily says at the same time I say, "Both. You still owe me your favorites."

With a smug grin and a particularly sharp snap of the scissors, Millie lops off the bottom of a stem and plunks the flower into the water. "I'm more of a why choose fan."

"Okay... that's going in the *stories for later* pile. Both the letter and your answer," I say.

Outside the flower shop windows, volunteers are stringing up lights across the square. The twinkling around the gazebo and the greenery cast an ethereal glow, like fairies dancing along the branches.

It's beautiful. If this were a romcom, this is the moment Mateo would appear on the sidewalk, holding large handwritten signs, declaring his love. Or a boom box playing a song just for me. Unfortunately, this is real life, and there's no point in daydreaming about him sweeping in to tell me that I'm perfect in his eyes. That he's moving here for good.

Once we've put away the questions, we help tidy the shop. We say our goodbyes, and Millie locks up behind us.

Delia and I walk home together, passing one lawn sign after another, each denouncing the Reynolds Group. I'm buzzing, from the caffeine and the sight. They're printed with phrases like *Keep New Jersey Weird* and *Keep PS Prices Affordable to All*.

My smile grows, and my steps get lighter. "Good, let those interlopers know how little the people here want their influence."

———

WYCLEF GREETS us as I pull off my boots. Once I've hung my coat, I pick him up and cuddle him to my chest. I settle with him on the couch and turn on the TV to fill the silence as I run my hands along his fur.

Unfortunately, none of it quiets my mind.

No, instead, those two voices that have been arguing compete for attention. My thoughts race one after another. About the script I created. About my friends. About what Ema said on Rosh Hashanah. That this year is about trusting others to fill in if I do less. Mateo wanted me to have fun. My friends and even Shae love when I let loose a little. My work is… meaningful, but in the dark, when I'm alone, I can't help but sometimes think that it's also run its course. Maybe it's time to rethink how much of other people's trauma I absorb.

But mostly, I keep thinking about the self-proclaimed reformed playboy who fell for someone he never expected to. He called her a smoke show who's out of his league. He's been missing from her life, just like Mateo and me.

Strangely, for as different as Mateo and I are, we share one very prominent struggle. We're both dealing with who we are expected to be and who we want to be.

I see it now, and I wish I could say something. I unlock my phone and navigate to our message thread. We haven't said a word to each other in weeks, and a tiny piece of me wants to restart the conversation. But I don't know how.

She's ruined me for all other women. That's what the listener said. It's romance hero stuff, and he knows how much I love that line.

Could it be him? Are we both waiting for the other to make the grandest gesture?

———

I WAKE up to a text that makes my blood run cold.

Group Chat: Bad Bitches
[Stef Carter, Lily Long, Delia Shane, Nessa Rabin, Millie]

STEF:

Hey, Nessa, can we talk? I'll be at The Featherweight this afternoon.

After two decades, I've finally broken the *framily*. I wouldn't blame her if she hates me. My heart sinks at the thought, but...

What's stopping me from being loved by them in return, other than holding everyone at a distance because of one worthless man?

It's time for me to take my own advice, no matter how difficult it is. I need to talk this out.

forty-three
Mateo

REYNOLDS and I arrive at The Featherweight at the same time, and despite his smug, disrespectful attitude, I approach him calmly and cordially.

"Nice to see you." I extend my hand.

He stands still, forcing me to inch closer, as though I'm beneath him.

That's okay. He won't rattle me today.

With the size of this group, they've sent us to what they call the library meeting room on the first floor. Liam—dressed in his Peacock Springs Fire Department T-shirt and work pants—stands with River. The rest of the Hendrix, Kelly, and Morgan parties arrive, each family sitting together at designated tables strategically placed in a U-shape.

As I take in the scene, a slight sadness creeps in. I wish Nessa was here. I want to show her I never gave up, and I hoped she wouldn't give up on me. On us.

When a small hand touches my shoulder, a zap of hopefulness courses through me, but when I turn around and find my sister and brother-in-law, I deflate.

"She'll be here," Stef says, shoulders back, chin high.

I try to absorb a little of her confidence. "Glad you're here," I say. "We're over there if you want to join me." I wave to my reserved seats.

"I have to wait for her at the bar," Stef says.

At the front of the room, a smaller table with three chairs has been set up. Gran walks over to the middle seat, taking center stage and scanning the room. "Thank you all for joining us. This is an important gathering for the Historic Families of Peacock Springs. While Jimmy tried to sway the community at the festival, this decision can only be made by the deeded property owners."

Eyes narrowed, she focuses on her grandson, then Grant, ending on Caleb.

"What?" Caleb lurches forward in his seat, his face red.

Points for me, yes!

"I represent the Kelly Family," she says elongating and emphasizing her position.

Walking over to the chair beside hers, Glenn says, "I represent the Morgan Family."

Last, River flanks her other side, making the tiny woman appear to have two large bodyguards. He finishes with "And I represent the Hendrix family."

"Thank you, gentlemen," Gran says, bobbing her head between the men next to her. "Please, everyone, take your seat. I'd like to call to order this unique gathering of the KMH Family Trust."

"Inside the folders on the table, you'll find the final proposals from the competing parties. Using town feedback, Mateo has made some updates since Jim's presentation."

As Caleb continues to turn redder, a confused Landan turns to Grant. "What are they talking about?"

Wide eyed, Grant looks to Jim. The blood drains from Jim's face, and he's left ashen and rapidly blinking.

Gran gives a haughty laugh, and looks at the trio, then says, "Landan, did you not know the ripple effect you and Grant set off? Grant's poor decision-making at nineteen had Glenn uncertain he was ready for this level of responsibility. Over the years, he has not earned the ability to fully take over the family business. You may have some financial benefits, but you do not have a say."

Glenn nods serenely as he looks at his folded hands on the table before him.

"This is ridiculous!" Landan screeches before storming out of the room.

Blinking, Grant looks from her to his father to the doorway his wife left through.

"Go after your wife, son. You'll be packing up soon, anyhow. Better to keep one wife happy in this lifetime." Glenn urges, maintaining his downcast eyes and shaking his head. "Our hope is that Mateo is granted permission to purchase the Morgan properties, while Cathleen"—he nods at Gran—"will transfer her shares to her grandson—"

Jim whoops.

"To my grandson, Liam," Gran cuts in firmly.

"Me?" Beside me, Liam's eyes go wide.

"You are a good man," Gran says with a warm smile. "And you already take good care of the farm. I'm too old, and your dad here will be retiring soon enough. It's time to hand this over to young blood. Will you be okay staying put?" she asks, a twinkle in her eye.

"I was never planning to go anywhere else," he says with a dip of his chin. "Thank you, Gran."

I catch Liam's gaze and raise my eyebrows as if to say *can you believe this?*

He gives me a stiff nod, answering, *of course—we're awesome.*

I try not to chuckle. This is the perfect future business partnership.

I glance at the doorway again, hoping to see her blond curls, but still nothing.

The room erupts into whispers over the announcements.

Caleb turns from red to purple, and his tantrum includes shouts that we are all a bunch of nobodies. I scurry to watch from the open doorway as he knocks over anything he can in his path, then finally exits through the front door and stomps down the steps.

Good riddance, asshole.

forty-four
Nessa

INHALING A STEADYING BREATH, I stare up the front steps of The Featherweight.

Beside me, Pru winks and presses a coin into my hand. "An agate worry stone so that you can be confident in speaking your truth."

"Thanks," I mumble as I turn the smooth stone in my hand.

During that moment, Satan stomps his way down the stairs, screaming about using every lawyer at his disposal. His face has turned an angry shade of maroon, his words venomous.

I hope this is the last I see of him. If it isn't, I'm ready to handle it the right way next time.

"Perfect timing, thank you. Pru, Gabe. Do you have the paperwork and notary kit to finish the transfers for our family and the contract between Mateo and Glenn?" Gran asks.

My dad and Pru unpack supplies as Stef slips her arm through mine and leads me to the bar. Lily waits on a stool, and Delia stands behind the counter with a towel slung casually over her shoulder.

"What else have you bitches planned?" The words may be

harsh, but the venom is gone. Instead, I sound childish. "You planted those letters," I huff. "I know you did."

"Matty organized it," Lee says as he pulls his wife close. "Did it work?"

With an eye roll, I dip my chin.

The four of them hiss a quiet cheer.

"Are you going to tell him?" Lily asks, leaning in, casting an eye-crinkling smile my way.

With a nod, I swallow thickly, my throat dry and scratchy.

As if she's conjured it, Delia holds out a glass of water.

Maybe we are witches, I laugh to myself.

"It won't be easy, and it won't change overnight, but I have to take better care of myself. I'm going to look for a new job. This one is too hard on my heart," I admit, feeling a mix of defeat and possibility.

"I think you should take a look at the final approved proposal," Stef says, her lips tipping up in a secretive smile.

With a deep inhale, I rush into the room.

Dad is packing up the signed and notarized papers. Mateo has his back to me, chatting reverently about the town with Liam and Gran.

The papers on the table are his revised proposal. Blueprints for a community center with health and mental health services, as well as a pool. There's also a page with a recommendation for a person to lead the facility.

I blink, my vision blurred and unwilling to trust my eyes: *Dr. Nessa Rabin, PsyD, Executive Director.* I'm shaken from my stupor when the girls shove me forward.

"I just wish Nessa could see this," Mateo says, oblivious to my presence. "I think she'd make an amazing executive director for a community center. She inspired a lot of the ideas on the list of services we hope to provide."

"I'm here," I rasp out.

Mateo turns slowly, and I rush forward and meet him in the

middle. He runs his hands through his hair, going for cool, though anxiety rolls off him in waves.

I try to apologize, getting out only, "I'm sorry. I—"

He pulls me into a bone-crushing hug. "No, I'm sorry. I really believed I had made my intentions clear to you. When that police officer said those things." He shakes his head. Our eyes meet, mine blurry and his filling with so much watery emotion.

"Then Delia said you went to your sister's, and I wanted to give you space. It has been killing me, but Ness, I'm not going anywhere. I am exactly right for you."

I bite my lower lip, trying to suppress a laugh. "Did you just quote Jacob?"

He gives me that big, goofy, grin. The charming one I used to think he wore to deflect. This time, it's accompanied by a little flicker of fear in his eyes. "Sure did, Ivy," he whispers. "I'm nothing without you. I need you to cling to me and grow with me."

A breath shudders out of me and tears crest my lashes. Fuck, I hate crying. Before that fact can set in, his thumb is there, wiping away the moisture. He studies me, his irises, the color of melting chocolate, swim with emotion.

"I love you, and your poison, Ivy. I'm not going anywhere. I'll be here to tease you, to support you, all of it, for as long as you'll let me."

With that, he claims my lips, and the rest of the room falls away. Our kiss starts soft and sweet, but when his tongue parts my lips, it grows fervent, our mouths dancing together making up for the weeks we've been apart.

Stef shouts, "Get a room you two," startling us.

Taking me by the hand, Mateo leads me out. As we exit, Lee asks, "Should we send River to our house to make this moment really full circle?"

———

BACK AT MATEO'S PLACE, we lock the front door behind us, then divest ourselves of our coats and shoes.

"They won't show up. Don't worry." I smooth a hand down his chest, laughing at the idea of River showing up to interrupt this moment. With a hand beneath his shirt, I scratch along his chest, pressing the material upward.

He yanks it over his head, then his lips are on mine again, his hands on my arms, neck, and shoulders. His fingers thread into my hair and force my face up.

With a low growl, he says, "I love you."

My heart flips, and my legs wobble, but before I can respond, he goes on.

"I told you that before. Remember when I said, mahal kita?" He backs me over to the couch, leaving a trail of my clothes behind until I'm in nothing but a simple pair of black underwear.

"Is that so? Mahal kita," I repeat. Though the words sound right coming from him, they sound funny from me.

I undo his belt in a swift motion, my mouth watering at the impressive bulge pressing against the zipper. As I cup him through his pants, he eases me back so I'm sitting on the couch.

Kneeling before me, he holds one breast, massaging above the heart that beats wildly for him. Deft fingers trace my nipples, bringing the rosy flesh to peaks, and he captures my lips for another kiss. Quick and pressurized, he trails his mouth along my jaw to the pulse point behind my ear. He takes his time moving down my neck and across the top of my collar bones before hovering above my chest.

I'm growing impatient, but before I can beg him for more, his mouth is on my breast, his teeth grazing over the beady point. He pulls ever so slightly and peers up at me. When I shudder in ecstasy, he does it again, this time harder.

A moan escapes me as he continues nipping, then laving over the bite to reduce the sting. He cups that breast gently, massaging as he turns his mouth to the other side.

The heat between us builds and settles heavily between my legs. I press my thighs together, desperately seeking friction. When Mateo sees this, he presses my knees apart, wrapping them around his torso and causing the ache to intensify.

Kissing his way back up my body, he whispers, "Do you still want to call the shots, or can I see how close I can bring you without touching that tight little cunt?"

Lost in a haze of lust, all I can do is nod.

He returns to my breasts, savoring the exploration, moving from feather light touches and nuzzled kisses to harsh plucks and teeth grazing, then back again. On one particularly strong press of his hands on my chest, a realization hits like a flash of lightning. When Jim said that cats believe the dominant one is the active one, while rabbits believe dominance is in being cared for, he could have been talking about us. The dominant one is the one who thinks they're in charge. I've insisted on calling the shots, on holding Mateo at arm's length because love meant inevitable pain. Yet the most punishing touches cause my core to clench exquisitely. The muscles there pulse and flutter around nothing, seeking resistance.

"More," I whine. Fuck, I've never been so turned on.

In response to that one-word command, Mateo swipes his hand across my panties and eyes me.

"Oh, gorgeous girl, you're drenched for me. Let me help you," he says before removing the fabric. He slides the panties into his back pocket with a mischievous grin and plunges two fingers into my core. The slick sounds of my arousal coating his fingers grows as he increases the pressure, curling the digits toward that spot inside me he knows will make me explode.

The throb intensifies, and my muscles pull tighter still. As the inferno between us reaches new heights, he lowers his face to my core and nips at my clit. With the same mix of nips and lick he used on my nipples, he punishes and soothes. Suddenly, a warm, wet heat washes over me, soaking my thighs, Mateo's hand, and the couch.

"That was fucking sexy." He holds his fingers to my mouth. "Taste how sweet you are."

As I lick along his long, smooth fingers, another gush of liquid coats my thighs and the cushion beneath me.

"Did I just... do we need to worry about... did I squirt on your sister's couch?" I cringe. Shit. This is one of Stef's favorite possessions.

"I'll buy a new one. I don't fucking care." He stands and shucks his pants, his long, thick cock springing free.

I sit forward and place kisses to the dark hair that coats golden skin.

"I know you did this once, but Nessa, you do not have to." His tone is hushed, full of care and concern.

That alone washes away any apprehension. I take in every defined muscle, the strength of his arms, the swell of his chest, and the cut of his abdomen. As I assess every inch of him, my hands slowly trace along his thighs getting closer and closer to his stiff cock.

"Condom?" I ask, cupping his balls and massaging them.

"Wallet," he says with an exhale, his erection twitching.

"Sit," I command him, then crawl along the floor to retrieve the foil from his pants.

His eyes rove over me as I pass the packet to him. I'm naked and on all fours at his feet, yet I feel incredibly powerful.

"Fuck, Ivy," he says, sheathing himself. "Please get up here."

With a wicked smile, I crawl up his body. I drag my nails along his skin, leaving light marks and a trail of goose bumps in my wake.

When I'm standing, he grasps my hips and pulls me closer. "Take, gorgeous, please. I love letting you take control, ride me, scratch me. I'm yours," he begs.

I'm not sure how it is possible for me to be more turned on, but I am. Sinking into his lap, I line his head up with my entrance. Inch by inch, I lower myself, watching where our bodies connect. I stretch around him, enveloping him in my pussy, and as I rock my hips, working him deeper, he tightens his hold. With an inhale, I rise up on my knees, then, as I blow the breath out, I slam down against him.

His head falls back with pleasure, a gasp escaping his lungs. Back arched, I set a pace that is fervent and punishing for us both. All the while, he holds me. I trace paths from behind his neck along the tops of his shoulders and back, then clutch his arms, accidentally pressing my nails in too deep.

He releases a guttural "fuck" and I let go on instinct, but he growls and tells me to do it again. So I grasp his biceps and sink deeper onto his shaft, my nails piercing his skin.

His length pulses inside me, and he grits his teeth. "I'm going to—"

A sense of power overtakes me, bringing with it a heady desire. He traces along my hip and thigh, then presses the pad of his thumb against my clit. The surge of electricity between us becomes too powerful.

"Mateo," I cry out.

"Are you going to come again, gorgeous?" he rasps.

My muscles have tensed, and from the feel of his grip on my hip, so have his. We're breathy, sighs and moans, lost in each other until we're shuddering and clinging to one another.

With his sweat slick brow against my forehead, he presses his lips to mine, sealing an unspoken promise to stick to the new path forward we've found.

forty-five
Texting Break Two

Group Chat: Bad Bitches [Stef Carter, Lily Long, Delia Shane, Nessa Rabin, Millie]

STEF:

<digital invitation> Christmakuh at my mom's, hosted by Nessa's mom & mine?!

NESSA:

<eyes emoji>

DELIA:

I'm in!

LILY:

We're in!

NESSA:

The moms planned this? This reeks of your brother...

STEF:

<shrug emoji> I was just told to send the invite.

———

BAD IDEA

<black heart emoji>: Did you have something to do with this? <invitation link>

NESSA:

I legit just said it seemed like YOU would... it's called CHRISTMAKUH

<group chat screenshot>

BAD IDEA:

...this has Lee written all over it...

NESSA:

Will there be red yarmulke Santa hats?

BAD IDEA:

I'll make sure of it.

NESSA:

I'm in <black heart emoji>

———

NESSA:

Ema! What did you do?!

EMA (DASSI RABIN ICE):

What do you mean?

NESSA:

You're throwing a party with Susan. We just started dating!

EMA (DASSI RABIN ICE):

And I know my girl. She'll want to be with her siblings on Christmas for a movie marathon and Chinese takeout, but she'll want to make her boyfriend happy and be at their party, so I made it one event <shrug emoji>

NESSA:

<heart eyes face>

EMA (DASSI RABIN ICE):

You'll be amazed what happens when you trust & let go, sweet girl.

forty-six
Mateo

ON CHRISTMAS AFTERNOON, after we've slept off the late-night Noche Buena with Mom's church friends, time seems to have slowed. I've been anxiously pacing, eager for four p.m. to arrive.

"*Brosef,*" Lee teases me as I wear a hole in the carpet, "I brought my supplies and sketches. Want to kill a little time?"

"Have you inked skin yet?" I ask. Either way, I want to do this. I just want to make sure he's truly prepared.

"I have marked every grapefruit in the greater Manhattan area, and also this." He slides his sleeve up, revealing a new design on his forearm. The delicate letters are immediately familiar.

"Did she write it first or did you free-hand?"

Stef appears, wearing a smile, and traces the words on his skin —*love you most*—with a glowing smile.

"Total surprise, but he took it from a letter I wrote on our wedding day."

After a heated look between them, she breaks into a wicked grin. "Also, you aren't Lee's first. I get that title."

I shake away the double-entendre while she slides her watch up her wrist to show me the two tiny hearts with the letters *L* and *S* inside.

I grin up at my brother-in-law. "Sweet, show me what you got."

Lee pulls out his tablet and scrolls through a few designs he's drawn up and images he's created that integrate the choices into my current sleeve.

"Hold up. Go back."

He does, and I take the device from him so I can study the image.

"Yo, it's this one. Think we can pull it off today?"

It's a simple design that I assume a seasoned artist could complete in the time we have, but I don't want to show her the unfinished product if he needs longer.

He slides Stef's watch back into place and eyes the time. "It's your lucky day, my man."

————

"NANAY, you got everything you needed from us?" I heave out a sigh.

Lee and I have been moving couches and tables for the last forty-five minutes.

"Looks good, tisoy. Thank you, boys. Stop stressing. We've had the Rabins over before. We've been to their house. This is nothing," she chides me.

"Not like this, though, Mrs. M," Lee teases.

Eyes narrowed, I growl. "I recall when a certain someone was sweating bullets as he asked the three of us for permission to propose."

"Permission? Nah. I just wanted your blessing," Lee replies, chin lifted smugly.

Yeah, I like having a little brother.

The doorbell chimes and Dad shuffles across the floor to welcome our guests. The bouncing sounds of greetings echo through the house.

Our buffet is made up of mostly our family recipes, though Lee has added to it. The first time he presented the list of ingredients for his grandma's casserole—including canned cream-based soup and mayonnaise, but very little seasoning—I thought my mom was going to throw him out.

Mom and Stef have made an outrageous amount of food, as well as pulling out the leftover lechon and pancit. They've already pulled out a full spiral ham, ginger-garlic roast chicken, and a series of sweet bibingka. Now Dassi directs her children to add potato latkes and a braised brisket to the smorgasbord. They also add a tray of jelly donuts and chocolate coins to the smaller table where the flan and Mom's creamy coconut fruit salad are set up.

The doorbell rings again, and a moment later, Lily and River enter with growlers of his latest micro-brew, followed by Delia, who carries bottles of wine.

Liam and Christian arrive with big smiles. Screams erupt from the women when they catch sight of the new silver bands both men are sporting. Looks like we have a wedding to look forward to next year. Before we can congratulate them, they apologize for forgetting to bring a dish. "It slipped my mind," Liam says, turning red.

Gran appears next, arm linked with Pru's and holding an apple cake like the one she taught us to make a few months ago.

"Did you boys really think you could get away that easily?" Prudence teases.

The moms invite them in, thrilled about the additions to the group, and plates are piled high. Once the crowd is settled around the tables and on couches set up facing the television, the moms giggle like schoolgirls together.

Both their husbands smirk, clinking whiskey glasses. They're all still as smitten as ever all these years later. That's when it all clicks. The room is loud and warm with the joy of what the girls call their "framily." It may be chaotic, but the room is filled with nothing but love. This is exactly what my life has been missing.

Nanay clears her throat loudly, garnering everyone's attention. "We figured that the perfect way to combine our family's tradition of karaoke—"

"Was to pick a movie we knew you would all be willing to sing along to," Dassi finishes.

A second later, the opening notes of a childhood favorite begins.

A half hour later, we're all focused on the animals dancing in formation around the future king of the jungle.

I whisper to Nessa to follow me, and we sneak upstairs. In my childhood bedroom, I immediately unbutton and remove my dress shirt, anxious to reveal my surprise for Nessa.

"What are you doing?" she hisses. "Everyone is here! They will absolutely figure out what is going on." Though she chides me, her eyes rove over my pecs and abs hungrily.

It takes a minute for her to notice the plastic bandage across my arm. When she does, she approaches slowly, her fingers raised.

"What did you do?" she asks on a laugh.

I remove the protective sheet to give her a clear view. In the open space below my existing quarter sleeve, Lee added a perfect, simple Loch Ness monster surrounded by tiny ripples of water.

"You are stuck with me now, little monster." I wink.

She places her hand gently against my bicep and plants a sweet kiss on my lips. "I kind of love it, kind of hate it." She shakes her head, but she's grinning, her blond hair flowing around her, picking up bits of the lighting overhead. She looks like an angel for a split second before something darker flashes in her eyes. "You really wanted to mark yourself permanently with an image that represents me?" she teases, lightly scratching across my arms, chest, and down my stomach. As her hand grazes the waistband of my pants, someone calls our names from downstairs.

"Shit." I pick up my discarded shirt and give her a quick kiss. "I'll go first. Wait a minute before you follow," I plead. I do not want to get into the "not under my roof" business today.

She nods in agreement, and with a kiss, I step out and close the door quietly.

Shit. I just left Nessa to snoop through all my embarrassing relics from high school.

With a shake of my head, I jog downstairs.

I find my dad in the kitchen. "Your buttons are uneven, son," he chuckles as he fills a glass for me.

"It's pretty impressive, Mateo. You may not have gone into the medical field, but you managed to bring home a doctor. Now you just have to do your best to keep her."

A bark of a laugh behind me has me spinning. When I do, I find said doctor wearing my old varsity jacket with a long forgotten fitted hat. She saunters by and grabs the microphone at the perfect moment to cosplay as me and sing about having no worries.

Gabe approaches, glass raised to clink with mine, and we watch her performance together. He leans over and says, "I don't give unsolicited advice often—"

"Liar!" Shae squeals.

"Okay," he chuckles. "I give unsolicited advice all the time. But if you're with Nessa, then you're one of my kids now. As the man who has kept the original version of that woman happy for the last almost forty years, let me make this clear: do not retaliate."

Unfortunately, I've never been considered a smart man.

When the movie ends, I cue up a hilarious Meghan Trainor song, one she sings to her future husband, and dance around like it's the Short n' Sweet Tour. Thankfully, Liam and Christian jump in, and our impromptu boyband shifts the focus to their marriage.

Though it's impossible to miss Nessa's salty smile. She's going to scratch me up good for this one.

forty-seven
Nessa

IT'S New Year's Eve, and tonight, I'll use comically large scissors and cut a ribbon in front of the library as the incoming Executive Director of the Peacock Springs Community Center. Construction won't start until the spring thaws the ground, but this truly feels like the start of a new life. As much as I'll miss Ruth Anne, I've learned to put myself on the to-do list. Though I don't often make it anywhere close to the top.

The women have all gathered at the house Delia and I share to get ready for tonight. It reminds me of Stef's wedding day and a sorority party rolled into one. I cherish the moment, realizing how infrequent they've become for us.

We take turns in the chair Delia has dragged into the living room, getting our hair and makeup done, laughing and discussing our celebrity doppelgängers.

There's a knock, and Shae appears at the front door. Her gown is in hand and she gives a gregarious hello to all. We've found a good path forward these last few months.

"I'll have you know, this is now your official Chanukah present." She points to the blanket on the couch.

"Fine." I shuffle over and pull her into a hug. "I'm sorry it took me so long to acknowledge your growth. But it's on a podcast, so it's really real now. Forgive me?"

"Always," she says, holding out a hand to ruffle my finished hair.

I dodge her before she can mess it up.

"No!" Delia says sternly, pointing the curling iron her way.

My phone goes off in my pocket, startling me. I nearly kick Wyclef, who's winding himself between my feet. I dig it out and reading to myself.

"Shoot!" I call out. "Mateo and the boys will be here in a few, are we almost all ready?"

The whole group peers around the room, eyeing the chaos we've created, and laughs. We take turns changing into shimmery new year's dresses in the bathroom and the bedrooms before taking a group selfie.

Delia serves as photographer, of course, having the longest arms.

The guys roll up in a pair of oversized SUVs and step out, all of them dressed in dapper suits and ties.

Millie grabs a box from the front door, and goes from person to person, handing over corsages and boutonnieres.

I chuckle to myself. It truly is like going to prom again.

Mateo slips a gorgeous oversized purple dahlia bloom onto my wrist before kissing my cheek. "I got us a room at the Honeybee Inn tonight, since my sister is back home," he says in my ear.

"Mmm. Why don't we just skip the party and go there now?" I tease a finger over his dress shirt.

"I think they'd notice if the primary donor and new Executive Director didn't attend." He kisses the tip of my nose and pulls back with a grin.

Lily pins a fiery tiger lily onto River's lapel, and then Delia and Millie, descend on Seth trying to pin a boutonniere to his jacket. Once they do, they slip blooms onto their own wrists, Shae too, and we pile into the SUVs.

Five minutes later, we pull up to the square. The energy at the party going on at the dance studio and library is buzzing.

Lily's studio is open for partygoers to dance. Outside the library, folks mingle beneath the twinkle lights, not straying too far from the outdoor heaters. It's beautiful, the way this town has come together. These people and this man are mine. There's no point fighting the swell of my heart, the love I'm filled with cannot be dulled. We spend the evening chatting and drinking and dancing.

As we get closer to midnight, during a slow song, Mateo leans into me. "What do you want to accomplish next year, gorgeous?"

"I think next year I want to get to love you for all three hundred and sixty-five days." I smile at him.

"I love you, mischievous girl. Have for a while. I'm glad you caught up." He winks, and when he smiles, that dimple pops, doing me in like it always does. As my knees weaken slightly and he pulls me closer, his lips are on my cheek, my chin, and finally my lips.

"What else, goal-getter?" he asks, his tone oozing with pride.

The crowd begins to count down and we enter the new year laughing, kissing, and holding each other.

From now on, I want every year to begin just like this.

epilogue
Mateo

One Year Later

MICROPHONE IN HAND, I stand at the front of the large room in the community center and survey the crowd, finding my gorgeous girlfriend, my sister and brother-in-law, and my friends—not just her friends, but mine—and a sense of accomplishment, of purpose, washes over me. This is home, and I'm so happy to be back here.

"Good evening, folks!" I finally say. "Thank you so much for giving me a moment of your time. I want to start off by thanking the generous donors who have made this dream a reality. The Peacock Springs Community Center is the product of the hard work and collaboration of many. Special thanks goes out to Christina Salvatore and her fiancé, Tom Sinicola, for rounding up some of the best construction teams in the tri-state area."

The crowd erupts into applause.

"Speaking of the Salvatores," I continue. "If you enjoyed tonight's appetizers, please be sure to thank Carmine and the team at the butchery. They are offering ten percent off select items for anyone who shows a ticket from tonight's event at checkout through the end of January.

"Our drinks came courtesy of the team at The Featherweight, be sure to thank River and Lily when you get a moment. Our head bartender, Kyle, created tonight's New Year's punch himself." I hold up my glass of the delicious concoction. "Please enjoy responsibly. If you need help getting home, members of the high school student council are here to drive or walk you home. Do not get hurt. Liam is off duty tonight."

The guys from the fire department erupt in a chorus of boos for that joke.

"Last, I want to thank the executive director and head clinician of the facility. You may know this local celebrity for her relationship advice podcast, but I simply get to call her mine. Nessa, can you please join me up here?"

The room explodes into a hearty round of applause as she approaches, her eyes narrowed on me.

Fuck, I love when she's feisty like this.

"Nessa," I say when she's at my side. "Eighteen months ago, you and I played a game of truth or drink and had a fair amount of tequila. Tonight, I have only one question for you, though I have two choices of shot glass. The one you get will be based on your answer."

She gives me an exaggerated sigh, crossing her arms and accidentally pressing those amazing breasts into a better view. She's trying to conceal her apprehension, so I widen my eyes, silently telling her to trust me, then lower to one knee.

Instantly, the room erupts into a deafening cheer.

"Nessa, you are the ivy that grew and wrapped itself around me, and there's no coming free from it. I am so much better because I have you, Wyclef, and our bunny, Karen Horney, in my life. Will you please do me the honor of becoming my wife?" I reach over to the tray and pick up the shot glass containing the three-carat oval diamond on a delicate band of pink diamonds.

With shaking hands, she reaches out past me and picks up the shot glass filled with amber liquid. She tosses it back, and with a heavy exhale, she gives me a Cheshire smile and holds out her left hand.

"Of course I will. I love you, you idiot!"

Once the ring is on her finger, she yanks me to my feet and presses her lips to mine.

Like this, the world around us disappears. The music fades, and people fade away. It's just us. I can taste the smoky and tangy liquid on her tongue, feel her soft curves against me. Then, she's grabbing my hand and pulling me through the crowd and out the double doors.

We run down the hallway hand in hand, and she drags me through the door leading to the indoor pool. On the deck, she drops her dress, and with a shriek, she jumps in wearing her bra and lace panties.

I shuck my clothes and follow her in, wearing nothing but my boxers. I don't surface until I've got her in my arms. Mouth on hers, I guide her to the edge and press her back against the wall.

She squirms and squeals, the jet behind her massaging her muscles in a way that makes her go boneless. I spin her around and prop her up so the rushing water hits the junction of her thighs and use my free hand to toy with her nipples through the lace of her bra. A soft moan leaves her, and I slide one hand into her panties to feel her swollen lips.

"Think you can come for me before we're discovered and we get kicked out?" I ask.

"Doubtful." She eggs me on, dropping her head back against my shoulder.

Always up for a challenge, I press firm circles against her clit.

She clamps her mouth shut to muffle the moans escaping her. I slide two fingers into her pussy, looping my thumb over her clit, and pump into her hard.

"More," she whines.

Obediently, I add a third finger.

She sighs and bucks against my hand. "Oh fuck," she grunts as her body trembles.

"That's it, baby. Squeeze my fingers. Let go. Don't fight it," I encourage her.

And she does. She gives in to her release, letting out small sounds of relief and ecstasy.

"Well, that was great," I say, sliding her panties back into place. "But what was your plan for when we get out of the water?"

She cranes her neck, peering over at the empty towel racks, and laughs. We're giggling like two teenagers when an actual teenage lifeguard comes in to test the water, and we freeze.

"Oh, sorry, sir. Ma'am. You really shouldn't be here without the lifeguards. I'll grab you some towels," he says, gaze averted, before turning on his heel to exit as fast as possible.

She turns, wrapping her legs around my middle, and kisses me, laughing into my mouth.

"Take me home and fuck me properly."

also by jordana blake

Flying

Flying Bonus Scene

before you go:

Holy Shit, babe—I did it. Again. You'll always get top billing because without you, I couldn't be here.

Thank you so much to every reader for coming (back) to Peacock Springs. This quirky fictional New Jersey town is everything I have ever wished could exist in life, love, friendship, and life. The walkability of Stars Hollow, the personalities of any Michael Schur sitcom, and people who get my references. If you enjoyed this book please consider rating and reviewing it online.

Revisiting what the concept of becoming viewed sexually highlighted three major areas for me. First, the shared Y2K culture of categorizing women as binary options like virgin/whore, slut/prude, etc. Next was the impact of the broader purity culture and how despite being in USY, a Jewish youth group, we were not exempt from American culture. Finally, the whiplash to my self image upon joining Delta Gamma in college. Each of these moments wove their way into Nessa's story, but they do not reflect on any of the people, places, or organizations I was a member of directly.

Amanda Beth, stepping back in time through this story was an interesting way to revisit our tumultuous time in USY (again). Thank you for being another loud, virgin, 'slut' that couldn't be contained. I'm sorry I tried to fight you at that bat mitzvah in eighth grade.

Elaine, you are the Helen Pai to my Amy Sherman Palladino. Thank you, and your mom, for all the help and support as I drafted this story. Whether it was pledge class shenanigans, shots at Queens, long nights at Club Alex, or frat parties, there is no way college would have been the same without you. Thank you for being my sister since 2006. Mahal kita, ITB, love you forever.

This book could not exist without the Bi+ Book Gang Saturday Morning Crit Group, the Smuttering, the Gold Star Good Girls, and so many more. Thank you, Sammie, Kayla Martin and Katie Van Brunt, for letting me anxiety and ADHD all over your DMs, text messages, voice notes, and smoke signals.

Beth, my goodness, Beth. I owe you for taking my imaginary friends words to the next level twice. I truly hope to be a better student in the future. This whole experience was longer, harder, and more intense than any penis you've had to edit the description of. Thank you for teaching me and taking all of my (many) anxiety-fueled voice notes despite being sick, at Apollycon, and so much more.

Emilie from Glitter Pen, thank you for cross checking this all. I am so excited to work together more in the future.

My alphas, betas, gammas, and sensitivity readers: Becky, Bekah, Britini, Dallas, Elaine, Jordan, Kayla P., Lexy, Megan, Melissa B., Melissa W., Riya, and Shelby. I couldn't do this without all of your kind words, questions, and holes poked along the way.

Specifically, my dear gammas–this book only ultimately exists for the reader because of you bringing me back from the brink.

Thank you for reviving me.

suggested reading
by Filipina & Filipina-Diaspora authors

Blackburne, Wren. *The Cage of Chaos*. Self, October 2025

Cruz, Elle. *How to Survive a Modern Day Fairy Tale*. Entangled, 2021.

Cruz, Elle. *Catching Feelings*. Self Published, 2024.

Elliot, Coco. *Now and Forever*. Self Published, 2023.

Elliot, Coco. *Sin Bin Bay*. Self Published, 2025.

Gaskell, Carina. *True North*. Self Published, 2024.

Gaskell, Carina. *Trust Issues*. Self Published, 2025.

Hopkins, Mia. *Thirsty*. Self Published, 2024.

Hopkins, Mia. *Trashed*. Self Published, 2019.

Hopkins, Mia. *Tanked*. Self Published, 2022.

Kinkade, Rebecca. *Streams and Schemes*. Davenport-Ridgeway, 2024

Kinkade, Rebecca. *Tips and Trysts*. Davenport-Ridgeway, 2024

Lim, Dominic. *All the Right Notes*. Forever, 2023.

Lim, Dominic. *Karaoke Queen*. Forever, 2024.

Miranda, Anj. *The Off Chance of Me and You*. Self Published, 2023.

Miranda, Anj. *The Odds of Happily Ever After*. Self Published, 2023.

Paige, Aurora. *Playing for You*. Smitten Ink, 2024.

Paige, Aurora. *Playing for Keeps*. Smitten Ink, 2024.

Paige, Aurora. *Playing for Us*. Smitten Ink, 2024.

Rockwell, Kaye. *Honest with You*. Self, 2022.

Rockwell, Kaye. *Forever with You*. Self, 2024.

Bookshop Affiliate Shopping

about the author

Jordana is a textbook Millennial: she has a Master's Degree in Social Work she'll be paying off in the nursing home, a history of changing careers, and obsession with 90s nostalgia, and cannot talk before coffee.